FRASER VALLEY REGIONAL LIBRARY

30083503745482

D0925957

LAND AND POWER

LAND AND POWER

Wallis Peel

CHIVERS

British Library Cataloguing in Publication Data available

This Large Print edition published by BBC Audiobooks Ltd, Bath, 2009.
Published by arrangement with the Author.

U.K. Hardcover ISBN 978 1 408 41255 8
U.K. Softcover   ISBN 978 1 408 41256 5

Copyright © Wallis Peel 1975

All rights reserved.

Printed and bound in Great Britain by
CPI Antony Rowe, Chippenham, Wiltshire

BOOK ONE

James Mayo

CHAPTER ONE

The clouds hung ominously low, bunched thick and grey as far as the eye could see. Everywhere was sodden. The leaves dripped and those which had already fallen lay underfoot in a squelchy mass of red and brown. Fields were half-flooded. Ditches gurgled over on to muddy tracks. The wind was sharp even for October, blowing from both north and east, squalling, the rain lashing like a whip.

Mid-day visibility was poor. The man frowned as he sat his bay cob, looking out over his best field. There lay his corn, sodden and useless, just a small fraction of what he had hoped would be a good harvest. Now it was ruined. Such rain. Who would have thought it possible?

James Mayo's face was bleak, his thoughts grim. Never had he known such appalling weather. Times were bad enough without the elements being against the farmer. 1816 was proving a disastrous year in more ways than one.

Way back at the age of thirty and as the recent inheritor of Mayo's farm from his father, the turn of the century had seemed a bright point in his life. The years following had been very good ones.

He had thoroughly approved of the Land Enclosures Act which had enabled him to expand his property. Many plots of rich Gloucestershire farmland were shrewdly added until Mayo's now extended over 500 acres of prime land.

He shifted in the saddle. A man of medium height he was built on gigantic lines. His wide shoulders threatened to rip apart the seams of his cloak. His muscular thighs strained against the material while his calves swelled in his boots.

His face was square, almost chiselled out of stone with jutting jaw and high forehead. Well-spaced grey eyes topped by black brows gave his face a frightening visage when he scowled. The skin was red with still only a few wrinkles marring what had been, in his youth, a handsome if slightly brutish face. He was hard, even cruel, and with the power of his land and tenacity of purpose he was also a feared man.

He feared no one, be it man or beast. He would fight happily and willingly, defeat never crossing his mind. He had waited patiently to inherit Mayo's farm, and his father's death had been a day of great satisfaction. Little love had been lost between them. The only son to survive, he had immediately thrust himself into often-thought plans.

He had not hesitated to fly in the face of ancient custom. No longer did the hired farm labourer eat at his table at night. Why should he house and feed his workers as well as pay them? That the young farm labourer, coming from a cottage of great poverty, enjoyed an increased standard of living when eating with his master, concerned him not at all.

He banished them, adding to their already abject misery but satisfying his own mood and further increasing his thirst for class distinction.

He also abolished the oxen, causing a storm of controversy in the county, and he cared not. He drilled his corn instead of broadcasting it. When the sheepdog tax was raised to eight shillings per licence he sold his sheep and concentrated instead upon his crops and horses. Fat wartime profits were shrewdly ploughed back into the land. His shrewdness enabled him to meet his tithes and still have enough money to buy more land.

But this year of our Lord 1816 was bad. Was it also the start of the rot? He had never, in all his life, seen the harvest decay in the fields, nor his well-kept ditches overflow. Neither had he seen such national unrest. It was only yesterday that news had reached him of rioting in East Anglia. His lips tightened into a snarl as he considered this turn of events. Quiet countryside was being terrorized by gangs of destitute farm workers who were firing ricks and burning down farmhouses under a dramatic banner of 'Bread or Blood'.

His snarl tightened, showing fine, white

teeth. Let them try such actions on his land. He would plunder and kill to hold his own. They should hang them, or transport them. What was the world coming to? Of what use was the Combination Act.

James Mayo's thoughts turned to his horses. He loved them best of all and had an uncanny knack for breeding. He had faith in them and was unable to visualize a life without them. But times were changing.

The Enclosures Act had brought a new type of riding into being. Hunting now included 'flying leaping' over fences, a somewhat dangerous pastime which many avoided if they could. When they couldn't the riders gingerly removed their feet from the stirrups. Mayo sniffed. He kept his feet rammed home tightly in the irons and no fence frightened him.

His thoughts switched back to his ruined harvest. If only there was some way to cut the corn quickly and beat the weather. It took six expert men many weary hours to cut just one field of corn, swinging their scythes in a rhythmic row, each man four sweeps ahead of his neighbour. If only there was some way to to cut a field in one day—he would never be at the mercy of such weather as this.

He ground his teeth angrily and urged his cob into a fast canter. The cold rain was sheeting down now. The farmhouse fire! Home-cured bacon, Home-brewed malt ale! He smacked his lips in anticipation and drove with his heels.

The cob breasted the rise and automatically he felt on the reins. The animal slithered to an abrupt halt in the mud and stood restlessly, dithering its hindlegs, anxious to be off again.

James Mayo stared down at the house. His house! He never tired of looking at it, admiring the beauty of the white Cotswold stone. For generations now the house was known by the name of the family who had owned it, and who, James vowed, would forever hold it. *It* and the land which he had so shrewdly added.

He scowled again and heeled the cob down the slope. A movement caught his eye and momentarily he checked while his grey eyes hardened and swept the man from hair to feet. A wet, utterly bedraggled man, walking hunched against the rain. A man of his own age who halted and stared up at him with blue eyes, hard as ice and full of hatred.

The farmer held the gaze and remorselessly stared the other down. Then, with a wry twitch at his lips, he dismissed the incident and rode on. Behind him, the other turned and watched. Loathsome hatred rippled from him in an almost visible aura, then shuddering and shivering with the cold he plodded up the slope again.

Mayo drove forward more quickly, anxious now to be in from the stinging rain. He cantered into the cobbled stable yard. The cob slithered to a halt, lowered his head and snorted. The farmer swung out of the saddle, tossed the reins to a boy, growled for the animal to be well rubbed down, and strode quickly into his house.

He slammed the heavy oak door shut with a one-handed flick which demonstrated the enormous strength in his arms, then stamped up the stone passage leaving a trail of water behind. The kitchen maid bobbed hastily to him as she ducked aside to let her master pass into the kitchen.

Although not gentry, Mayo expected and received subservience from both house servants and hired labourers.

Mayo swung his eyes round the large kitchen. It had a high ceiling supported by two oak beams darkened with age and smoke. On one side were the bacon flitches while on the other pans hung in neat rows. A cauldron bubbled over the roaring wood fire and he sniffed in anticipation, saliva filling his mouth.

He liked this room. Since a boy it had always been his favourite, always warm and cosy yet filled with never-ceasing activity. It was the very hub of his farm and land.

Land was power and power was all!

Even the gentry were nothing without land. Take the squire—what had he to show for his position? Not half as many productive acres as the farmer and all because he had been too slow and sentimental to take land when it was going cheap. Why bother about those who lost their possessions? They were fools who had taken neither precaution nor opportunity when it came. He sniffed. He despised the foolish and weak. Land, power and strength made up his sole creed. *He* worshipped nothing else.

The kitchen maid came back into his vision, nervously ladling some of the thick meat soup into a bowl and placing it on the well-scrubbed white table before him. He started to eat, still busy with his thoughts.

His wife was ailing again. That she was with child once more did not please him. There had been too many births. Too many rapid deaths immediately following. So far his twenty years of matrimony had produced one living son— on the right side of the blanket. But what a son! His eyes softened, his face mellowed.

His fine boy was seventeen years now. And a strong forceful replica of his sire. One day Mayo's would be his to hand on in turn like any monarch's crown.

He thought about his wife again. If she managed to come to full term would the child live and be normal? He had chosen badly when he married her. A poor breeder. His one great mistake. But who would have thought that a farmer's daughter from such strong stock would turn out to be a weakling who could not breed true? His own father had approved the marriage. From where had the weakness come? Certainly not from the Mayos.

His mare though was strong. His mare! Now *there* was a bloodline! Strong, sure and lasting. The farmer knew her breeding went back to the fantastic Alcock Arabian, sometimes known as Mr Pelham's Grey Arab. Now *that* was a horse. He remembered how his father had always wanted to have a grey from that line but it had fallen to him to buy the mare at a fantastic price.

Only a few diehard fools still worked the slow oxen. The demand for horses was endless. Were they not a better investment on the land than ruined corn? He ate thoughtfully, belching now and again as he considered the economics of changing from crops to animals. He keenly weighed the various pros and cons. Perhaps it would be better to have both until the times were more settled. Look how corn had dropped in price! During the war wheat sold at 100/- a quarter and was now down to a miserable 66/-. The farmers were being ruined. At least the recently passed Corn Laws helped a little.

He finished his meal, drained his pewter tankard of ale and thought about what to do next. He supposed he should go and see his wife. The thought dampened his mood again. John! Where was his son? Out with their cherished mare, he guessed, suddenly pleased again. *What* a son! The same thoughts, the same interests. Land, power and horses. The Mayos always bred true and strong in the male line. Was it too much to hope that his wife might manage to produce another sound, living son?

He stamped slowly out of the kitchen and headed towards the wide, wooden stairs. He passed another serving wench and a thought nudged at him, making him halt in mid-stride. Where was that Betty girl? He realized he had not seen her since yesterday and, as he thought of her, so did the picture of the hating man cross his mind again. He dwelt upon Joseph Howard for a few seconds then shrugged his shoulders. He owed him nothing. Why should he? He had given work to Betty Howard when there was no actual need. Because Howard was a weak fool why should he care what happened to him now?

He flung open the door to the cold bedroom, strode in and looked down at his wife. His eyes asked a silent question.

Mary Mayo looked up at him. She had heard his heavy tread and flinched down beneath the sheets. Once, long ago, her love had flowed wildly for this strong, virile man but it had slowly been stifled as her spirit had been quenched.

It was not that James ever hit her. To give him his due he had never struck any woman. There was no need. When he lowered his brows and turned the full force of his dynamic

11

stare on her she had never dared oppose him. His spirit and personality overpowered any resistance she might have had.

For so long now life had been a dreary game where she had tried to please him by word and deed; to win a smile or touch of his hand. Long ago she had suspected that James had other women but there was nothing she could do about it. He was far too strong a personality. And she knew she was much too weak to fight him. John! Her son! The only truly wonderful spark which had come from her marriage. Although he was the double of his father he was her son too. There was a great bond of love between them. A love that was pure and simple in its depth and which not even James recognized.

For the thousandth time Mary asked herself why so often she had to fail in childbirth? If, perhaps, there had been other children James's attitude might have been different. Their solitary son was a reproach to his manhood when large families were so common. Although Mary knew few facts of the bastards which were in evidence she had guessed. James had to prove himself. And with his proving she had shown her inability to make a family.

Sometimes she felt tired to the bone with life itself. Surely her world could hold more than this—or was that only for the gentry?

On her wedding day she had been bonny to

the point of prettiness. Yet her once curling dark hair was now liberally laced with white. Her cheekbones stood out in stark relief and always in her grey eyes was a hunted, wary look. She had thinned down after each birth. Now, even when fully dressed, she was gaunt as if starved.

As usual, she was being horribly sick in the mornings with a nausea which left her limp and wan. Reluctantly, she had taken to her bed, leaving the management of the farmhouse in the hands of the servants.

She flushed suddenly, remembering the girl. Betty Howard.

'What's to do?' Mayo asked her suddenly. He had studied her for several moments. He could read her like a book. His bass voice rumbled from the depths of his broad chest.

Mary writhed uneasily. 'I'm all right, James. I'll be all right this time. I know I will if I go carefully!'

James frowned. Why the flush? Certainly it was not for him. He waited, holding her eyes with his own, forcing her to answer him.

'That Howard girl, I had her sent home,' she told him, the words tumbling out in a rush.

His nostrils flared but he said nothing. His silence stabbed down at her.

'She's with child!'

There, it was out. She flopped back on the pillow, sweat tracing her forehead. She knew she was terrified of her husband and she did not understand why. If only there was not this horrible iron wall between them.

So, thought James, Howard really will hate my guts now! His girl out of work and him only doing odd jobs. They'll have to go on the Parish if they don't watch out. Not that it would be any of Mayo's concern if they did.

'She said it was our John!'

He stiffened to attention, watching her carefully, considering this information with interest. His son! Well! It was possible of course. Young, hot-blooded and all male, the lad had to start sometime, somewhere—but with Howard's girl! Would this make trouble?

He turned and stared out of the window thinking rapidly, then shook his head, smiling to himself. What trouble could Howard make for *him*?

'Have you spoken to John?' he barked at her. She was the mistress of the house. Why couldn't she control the females? Weak, as usual.

She watched the sneer cross his face and knew exactly the line of his thoughts. Wearily, she turned her head and stared at the wall.

'No, I've not seen him since I found out and sent the girl home.'

'Leave this to me then. More than likely it's a wild invention and if not, who's to say that John was the first?'

He walked to the door, paused and looked back at her. She *was* his wife but he would not, could not ask a sentimental question about her health. She did not now interest him that much. And he had grown too hard. He shrugged his shoulders and clomped back down the stairs. The cook was busy in the kitchen, making what seemed an unnecessary clatter while he paused a moment to watch her. Two serving girls silently worked under her orders and he nodded approvingly. The cook also doubled as the midwife. It suddenly crossed his mind that perhaps, this time, he should get some other and perhaps more experienced person for his wife's birthing!

John! He must find him and sort out this Howard business.

Mayo stepped into the long cobbled passage and immediately his mood changed. It pleased him to see the long lines of horses contentedly eating, each tied from the head in its individual stall.

The heavy working horses, proud with the blood of the Shires. The lighter boned riding animals, and the arrogant coach horses half-bred from Cleveland stallions.

Each animal stood in solitary state. Each wore a heavy leather collar whose buckles shone from polish. Each had a manger and above this an iron hay rack. Underfoot, long strands of wheat straw made a thick bed.

He walked down the line of animals, ignoring the stablemen as he considered his horses. They represented a lot of capital but more, they pleased his eye.

He reached the passage end and opening a door stepped into his latest innovation over which many in the county were laughing at him behind his back. It was a stable in which a horse could roam free. Mayo called it a loose stable.

The grey mare looked at him and nickered, then turned and came to him, ears pricked, eyes bright, bold and friendly. His prized and precious mare! Her Arab blood was strongly shown in her dished face, tiny ears and eyes spaced well apart. By her side, a gangly legged filly foal trustfully nuzzled the man's breeches.

As expected, his son was there too. Young John Mayo leaned against the mare's manger. A smile creased his face. He was built on the same lines as his sire. Not over tall but constructed with a framework of large bones. His face was a replica of his father's without the age lines and with more humour and good temper apparent in calculating eyes just below an intelligent forehead.

'That's the best she's ever bred!' said Mayo senior, thoughtfully eying the inquisitive foal.

'And no matter what colour the sire she still throws back to grey,' his son replied.

'You must always have at least two of her stock on Mayo's after I've gone,' the father said firmly. 'Always remember, this is a rare and unique blood line. There were not many foals from that stallion. My father tried all his life to get a mare from that stock. Never let Mayo's be without a grey from this line. When the greys go, then so will Mayo's!'

James looked at his son, then frowned as he remembered the object of his visit.

'I've just seen your mother. She's sent the Howard girl away. She's with child,' he said quietly, adding, 'and the girl names you as the father.'

His son stared back thoughtfully, eyes open but hardening.

'Are you?'

John thought rapidly. Between him and his father was a deep affection which stemmed from a similarity both physical and mental. Not the same type of attachment that he had for his mother but, nevertheless, a close bond which amounted almost to friendship.

John knew the hatred of Howard; he had been told the reason long ago and, like his sire, he despised the foolish or short-sighted. The girl? She had been most amusing, fresh and a challenge but nothing else. If she had fought too hard he would have desisted and gone elsewhere. A rich man's son was never short-served in that direction.

John shot a questioning look at his sire.

His father! What kind of answer was he expecting? More to the point, what would be his reaction? He eyed him carefully. At a very early age he had learned James Mayo was a disciplinarian.

17

'Could be,' he replied evenly.

His father smiled. The answer was the correct one. Truthful, short, unconcerned. 'When and where?'

John considered. 'At the end of hay-making. Remember that one really hot day we had? She came over with the ale and stayed talking too long,' he replied grinning.

'Howard should look after his own. But he never could look ahead—no imagination and see where he is now! Forget it, what's one by-blow anyhow?' Then his voice deepened further. 'But lay off the other wenches in the house. There's enough uproar with your mother lying-abed sick. I don't want to be continually looking for fresh girls for the cook to train on. Get off round the villages for your sport. Now be off! Ride the grey mare but look after her!' and he slapped his son on the back.

James slapped the mare's neck affectionately. 'I've been thinking about going in for more horses. Corn growing is too much of a risk with the rain and anyhow, at the low price of wheat now it's hardly worth the trouble of growing.'

John pricked his ears. 'Do away with corn altogether?'

His father shook his head. 'No! Grow enough for our own needs and a little over to sell if the price should go up, but get more horses. People always want horses and now the roads are getting better they'll travel more.

Not just in coaches but actually drive themselves,' he predicted shrewdly.

John nodded. 'And the gentry always want to hunt. They say that flying leaping is now called jumping in the Midlands and is a big thing. They'll pay any price for a horse that can gallop and jump well.'

The two men fell silent, each considering this proposed enterprise.

'I have heard that the Squire has his eye on the mare's foal,' John added quietly.

The farmer stiffened. 'Oh, he has, has he? He can remove it then. She's not for sale—not at any price. Nor is last year's. I'll not have him cut either. We'll make him into our stallion, cross him with the mares and we'll get fast riding animals for the gentry.'

John patted the mare's neck, eyeing this latest foal. 'You'd not breed her back to the colt, surely?'

James shook his head. 'No! That would be brother to sister. The blood lines would be too close, son. But remember what I said earlier, always keep two of this breed, colt and filly, and Mayo's will never lack for money. Now take the mare out. Ride her gently and rub her down well when you come back.'

'And mother?' asked John, as if it were a logical progression.

James shrugged. 'She's ailing, which you know, but she says she'll go to term this time. Let's hope you'll have another brother to bring on. Though Mayo's will go to you,' he reassured his son.

John thought about this then frankly regarded his father. 'But if I were a younger son I'd want land too,' he pointed out.

'There's no need to fret about that point when we have so much land. If you have a brother he will have some acres but you are my first born. You are *my* son. Remember John, respect the land. Without it you're nothing—always remember Howard,' he warned.

John slowly shook his head. As if he could ever forget Howard and his stupidity or his daughter, come to that. If things had been different, Howard's girl could have made him a good wife. The stock was sound, it was just that fool of a Joseph Howard.

John Mayo, like his father, had a streak of hardness inherent to his nature but unlike his father he also had some sentiment which he carefully kept to himself. Betty Howard, just a year his junior, aroused strong feelings in him, not altogether dominated by lust. He liked her. She was pretty and well made. She laughed easily and was good company to be with. He knew, in his heart, the child she carried was his. If things had been different, they might have made a good match of it—but now—the Mayos were rich and the Howards so poor.

With his father gone he fondled the mare, thinking of the girl. He must see her, talk to her. She would be frightened. Perhaps she would hate him! There must be something he could do. Marriage was out of the question. His father would never countenance it and neither would Howard. Too much hate came from that direction and too much scorn from his father.

That summer's day was so clear to him.

He had only intended a romp and tumble but somehow things had got out of hand. She had been bewildered and alarmed to start with but never afraid.

And he had been the first. That was why, come what may, he could only ever be tender to her. She had been so sweet, not crying out in distress afterwards, neither had she clung to him. She had just accepted what had happened and taken pleasure in his enjoyment.

Now that soft, white belly would soon swell with his seed. What would it be—boy or girl? A father? The enormity suddenly hit him! Him—a father.

Betty! Alone in that place with that father of hers. Joseph Howard—what would he do when he found out? Once a gentle tempered man, he had changed over the last five years. Bitterness ate like cancer into his soul.

Surely though, he would not vent his spleen on his only surviving child? It was odd, thought John Mayo, that in a day and age of large families, both the Mayos and Howards had only the one child apiece. Disease, ignorance and sheer bad luck had killed so many babies.

Sarah Howard, a tiny spit of a woman, once used to the good things of life, would stand up for her daughter. That John knew, but Howard could be an ugly devil when roused.

He made a swift decision. Howard would not yet know. He had being doing casual work on the parish. Betty had only gone home this morning. He must go over there, see her before her father came home. There must be something he could do. The coming child *was* his and though Betty could not be his wife, nothing must happen to her.

CHAPTER TWO

Joseph Howard made the top of the slope. He stared back to where rider and cob had passed. The rain squalled around him, but his bubbling hatred was a cloak of armour.

James Mayo! His one-time friend and neighbour! James Mayo, the enemy in the dark. James Mayo—boyhood friend and now? James Mayo the rat!

His thoughts turned back the years to his schooldays. Joe and Jim, bosom friends, inseparable companions, farmers' sons, respected equals—had that been possible? Friends and equals? It was so many weary years that Ferndale, owned by the Howards, had run side by side with Mayo's.

The latter had always been the slightly larger farm but Ferndale had the edge with better soil. Both Mayo and Howard senior had been careful farmers; the only major difference being that Howard had tenants on his land while Mayo hired labourers from the nearby village.

Howard rented a small parcel of land to each tenant who, apart from paying a nominal rent, also worked two or three days a week in exchange for his cottage and plot.

Because of the very great difficulty in feeding the cattle during winter months it had become established custom to slaughter the majority in late autumn. This left a small nucleus for the spring breeding.

Those had been good days. Both boys had learned their letters and figures at the village school, thinking nothing of the five-mile walk each way. They had played together, fought and yet been the best of friends. Healthy young animals never still for more than a minute.

Ferndale's kitchen had been a never-ending scene of feminine activity and, as a boy, young Joe had loved nothing better than sitting on the kitchen stool watching his mother kneading the bread. Her plump reddened cheeks had pursed with effort as she pounded and beat the dough to her satisfaction.

Those were good days. Life revolved around the farmhouse and the nearby village. The war with America meant nothing. All was centred on the constantly noisy brood that made up the Howard family. The laughter and bustle of many daughters, long since married and departed; the strength and bantering of the working sons—his brothers now gone to God knew where. All this was past . . . lost forever.

As eldest son, and therefore the heir, as well as being last to marry, Joseph had spent much time with his father, Old Joe. He had been carefully taught the work of the farm in preparation for when it was his.

Old Joe was conservative. He was slow to try new ideas. Unconsciously he handed this fatal reticence down to his son. It took him many years to agree that dibbling corn brought better results than broadcasting it. As for Tull with his weird machines, the man's name was a positive anathema to Old Joe. What had been good enough for his father before was good enough for him and should also do for young Joseph.

Old Joe died suddenly and quietly in his bed and at twenty-five years Joseph took over the running of Ferndale. He installed his beloved childhood sweetheart Sarah as wife and mistress of the house—his mother having died from a pox when he was still a boy. With his brothers and sisters all flown Joseph Howard settled down to raise himself a family and to enjoy life to the full.

In 1793 came the start of the war with

France. Suddenly change was in the air. The Enclosures Act and Pitt's Combination Act shattered his life. The common land was fenced. Bereft of those extra acres things became bad. They were worse for his tenants and he was reluctant to press for rents owed to him. Sentiment stayed his hand as he watched. Men he had known since boyhood struggled to find work, to get food, even just to live. Without the use of the common land they were doomed. No land meant no food and no life to many.

Families starved. He could not stand by and watch. From his rapidly diminishing supply of both corn and money he tried to help. Others, shrewder, harder and more ruthless took their advantage. James Mayo started taking land. When debts were owed he had no hesitation in pressing his claims. Slowly and remorselessly he drove the debtor out. He increased his holding until only Ferndale stood between him and 500 acres of prime Gloucestershire farmland.

Joseph Howard just could not understand this change in his boyhood friend. To own land was something any self-respecting farmer understood. To hound people to get it was another matter. A gap widened between them. Suddenly it became a gulf one morning when Joseph Howard realized he was in bad straits. He owed money to Mayo! He had none.

Howard was forced to remove his tenants,

repossessing where necessary until one frightful day he realized he could not go on. Somehow, he never knew how it had actually happened, he could not pay : but Mayo did not want money. He wanted land! His land— Howard land!

Howard went and saw his friend. Begged for more time, asked for help but he came up against an inflexible wall of resolution. The determination of one man to found a dynasty and reign like a monarch. To stand, feet apart, daring man and the elements to dislodge him. It would have taken a better and much cleverer man that Joseph Howard to beat James Mayo.

He realized he had no chance but he had tried for the sake of his family. He learned much in that half-an-hour at Mayo's. He had, above all else, learned that he was despised. The shock had pole-axed him and removed the last vestiges of self-respect.

With breaking heart and streaming eyes, Joseph Howard had been put from his inheritance. With a few miserable possessions, he, his wife, his eldest child Betty and three little ones had walked from their land. They sought shelter and work—anywhere. In those bitter, hard days, there were too many unemployed, too many starving and homeless.

The lessons were bitter to the broken man. Only slowly did it dawn on him that the carefree James Mayo had grown into a ruthless, forward-thinking farmer.

Howard shook his head as he remembered back. He had smiled when James Mayo drilled his seed, but the resulting larger crops had paid off mighty dividends. His quicker horses against the slower oxen had enabled him to cultivate more land. Why had Joseph not been able to see this?

Where was he now? An odd-job labourer, glad to take any work offered for a few pence to try and keep his home together. Home! He sneered at the thought. Who could call that miserable hovel a home?

A mud and straw shack with rags blocking the one window. An earth floor with a few miserable sticks of furniture. And food—when had he last eaten well? It was difficult to remember, though Sarah was a wonder to keep them alive at all. Even so a man became tired of starting work on a mess of cold potatoes or a bowl of thin soup.

Only his girl Betty was safe and sound—but working at Mayo's! The sheer desperation for the extra shilling or two had allowed him to let his daughter go to that man's house. Beggars—and heaven only knew that meant him—could not be choosers.

It seemed nothing further could possibly happen to the Howards. But disaster again struck with explosive force. Within 16 terrible days the Howard family was reduced to the parents and the girl Betty. The smallpox had raged furiously throughout the area. Small children, ill-fed and poorly clothed had little resistance against any illness let alone the scourge of smallpox. They had died and been buried at the Parish expense in a pauper's grave. And that had been perhaps the most bitter blow of all to bear. His children dead and he couldn't afford them decent burial. Him—once a landowner relying on the charity of others even unto death.

Betty was unaffected. The foresighted James Mayo had, long ago, arranged the new vaccination for all of his family and workers, thus safe-guarding them.

Why did everything strike at him? All Joseph Howard knew and understood was that he had gone hopelessly down in the world. James Mayo had gone upwards—and at the Howards' expense.

*   *   *

Sarah waited for her man with tight lips and worried eyes. Her grey hair—far too premature—hung limp in damp strands. Her once laughing features were rigid, hardened into a mask which rarely cracked to display emotion. Long ago, she had learned to stifle her feelings. She had found that she must be the rock of security. When the waves of disaster threatened to drag Joseph down at the knees it was she who had to produce the inner strength to keep them going. At times, she had been wearied to the marrow of her bones. Surely it was in the order of things that the woman turned to the man?

For all that though, theirs had been a good marriage. He had never turned to another woman. She did not love him now. Very few couples could undergo their misfortunes and still be in love but feeling and affection, of a kind, were still present. They needed each other; they were used to being together. If things had been different, what might not their life have been?

Right now she was desperately afraid. Fear churned her belly until it lurched ominously but this she dare not show.

She stared at her daughter huddled on the old wooden chair, head low, cheeks stained where tears had run through dirt. Her long, dark hair was dishevelled, her tall full figure was a heap of shocked misery.

Sarah's fear was also coupled with pity and anger. Each emotion separately attacking her heart as she frantically sought for an answer to this latest catastrophe.

Those Mayos! Joseph was right. They were bad, through and through—with perhaps the possible exception of Mary. It was because of her old regard for Mayo's wife that she had allowed Betty to go and work there. Joseph had ruthlessly opposed this but Sarah had cunningly pointed out the advantages of those

29

extra shillings. She had won but knew the deep resentment Joseph felt that his girl was in the camp of the enemy. Just how would he react now?'

'Betty, how could you?' she reproached gently.

The girl lifted her head, eyes swimming with tears of self-pity and apprehension.

She had lost her head. That she admitted, but also she had felt and cared for young John Mayo. It had never entered her head that the enmity between the families would not allow them to marry. With the thoughtlessness of youth she had been an agreeable partner.

'Do you care for him, lass?'

She nodded miserably. She had always been close to her mother but never more so than at this crisis.

'But you must have known you couldn't wed? You know what your father thinks of them Mayos. They took our land! They ruined us!'

Spirit flashed in the girl's eyes. 'It's been our dad's fault too! He should have looked after us in the first place and not bothered so much about others. We'd not be in this mess now!'

'Betty!'

'It's true! He could have been more go-ahead like Mr Mayo—'

'Stop it! That's enough! Don't you speak about your father like that. He did what he thought was best at the time. How dare you!'

But she's right, Sarah told herself silently. Why couldn't Joseph have looked ahead? Why didn't I? We are both to blame. Dear God, where is this all going to end?

Betty stayed silent. She knew she was being disloyal to her parents but she had not spent months working at Mayos without hearing things from the other servants. Why, they were the joke of the village. From being well-set-up farmers, they were just about paupers. They lived from hand to mouth, on what casual work her father could get.

James Mayo was respected even if disliked. Joseph Howard was pitied.

John! Her heart beat quickly. She loved John Mayo. What had started as a summer game had developed into the real thing for her. Her first and only true love. Oh! Surely there was some way they could marry?

Her mother moved restlessly. She stood listening to the rain. Joseph could not work in such weather.

How best to break her news? She was not afraid of him. What she lacked in size she more than made up for in her fighting spirit but they were still a family. They had to live together in peace. She sighed.

'And why can't we marry? John does love me, he told me so!' the girl asked suddenly.

'You little fool! You can't marry because you're too young in the first place to marry without your father's consent and you should

31

know what he thinks of the Mayos by now. And in the second place what about James Mayo? He's got his own plans for that boy of his and you don't think they include marrying you, do you? Saying John loves you! What rubbish. They all say that, 'til they've got what they wanted in the first place. It's the oldest trick in the world. You fell for it, my girl. I thought I'd brought you up to have more sense. Just because we live like this now doesn't mean to say we are low. We're someone! We come from yeoman stock. Just you remember that! Our day will come again!' Sarah said firmly.

'And what about my baby?'

'You should have thought of that before!'

Betty started to weep.

Sarah hugged the girl. She tried to think. Joseph would go wild when he found a bastard was due in the family. He had always had high morals. With a Mayo as father . . .

They'd do nought to help. The lad might want to. His father would never allow it though.

She patted the girl and forced her shoulders straight.

'You'd best not be around when your father comes in. Let me break the news to him. He'll be home soon. With weather like this a man can't fence or ditch.'

'But where shall I go?' Betty asked, wild terror catching at her voice.

Sarah thought rapidly. The hovel only had the one room where they lived, ate and slept. It would never do for Joseph to find his daughter here when supposedly working at the Mayo's. She must have time to talk to him first. If only this news could have waited one more day. Tomorrow was Sunday and Betty came home on her monthly half-day off. She gritted her teeth.

'You'll have to go out!'

'But it's sheeting, ma!'

'I can't help that. It'll be sheeting in here if your dad catches you home before I've had chance to talk to him! Here! Take this old cloak and go into the woods. You know that big oak? Good, you wait there. It'll shelter you a bit from the rain. I'll fetch you when I've had my say. Now mind my words, don't you come back until I tell you!' she ordered, wrapping the thin material around the slumped shoulders.

Sarah pulled aside the sack which composed the doorway. The rain did seem to be easing a little and she held Betty's arm, squeezing it affectionately.

'Of with you!'

Sarah came back into the hovel, sank down in the one decent chair left to them and mentally started composing a story. She had to make Joseph understand that, terrible as this was, it was not the first time it had happened and it certainly wouldn't be the last.

But with John Mayo! She shuddered in anguish. Joseph would be tired, hungry and wet through. She anxiously thought about food, their biggest never-ending problem. All they seemed to do was exist upon potatoes, turnips and whatever scraps she managed to get. She had not eaten white bread or good meat in four years. She did have a small knuckle of bacon bone which had been given to her in the village for scrubbing a floor and this she was saving for their Sunday meal. With some turnips and a few other root vegetables she might be able to conjure up a thin broth.

Joseph, if lucky, brought home seven shillings for a hard week's work. It was just enough to keep the two of them alive. With Betty home now and a baby coming—her thoughts appalled her. To go on the Parish relief, to enter the workhouse—she gritted her teeth. Not while a drop of red blood flowed in her veins. They were yeomen, not paupers. They would rise again. They had to!

She heard the footsteps squelching through the mud and her heart started to thud. She composed her face, sat firmly on the chair and faced the wet sack. Slowly it moved aside and Joseph Howard stepped into the gloom, shoulders hunched.

His lined face streamed with water. His clothes clung to his body, etching the frame of a once powerful but now wasted and hungry male.

Slowly Joseph Howard sank down on a three-legged stool, lowered his head and studied his powerful hands.

He raised his head, suddenly aware of his wife's silence. Her still face, tightly composed lips and narrowed eyes made her silence ominous.

'Joseph!' she began nervously, then stopped. This would not do. She must speak clearly and calmly as if the event were of no importance.

'Well?' he asked her. What was up now? When his little Sarah stuck out her chin like that and bristled like a game-cock there was usually a good enough reason. He wondered, for one uneasy second, if he had done something.

'I've something to tell you,' she began again.

He waited patiently.

Sarah groaned inwardly. He was not going to help her. 'It's about our Betty!'

He stiffened now. All alert.

'What about her?'

Sarah shook her head. She lost courage. How *did* one break such news gently?

'What is it then? Tell me woman!'

'Our Betty's with child!'

He stared at her, stupefied in horror.

'But she's only a child herself . . .!' his expression changed, hardening as he stood, and towered over her. 'Where is she? Who did it?' he shouted.

Sarah also stood. She moved to put her back

35

to the hovel's one exit.

'I sent her out a bit!'

'Out? You mean she's come back from Mayo's?'

Sarah nodded. 'Mary Mayo sent her back when she found out. You'd have done the same.'

He lifted a fist and smashed it into his other palm, grinding his teeth, his eyes flaming.

'Who did it? Tell me woman! He has to answer to me!'

'Joseph! Sit down! Let me talk to you—please!' and she pushed him back on the stool.

'Who did it?'

His voice was coldly quiet now. The rage was suppressed. This frightened her more than anything. She would have preferred him to storm and rage.

He looked at her. 'I'll only ask you once more, woman! Who?'

'Young Johnnie Mayo,' she whispered. There, it was out now!

Before her appalled eyes, he changed. His face and neck went bright red. The muscles stood out in rigid bands. His eyes narrowed and, with flaring nostrils, he breathed in short bursts.

Sarah touched his left arm, the muscle was like a stone beneath the wet clothing.

'Joseph?'

He did not hear her. Weeks, months and years of cruel misfortune had sent the hate cancer deep into his soul. Even Sarah could not reach him now. She had no idea of the extent of his loathing for the name of Mayo. This bitter news was the final blow.

He did not feel her touch his arm; he did not even see her now. With a snarl of obscenity he swung her aside and stormed from the hovel. He stood a second. The damp air clung to his body. Then with large strides he vanished from her sight and strode towards the trees.

His mind still functioned enough to remember what Sarah had said. He guessed Betty had been sent to hide while the news was broken. There was only one place for her to hide. His ears picked up the sounds of muffled sobbing.

Moving with surprising quietness he skirted two bushes and approached the oak tree. He caught a glimpse of a torn skirt and a soiled cloak. It was Sarah's.

He walked softly round the tree and gripped the girl's arm. She jumped with shock, uttering a shrill scream. Then she relaxed for a second as she recognized him. Her hand went to her mouth and instinctively she tried to draw away. Fright expanded the pupils of her eyes: fresh terror constricted her throat muscles.

'It's true then?' he growled down at her. 'That Mayo pup has had his way with you?'

'Answer me, blast you!' He shook her.

She struggled futilely. Then she nodded.

A look of disgust crossed his face. He smashed his hand across her face, and back again in two viciously stinging blows. Her head rocked with pain and shock. Her eyes bulged. Then nature stepped in and she fainted.

He looked at her for a second or two, lifted his head and turned peering through the trees. He thought he had heard a sound. His rage bubbled more fiercely now that he had used his hands. The two blows had been satisfying but his revenge demanded more . . . much more.

He thought about James Mayo. What did he value most? His son and that grey mare. Mayo had to be hurt as *he* had been hurt. The pain had to be enormous to cover everything which had happened in the past few years. The blows he would strike now must knife into that stone heart. No matter how long he lived Mayo would never recover.

The clouds had lifted slightly. Sniffing at the air he guessed the rain would ease off for a few hours. He knew the movements of the Mayos. That precious mare would be sent out for exercise and he guessed that the rider would be the boy. Where would he ride? He considered this, brain working furiously. Then he glanced down at the girl. The boy would know she had gone. He would guess why. If he had any spunk in him he would come to see her.

Joseph Howard looked to the left. The trees

were thick here, divided by a wide ride which in turn led to Mayo's place. Surely if the boy came it would be from that direction? He sprang forward, breathing hard now with anticipation. The ambush must be good.

Joseph Howard stopped, eyeing his position. The ride had narrowed because of the pressing trees. For four hundred yards it was a strip barely three feet wide. It presented him with an ideal situation. The grass was such that, rain or not, any horseman worth his salt would canter if not gallop down its tempting stretch. Directly opposite him, two stout trees faced each other. One was a birch the other a younger beech.

Coldly, calculating now, Joseph eyed the trees. He stooped, drew an imaginery line with his eyes then, feeling in his pocket, removed the strong ball of twine and knife he always carried. Working carefully, with complete concentration, he fastened one end of the twine to the beech tree. Backing up, he left the other end lying on the earth behind the birch. Listening intently he worked swiftly to cover the twine with dead leaves, twigs and patches of mud. Then stepping back to one side, he eyed his work. The twine was almost invisible to his eye. No horse-man could possibly see it.

He picked up the loose end and squatting on his heels in the gloom he waited. There was never a thought that the boy might not come. He would come. The woods were a fair place to ride on such a day. Rider and animal were sheltered from the biting wind and there was little likelihood of other persons prowling around in such weather.

He waited with the natural patience of the killer lion after its prey. His appetite for revenge was the most consuming passion he had ever experienced.

CHAPTER THREE

The mare picked her passage daintily. From a distance her pure grey colour blended with the overcast sky. She champed on the snaffle bit, one ear going backwards and then forwards, intent upon her rider and his mood. She felt a tiny nudge at her flanks. Instantly responsive she swung into a rolling canter. Ears pricked now, eyes bold and bright, small head with flaring nostrils and dished nose—she carried herself with the regal pride of the pure bred Arabian.

John loved the grey mare. No other horse even remotely compared to her but, for once, he sat oblivious to the charm of her ride. He was too engrossed in his own thoughts. A few hours ago, the knowledge that a wench he had loved was to have a child was interesting but not startling. Yet quite suddenly his emotions had transformed. This was not just any serving girl. This was Betty Howard. Sweet, gentle Betty who had shown no fear or hesitation for him. A Betty who would make a loving wife. A wife of his own choosing.

He wondered at his past, callous stupidity. Why had it taken him so long to analyse and understand his feelings? He loved Betty. He would never love anyone else. A life without her at his side was plainly unthinkable. The problems ahead appalled him.

That his father would approve such a match, he knew to be out of the question. Even thinking such a thought made sweat appear across his forehead. His mother would side with him, but her feebleness would provide little real tangible help. What he had to do he must do himself.

'Wed Betty Howard I will—if she'll have me!' he vowed.

This new thought made him draw back on the reins. The mare slithered to a halt and stood patiently waiting.

'What if she turns me down?' the thought horrified him. 'Betty left Mayo's under a cloud of disgrace and fear. She might loathe me, despise me, scorn me!'

He ground his teeth together, cursing himself soundly. Why had he not understood his feelings before and spoken sooner to Betty?

His father! John Mayo frowned. There would be a row if nothing else but, his mind decided, nothing would make him deviate from his chosen path now.

A baby! His child! He touched the mare with his heels and she bounced into her springy canter again. They rode up the fields heading towards the woods and the direct and shortest route to Betty's home.

He slowed the mare back to a walk. Under her hooves the sodden ground squelched. The mare snorted slightly. The grass was ticklish to her feet. She wanted to bound forward and thrash along in a gallop, but she was too well trained to disobey her rider. She jingled fretfully at the snaffle and twitched her tail with impatience.

The trees gradually thickened, bunching together in groups then extending in an unbroken line of dark trunks. Overhead the branches reached out and touched each other, murmuring in the wind. Old leaves tumbled down, thickening the rich carpet underfoot.

John turned the mare to the left and nudged her into a canter. They were on the ride. Now for a gallop!

The mare felt his change of mood, swung up her head and danced in excitement. She bounded forward. Eyes sparkling, nostrils flaring extra wide, ears pricked forward, keen and alert. Her legs thrashed down as she increased speed. Her neck extended, her tail flowed out almost horizontal.

The boy eased his weight out of the saddle.

His knees gripped the saddle flaps, heels low, hands just feeling the reins each side of the mare's neck. His hair tumbled forward, his cheeks reddened and he laughed wildly. This was the way to live. This was the supreme joy, being on the best horse in the world, going at a flat-out gallop to see the girl who was to be his wife.

He yelled with excitement, drummed with his heels and the mare increased her speed yet again. They were moving fast now, chunks of mud flew in every direction, a thin line of sweat could be seen dappling her grey coat.

The grass ride narrowed until the trees allowed just enough passage for a rider. They flew over the rich green carpet, hurtling down to where two trees stood almost parallel to each other.

The mare suddenly twitched one ear. She raised her head an inch and looked to the left. Her nerves tensed as her instinct warned of danger but it was too late to halt their wild pace.

With exact precision Joseph Howard jerked the strong twine inches from the mare's flailing hooves. She saw it and, at the last second, endeavoured to jump. The powerful hocks thrust downwards but her hind hooves slithered unable to make a purchase on the mud. Then the twine slapped against her knees as rigid as a stone bar.

The mare felt herself falling and tried to

turn her head sideways. She had no time. She fell forward, straight and true, throwing the boy from the saddle. Her dainty muzzle touched the mud. Her fast, moving body ploughed on and, unable to stand such strain, her neck snapped. She was dead before the whole of her body landed.

John Mayo had no idea what was happening. He felt the mare going under him then his body was leaving the saddle, arcing into the air. He caught a floating glimpse of a dark figure standing behind a tree, a dark line of something under the mare's legs, then the ground came up hard and fast. He hit the wet grass with a bump and rolled over and over. His body carved a trail of torn grass, water and spray before he lurched to a halt and lay spread-eagled on the ride. For five seconds he lay still, his mind bemused. Then, with the quick resilence of youth, he scrambled to his feet and stood swaying slightly. He looked back down the ride trying hard to understand what had happened.

The mare lay ominously still and in a flash he knew she had broken her neck. Now he remembered a sharp crack as he flew through the air. The mare dead! Horror and misery snatched at his throat. He felt a dampness behind his eyes. The mare dead? It couldn't be true!

Then he saw the man. A muddy, soaked figure who, at first, he did not recognize.

Slowly, recognition came to John. Howard stood watching. In one hand was a tangle of twine. John refused to believe what he saw. The whole thing was too horrible to be true. A person didn't deliberately set out to kill a horse—or did they? He raised his eyes to Joseph Howard who had started advancing towards him with slow, deliberate steps.

There was a look about him which John Mayo recognized. It promised violence and revenge. It was meant for him. The man was snarling, teeth bared, like a wild animal. His eyes were hot pools of red fire, fists balled into bony clubs.

The boy sprang forward, trembling with fury. The man sprang at the same time. They clashed in a whirl of flailing arms, kicking legs and snapping teeth. They fought like two dogs over a bone. Neither was human. The man struck with his great fists, hammering the boy's face, splitting the lips and bursting both nostrils. The boy fought back in wild desperation. He, too, hit, kicked and gouged in his fury. With his youth he was everywhere.

To the older man he was a wraith of energy and activity. Howard fell back a step, arms in front of his neck and face, while his narrowed eyes watched for an opening. He had the strength, he had the wisdom gained from other fights in his youth. The boy could not keep up this pace for long.

John sprang forward again, his right leg

coming up in a vicious kick aimed at Howard's crotch. The man grasped the foot, twisted and flung all his strength into throwing the boy off his balance. Then, with surprising speed he jumped on him, both hands straining to grasp his neck.

John Mayo felt sudden fear. His first wild rage had abated. He was now fighting in a cold fury but on the ground, under the heavier man. He realized his disadvantage. They fought in complete silence.

The boy felt two hands slide round his throat. He struggled to move, kicking with his legs, his hands working like pistons in the man's face.

John suddenly knew the fear of death then. He stopped hammering with his fists and struggled to break the grip of the fingers round his neck. His eyes bulged. His chest swelled for air and, quite suddenly, he knew he was going to die.

The man's fingers tightened even further. Pain of an unbelievable intensity exploded in the boy's brain, shattering all his senses in a bang. His lips strained to form a word. His throat gave one last contortion of protest and he died.

Joseph Howard slowly released his grip. Breathing hard, he stood, leg muscles twitching. The top half of his body was covered with his blood and that from the dead boy. The woods were still. Not a leaf moved or bird called. He turned aside as pains retched in his guts. He vomited, uttering gasping moans. Slowly, the paroxisms ebbed and, leaning against the beech tree, Joseph Howard's brain cooled. He returned to the land of the sane.

As the drumming in his temples receded, his breathing steadied and he turned and coolly looked down, first at the dead boy and then the still mare. This *was* revenge! The sweet taste for which he had waited so long. The dirt, blood and fury had been like a drug. Now he was cooling rapidly. Reason overtook passion with a burst of clarity that left him appalled.

'What have I done?' he cried in anguish.

Slowly, moving with infinite care, he bent over the body. Carefully he touched the boy's cheek. The face, now a grotesque mask with a swollen and protruding tongue, nauseated him.

'I have done right! I have done right! I have killed a monster!' he shouted.

In vain he fought to convince himself, yet growing larger with every second came the realization of the enormity of his action. He had murdered!

The sweet and sickly taste filled his mouth again as his bile rose. He turned away and stared at the dead mare. Now flat and covered with streaked mud she was ugly and repulsive.

He leaned against a tree, rested his forehead on his hands and shuddered. Great sobs racked his body until his shoulders shook.

47

He cried like a child.

Slowly, the sobs diminished and wiping his eyes with his dirty hands he turned back to look at the scene. For this they would hang him. He was doomed. No matter where he went or what he did, they would find him. They—James Mayo—his vengeance would be too terrible to contemplate. Sarah! Betty! They must live without him.

He heard a sound, whipped around, then darted behind a tree. His heart sent fresh waves thudding into his ears. The wind brushed in the tree tops. It had started raining again. There was movement.

'Joseph! Joseph! Are you there?'

He flinched. Sarah! Of course, come to find him and Betty. He hesitated, not knowing whether to run, hide or stay. While he dithered she came into view, pushing her way through the trees on an animal track. She stepped into the ride and halted. Horror chased over her face. One hand covered her mouth as she took in the scene, read the signs and looked at her husband.

Joseph made towards her.

Gently, he touched her hand, his fingers begging, his eyes beseeching. She looked up at him, mute and frightened. He drew her onto his chest, kissed the top of her hair, then held her at arm's length.

'It had to be,' he said quietly.

'But to kill him! Oh Joe, they'll hang you for

this!'

'I expect they will but I'll give them a run for their money first. Sarah, you're on your own now, you know that?'

She looked at him too bewildered and horrified to grasp the full truth.

'Listen, I've not much time,' he told her urgently. 'I'll come back with you. Let me have a crust then I'll be gone.'

'Where will you go?' she asked him terrified, clinging to his arm.

'Go? I'll go to Bristol. Easier to get lost there. Then I'll try and get on a ship to America. I'll send for you.'

'Oh Joe, you'll never do it. You know you won't. And me and Betty . . .?' She started to weep.

He soothed her as best as he could.

'When I'm gone go see the Squire. We got on all right in the old days, me and him, and I know he doesn't think all that much of Mayo. He'll help. Get you a little cottage somewhere. Have Betty with you. Look after her—and the baby,' he said quietly, knowing he would never see his grandchild now. He also knew instinctively that with his going Sarah might indeed be better off. A woman and daughter left alone in his family's circumstances would engender both scandal and pity. With pity should come practical help.

'Are you listening? You'll have to get work, regular work too, but maybe the Squire's wife can help out there. At least you'd not have to go to the workhouse. I'm sorry, Sarah, lass. I love you. Why did it have to come to this?'

She comforted him now, suddenly philosophical for the future. This was the end for her. Life could never be the same again. What James Mayo would do horrified her. What had so recently happened appalled her. But Howard was her man. In these last precious minutes their love for each other was as strong as at the beginning.

'Oh Joe! Joe!'

'Where's Betty?' he asked.

She nodded to their rear.

'I sent her back to the hut,' she told him. They walked, arm in arm for the last time.

*　　　*　　　*

Inside the hovel she hastened to wrap the little food she had, tying it in a rough square of cloth. Joseph looked around him. This filthy wet hovel was suddenly so very precious. He watched Sarah, bustling about making too many nervous actions with her hands. He could see she was trying to hide her fear while Betty huddled in the corner, staring at him in terror.

'Betty girl, what's done is done,' he said to her awkwardly. 'Don't think too badly of me?' he pleaded, but the girl was in shock. She just gazed back at him in awe.

50

'Here Joe, take it and go!'

'Sarah!'

Then she was in his arms, crying softly, her heart breaking. He felt a lump block his throat. A salt taste ran down his cheeks into his bloodied lips.

He gave her one last gentle kiss, looked at his daughter, ducked under the sack and vanished from their sight.

Sarah rushed to look out but already he was gone, melting into the rain and gloom as evening approached. In a daze she sat on the chair. Reaction was setting in.

The rain streamed down again, splattering at the hovel's inadequate roof. Life without Joe—how *could* she carry on? They had been through so much together. Without him life would be sterile because she knew she would never never see him again. She dare not think of the future. She just sat, huddled, frozen and waiting.

*   *   *

Joseph Howard ran wildly for half a mile then stopped to catch his breath. Already it was quite dark. He would have the whole night to put distance between himself and those woods. He must hide by day.

He considered his position. It was hopeless. When he had told Sarah he would go to America it had been a foolish statement to try

51

and bolster her morale.

To the north were the Cotswold Hills. High, wide open spaces. No place for a man on the run. To the west was the width of the mighty river Severn. If he could only cross the river and get to the Forest of Dean his chances would be brighter. He had no money for a ferry and no man could swim that treacherous river and live. To the east the town of Chipping Sodbury with the turnpike road to Bristol through Iron Acton.

He hesitated. Which way to go for the best? While he thought he ate the little food then wrapped the cloth around his neck. Somehow the soaking material seemed to hold Sarah's touch. He was miserably wet through to his skin and cold to the marrow of his bones.

He made up his mind. Bristol it must be, over the country. Perhaps, if he were lucky, he could hide up tomorrow and steal into Bristol during the next night.

He walked on, forcing himself to keep a steady, brisk pace. He waded through the water-logged fields, slipped into over-flowing ditches. He started to warm up with the exertion.

'As long as I keep moving,' he muttered to himself, but he was tiring. The fight and emotional shock of the whole dreadful day were hitting back at him.

He halted as he came upon a wide track. He guessed it led to a farm and there would be dogs around. He turned away, wondering at the time and how far he had come.

Faintly a greyness smudged the sky as dawn approached. So soon! He thought he must have come six miles but it was difficult to estimate. He started looking for somewhere to hide. He must rest and sleep. He could go no further. His limbs were trembling. He reeled as he walked.

Half a mile ahead he saw a cluster of trees. He headed slowly for them, his spirits lifting as he realized this was another wood. It was dawn now and he hastened to reach cover, driving his aching legs forward relentlessly.

He pushed his way in among the trees, sighing with relief then started hunting for a hide. The growth was not thick enough and the trees stood too far apart.

The bushes would not give cover to a mouse. He started to fret with worry, then he saw the tall oak. It was an old tree. Its lowest branch just above his head. The foliage was still relatively thick and he saw a fork where he could spend the daylight hours.

He staggered around, studying the tree and also noting his footmarks. There was nothing he could do about them though. He must hope for more rain to wash his tracks away.

He bent at the knees and eyed the lowest branch. With a wild spring, one hand grasped the wood and he scrambled at the trunk with his feet, pulled with the other hand and hauled himself inelegantly into the boughs. He leaned against the trunk, shaking and trembling with fatigue.

As he settled down in the fork, his arms were twitching as his eyes closed. With one hand clasped around a comforting branch he drifted into an uneasy sleep. The cold stole into his joints, numbing them, freezing his skin. Even asleep, he shivered in gentle spasms.

CHAPTER FOUR

For the rest of his life James Mayo was to remember the horror of that October day. Not until evening when it started to get dark did he begin to wonder. His son, after seeing to his mount, always came in to find his father and talk with him. It was odd that John was so late. Perhaps he was fussing with the mare. James Mayo debated whether to walk out and find him but the fire was comfortable.

He awoke with a start. It was quite dark and he pulled his large turnip watch from his breeches pocket. Where was John? He wondered if he had gone upstairs to see his mother first. Puzzled, he stood and went into the kitchen.

'Have you seen Master John, Martha?' he asked the cook as she skilfully turned the meat.

Fat, red-cheeked and hot from her work, Martha wanted no interruption at this crucial stage of her cooking.

'No, master. Maybe he's out in the stables still,' she suggested, knowing John's love for the horses.

Like all the workers she had a soft spot for the boy and even some regard for his father which, though, she never showed. She had come to Mayos as a serving wench when the master himself was but a boy. They had grown up together and she understood him more than most other people. She also admired him. Martha was a sharp woman. She knew how things stood between the master and his wife. And she had a good idea why Betty Howard had suddenly departed.

James Mayo grunted to himself. Most likely the boy was in the stables. He would go and see for himself. Then the door had opened and one of the older grooms stood looking up at him, anxious and scared.

'Master, the grey mare isn't back yet with Master John!'

'Not back yet!' snapped James Mayo, feeling a prickling at the back of his neck. The pair had been gone for hours now. They should have been back long ago. There must have been an accident. John was hurt.

'Go get the men. Saddle my cob! We must look for my son. Martha, say nothing of this to the mistress,' he warned, mindful of the latest pregnancy.

He hurried into thick clothing. The rain was streaming down again. He whistled to the house dog; a large brute of indeterminate breeding whose teeth and scenting capabilities he respected. For the first time in years he felt fear dab at his heart.

John was far too good a horseman to be thrown easily and the mare was a gentle ride. She had never thrown a buck in her life. Yet John must be lying injured somewhere—and on a night like this!

It suddenly occurred to him that he did not know where to look. He bit his lip, thinking quickly. The best thing would be to split into parties unless he could guess where John might have ridden.

He thought back to their last meeting, going over their talk. Betty Howard! Would John have ridden to see her? No, why should he—but—a doubt lingered. Young blood was still hot blood even on a day like this.

He hurried outside and sniffed up at the sky, trying to gauge the rain's mood. Would this downpour last long? The lanterns were lit. He mounted his cob, issued terse instructions to his men and rode out into the night still busy with his thoughts.

John would have ridden through the trees in the woods. That was the quickest way to the Howards and also the best riding turf. He

56

headed purposefully to the left, his men clomping after him.

They did not have to search for long but in that weather they tired quickly. The men had strung out in a long line, their lanterns dancing blobs of yellow in the rain. James halted the cob when the voice knifed through the air slightly ahead of him and to one side. A yellow light moved from left to right and he trotted in that direction.

They had been found at last! Relief caught in his throat. He saw it was Barker, his cowman.

'You've found them both? They're all right?'

Barker looked up at his master. His face ashen with shock. The words caught in his throat. He could not speak. 'Well, answer me man!'

'Yes, master, we've found them all right. Deep in the woods,' and Barker's voice dried up again.

James Mayo felt acute apprehension. 'What is it? Confound you man, have you lost your tongue!' he roared in worry.

'The boy's dead and so is the mare!'

James Mayo stared down at him, uncomprehending. His mind reeled with shock. Dead? John dead? What fool talk was this? Then he closely studied Barker's face. The white cheeks and trembling lips. Even the suspicion of moisture in his eyes. Everyone had loved his son. The hand holding the lantern was trembling strongly.

A horrible doubt rose in the pit of his stomach to gag in his throat. There had to be some stupid mistake. Other lanterns were visible now, clustered together as if a group of people were frozen.

He heeled the cob forward. His men looked up at him not daring to speak, too horrified by their find. One pointed with his hand and led the way with his lantern. The others followed in a silent group at the cob's heels. James Mayo's heart thumped with terror. Dear God, what were they going to show him?

The ride narrowed. The lantern stabbed the gloom like a yellow knife. The rain lashed down, beating on the leaves. The wind had started to moan through the branches. It was eerie, enough to frighten any man.

He stopped as he saw them. The shock hit him in the guts. Then like a robot, he dismounted.

James Mayo walked forward and slowly knelt by the body. Stone cold, wet and quite grotesque with thick, swollen tongue and distended eyes. He picked up the cold hands in turn, noting the split knuckles and gashed skin. At least his son had gone down fighting. A Mayo to the bitter end. He would have marked his murderer.

Dear John, what a way to go! And at his young age! Lying here in the mud and filth waiting for his father to find his body. Waiting for his father to come and avenge his premature death. His beloved son dead! He bent his head forward, a groan tearing from his lips. Tears burst down his face. Who, when and why?

Slowly, he controlled himself. He looked towards the mare. Something was wrong. That queer angle of her neck.

'Broken!' he muttered.

A hand touched his arm gently. So strung were his nerves he actually jumped.

'Master! Look! Some twine was tied to that tree. Someone hid behind this one,' Barker informed him, pointing with his free hand.

James Mayo nodded to himself. It had all been so diabolically simple, but who and why? An uneasy thought nudged at him. A pregnant girl, the daughter of a man who hated him. Surely not even Howard would take such a revenge against a mere boy? But the thought started to harden. His face changed. Fire blazed in his eyes. His lips and jaw froze and his neck muscles stood out in iron bands. His men watched in awe. They did not really like him but they certainly respected their master. This murder of his son was too much for them to stomach. To a man they were behind him.

'Make a litter and take him home,' he told them.

Mary! How to break such news to her?

'One of you go over to the Squire's and tell him what's happened. Barker, I'll want a fresh horse as soon as dawn comes. The rest of you men go home and rest. We go out again in the morning.'

'Master, who?' and Barker stopped nervously.

'I don't know for sure but I'll soon find out. Look, Barker, go over to the Howard's place and see who is there. Don't say what you've found here to start with then come straight back to me. Talk to no one else!' he warned him.

At fifty years of age Barker was his senior and most reliable worker, having been on Mayo's as long as Martha. He was both loyal and close-mouthed.

Barker nodded quietly, turned and vanished, his thoughts whirling. He did not like this errand but his personal fancies were of no concern where murder was concerned. The young master dead! It was horrible.

The trouble was Barker also liked the Howards. He remembered back to the good old days when they were well-to-do farmers in their own right. If Joseph were involved—and his heart quailed. He could be mean could Joseph and coupled with his natural Howard bitterness he could turn ugly.

Was there more to this than he knew? He shook his head, ill at ease, afraid of what he was to learn.

The other farm hands made a crude litter for the body. James Mayo watched them, choking with grief and cold fury. Someone was going to pay dearly for this day's work if it took the rest of his life to catch him. He walked round the mare, studying where she lay, then he back-tracked up the ride. Squatting he read the story. A flat-out gallop, his son probably laughing with fun, then sudden, unexpected death. He noted the mare's last tracks, the skid mark from her hind hooves. So she had sensed danger at the last and tried to save herself.

He rode back slowly, the cob quiet as if sensing his mood. He sat rigid and straight in the saddle. Shoulders square, head high, brain churning, his grief gradually giving way to an implacable rage. It *had* to be Howard—but he knew he must wait for Barker's return.

The farmhouse was ablaze with lights as he rode into the yard and dismounted. They had taken his son inside. He found the body lying on a couch, gently covered with a clean, white tablecloth. Martha stood at the boy's head, tears streaming silently down her face.

They looked at each other. Master and servant. And suddenly their gulf in class had gone.

'You haven't told her?' James asked, nodding upstairs.

Martha shook her head. 'I thought it had better come from you. Who?' and she nodded to the body.

'I'm not sure yet,' James Mayo told her slowly.

Mary. Now she had to be told. With heavy heart and slow tread he walked towards their bedroom. Outside, by the door, he paused trying to marshal his thoughts. Just how did one break such news to any mother—let alone one expecting another child?

Mary lifted herself up on the pillows as he entered the room. Her heart stopped beating, of that she was quite positive. She had never seen such an expression on her husband's face. She knew with maternal instinct.

'It's John!' she cried. She saw rage on his face, weariness and anguish.

'James!'

He turned to her. However he put the news she would receive a shock. She must have this baby safely now.

'John's dead!'

Mary stared at him, frowning, her lips parting slightly, her eyes widening. Turning she flopped back on the pillow, looking up at the ceiling, coldness stole over her heart.

Her dear boy dead!

'How?' she whispered watching him.

She saw his brows knit and the rage flash in his eyes.

Slowly, choosing his words with great care, James Mayo told her what he thought she should know. He omitted the more horrific details. He watched her like a hunting hawk. What would this shock do to the baby? Mary was too old to be sure of conceiving again.

This child must live! Mayo had to have an heir.

'But who—and why?' she asked him, falteringly.

James paused. There had been friendship of a sorts between Mary and Sarah in the old days.

'I don't know,' he told her truthfully. 'But I'll find him and he'll hang for this day's work. Mary, don't you fret now. This is my job to clean up. You must think of the baby.'

Mary flashed him a sharp look. Of course, the baby! The unborn child was of double importance now! Was she nothing but a brood mare? Sudden resentment surged through her. As if she cared about the baby when her dear boy lay dead downstairs.

Johnnie dead! Dear, sweet Johnnie, who had been everything a mother could wish for in a son. Kind, considerate and gay. A wonderful spirit in the home. Tears started to flow in two silent rivers down her cheeks as her heart swelled with grief.

'I want to see him,' she said, sitting up again.

'No!' he snapped too quickly. She must not see that ugly body.

'Why not? He's my son, too. I bore him— not you!' Mary cried, as for the first time in her life her spirit rose against him.

'I want to see him! I will see him!' and now her voice had risen high into a hysterical scream.

He held her shoulders. 'No, Mary! You must stay here!'

63

'But why? Why. *Why?*' she cried, struggling against his powerful grip until his fingers were pinching her shoulders through her flannel nightgown.

'Why don't you want me to see him? What does he look like then? What *has* happened? You've not told me everything and I am his mother!' she accused.

He bowed his head and sighed. She did indeed have the mother's right to know all. Slowly, he told her every detail even including his suspicions about Joseph Howard.

Mary listened to him quietly. Her hysteria abated as an inner strength she was unaware she possessed took control of her mind. This was the truth. Every foul and sordid detail of John's last day on earth.

With unusual tenderness he put his great arms around her slight shoulders. She stiffened and held back for a second, unaccustomed to such a gesture, then love flared. Feeling which she had thought long dead returned to her as their eyes met and locked. For the first time in many years Mary saw the James who had courted her so long ago. The hard, cruel look was gone. It had been banished by grief. He wanted *her* now. No one but her! With flaring instinct Mary knew that their positions were irrevocably reversed.

John! she cried out silently, but only James was there. And love flared again.

They were closer now than they had been in years.

'Why does this have to be?' Mary thought.

James sensed her feelings on identical tracks to his. He could not last remember when he had felt so genuinely affectionate towards his wife. He held her at arm's length, looking at her face and studying her eyes. She returned his look then wanly smiled up at him.

'Oh, James! What happened to us?'

'Whatever it was won't happen again!' he told her firmly, meaning every word. He stood, one hand holding hers. 'You stay here, wife. This is man's work now.'

'Are you sure it was Joseph Howard?'

He sighed. 'If it wasn't him, then God only knows who killed John or why. I've sent Barker to find out what he can. I'll be leaving at first light with the men. Whoever it was won't get far.'

'And his child yet to be born!' Mary remarked thoughtfully. 'From what that girl told me it will be born about the same time as ours.'

'What a stinking, foul mess! I never thought my first grandchild would arrive like this. A bastard and his father murdered! He or she will have no claim on Mayo's though. Our own comes first, Mary,' he said grimly.

'There, I think I hear Barker. Try not to fret too much. I'll send Martha up with a toddy.'

He left her reluctantly. Barker looked up as

he came into the kitchen.

'Well?'

'I've not much to tell, Master. Joseph Howard isn't there. But the girl and her mother are. They've both been crying a lot. Sarah wouldn't tell me anything and she wouldn't let me speak to the girl either. She just sat there, looking right through me as if I was the devil himself.'

'I see!' and James rubbed his jaw thoughtfully. 'We'll set out at first light. Take all the dogs in a pack. Go back to the woods and try to pick up some kind of a trail. I want you men armed though. Remember, I want this killer alive. I want to see a hanging!' he spat deliberately.

*   *   *

They left at first light, James Mayo mounted on a big, angular bay mare with a fretful eye and a humped back. The men followed his lead, on foot and mounted, the dogs snarling around the horses' hooves, making them rear and snort. Every man had a cudgel.

The wind had dropped a little but was still fresh, blowing straight down from the Cotswolds and the North. It was cold, stabbing into the men's clothes. They shivered with it and the anticipation of the hunt to come. This was something that would be talked about for generations.

The farmer led his men to edge of the woods and loosened the dogs. They bayed in and around a circle, not sure of their quarry. Something caught one hound's nose. He sniffed, showing keen curiosity, howled with excitement and ran forward eagerly. The rest followed in a noisy bunch.

The men brought up the rear, careful not to go ahead and foul the fragile line of scent. The dogs stopped frequently to cast around and once Barker shouted, pointing to a muddy footprint. James Mayo nodded as he studied it. Whoever made that track had been in a hurry. They found other prints here and there. It became obvious, after a while, that the track's owner was tiring. His trail became erratic and though the dogs frequently lost the poor scent the men had no trouble in following the trail.

James shouted to Barker, who was riding a thick-set pony. 'He's heading towards Bristol, cross-country!'

The dogs had started to lope ahead quickly now, barking eagerly. Their blood was up and, in full daylight now, they passed a farm and headed for some woods.

The leading dog burst among the trees, the pack at his heels. The riders slowed their horses to a walk. The woods echoed with noise as the dogs set up a frantic row.

'They've found him!' Barker shouted in excitement.

The dogs milled around the large tree, two

of them stood on their hind legs, pawing at the trunk. The men gathered round in a circle, dismounting with the exception of James Mayo.

'Treed!' the farmer murmured to himself, then he turned to Barker.

'Whoever it is up there—get him down. Call off those dogs. The rest of you men be ready to hold him. It might not be who we want,' he added, but a rapid surge of blood crimsoned his forehead. This was the killer. With this knowledge he also knew instinctively it would be Howard.

Barker disappeared up into the tree. There was some kind of a tussle then rapidly a man came slithering down to drop on the ground. He trembled as if he had the ague. The dogs howled, eager to bound forward but three of the men beat them back. The rest stood around in stony silence, waiting a cue from their master.

James sat square in his saddle, unable to remove his eyes from Joseph Howard. He took in the bloody face and torn hands. The man on the ground looked back up at him, lips bared in a defiant snarl.

He felt hands dragging him roughly to his feet. Men he had known all his life; men whom he had numbered as friends, but now he saw their open hostility. He was beyond the pale. They stood with the farmer.

Staggering a little, he faced James Mayo,

eyes burning with hatred. Saliva trickled from the corner of his mouth. He faced the farmer in cold rage, holding his eyes.

'I made one mistake only, Mayo. Just one mistake! It should have been you and not that whoring brat of yours!' he snarled, then spat. All the evil of the world was in that gesture.

James Mayo waved one hand. 'Take him!' he said in a low, cold voice. Without more ado he turned and rode back through the trees to his home. His mind was a racing whirlpool of thoughts. How exactly *had* such hatred been incurred? Surely not the land? He had only been astute! Howard could have done the same.

He thought of the girl and her mother. James Mayo was no coward but he flinched at telling Sarah. She would have to know though, and the better such news came from him.

What would be the outcome of all this?

Betty he thoroughly disliked. He had seen too much of her father in her. She had always made him uneasy when at Mayo's.

*   *   *

He halted and dismounted, holding the reins in one hand. The hovel was as silent as the grave. To his annoyance he felt fear touching his heart. Swallowing hastily, he called:

'Sarah!'

He waited, then slowly the sacking was

69

pushed aside and Sarah Howard faced him. She was white-faced and haggard, but her head was high, jaw tilted, gaze steady.

He hesitated, not knowing how to begin. She stood still, not moving an eyelid, eyes unblinking. This silence further unnerved him. He blurted out words, forgetting the little speech he had been carefully rehearsing.

'We've found your man. He killed my John. He'll be taken into Bristol and hanged.'

Her expression changed. The flicker of hope in her eyes died. Her shoulders sagged and her mouth twisted.

'James Mayo! You've done a bad morning's work! No! You'll hear me out this once, then forever keep out of my way. I curse you and yours. I curse you now for generations to come. This—all this—is your doing. You hounded my man. When times were bad you could have helped. My man in turn tried to help those worse off than us. Did you? No, all you thought about was getting the land while it was cheap. The land and the power that goes with it! You were richer than us, Mayo. You could have lent us money to tide us over. You could easily have ignored what we owed. You drove us down to this!' and she spat the words out, pointing to the hovel. 'Then, not satisfied, your boy takes my girl. I thought, at least, you'd have the decency to protect her under your roof. But you don't care. You're as randy as that brat of yours. Oh, yes, I know all about your meanderings and other women. Your poor wife! And where's it got you? Where do you stand with your lust for money, land and those grey horses? Well, I hope you're satisfied now! You've still got your money—and the land, too! But you've no mare, no son—and your wife's a bad breeder. I hate you, Mayo. Do you realize just how much?'

A trickle of ice had encased his spine while his face had turned scarlet. No living person had ever dared speak to him like this.

'But Sarah, I'll help you and the girl. I've nothing against either of you and she's carrying my grandson!' he remonstrated hurriedly.

'Your grandson!' Sarah stormed, advancing towards him. 'What right do you think you'll ever have to a grandson? I'll see that the child knows who you are and what you are. I'll teach hatred that will make you turn in your grave if ever you get that far and don't burn in hell, where you belong!' she raged up at him.

'But woman—!'

'You are evil, James Mayo! There's a bad line in your blood somewhere. I'll make sure I'll stamp it out in this child. Your grandchild indeed!' Sarah laughed hysterically.

'Think about that! Imagine, a child brought up to hate its grandfather. How does that feel?' she jeered at him.

He flinched, averting her gaze. His face white. He could actually feel her aura of hatred.

71

'But you have no money. I'll—'

'You'll what? Give charity? Oh, we're not much nowadays, Mayo, I grant you that. But I think we might still have some real friends left. Friends who don't make war against women. I'll tell you something else, Mayo. You'd better guard that precious land of yours. Guard it and hold it tightly because I'll do everything I can to take it from you. If I can't do it then I'll teach the child so that he can teach his children. And when you lose the land think—it will be coming back to its rightful owners. Your land and your precious horses. Everything comes to him who waits and the Howards will wait for what is rightfully theirs! I hope I live to see that day. If I don't, some Howard, sometime, somewhere, will take back what is rightfully ours. I loathe you, Mayo. I hate your name and everything it stands for. You are evil and dirt. My Joe had his faults but he never ground another man beneath his boots. He's dead—oh, no—I don't mean really dead because you'll see to that, won't you? You'll want your fun at a hanging. To me and my girl though he is dead right now. You can do nothing more to him or me. What is done in the future will be on you and yours. Now get away from me!' and lifting her head she spat up at him.

James Mayo felt his anger rising. She was making a fool of him when he had only come with the world's best intentions.

Flustered, undignified, he scrambled into his saddle, turned, opened his mouth to speak, saw the look in her eyes and decided to depart.

He left, feeling two icy eyes boring into his back. What a fool he had been to come. He should have left the job to Barker. He had allowed that woman to say things to him no one else had ever dared. To hell with the Howards. Let her bring the bastard up against him. What did she think she could do? He was James Mayo of Mayo's, powerful, strong and quite unassailable. Mustering his shredded dignity he rode home.

CHAPTER FIVE

They took Joseph Howard into Bristol to stand trial for murder. He went in chains, heavily guarded like a wild animal. He never saw Sarah again. He knew she might try to come and see him so he sent a message to her, ordering her to stay away. He did not want her to see him chained. She understood. Sarah also wanted to remember him as in the past.

He never stood his trial. Joseph Howard contracted the common gaol fever and, having no further wish to live, allowed himself to die. They took his wasted body out and buried it hastily in an unmarked grave, glad to be saved the expense of legal proceedings. He died unmourned.

James Mayo felt cheated. He had not bargained for this. He had wanted to see his son's murderer hang. There would have been satisfaction. As it was, the whole event had a hollow ring which certainly failed to appease his blood lust.

Young John! Dead two months already! It seemed impossible. All the time James Mayo kept thinking he'd see his boy again. Mayo's was lost without that young, carefree spirit.

There was perpetual gloom in the house itself. Would life never revert back to normality? He would always miss John—and Mary had been affected far worse than he had, at first, thought possible.

There was nothing wrong with her physically. For the first time in many years she was carrying her unborn child superbly. Her morning sickness had stopped abruptly. Ceasing indeed on the day of John's death. James Mayo puzzled about this, failing to see the obvious.

Mary knew she was now the most important person in miles. After many years of being a second-class citizen in her own home she had, at last, attained the status of a queen. Her husband watched her well-being down to the last detail. Nothing was too good for her.

Mary had quickly understood. With her age this would most likely be the last chance to conceive. She was carrying the one and only—

legal—heir to the great farm.

She thrived, enjoying every minute of this pregnancy, and while she thrived she planned for the future. No more second place for her. She was a queen! Her husband no longer aroused fear and awe in her. She was as good as him if not better. He could not produce an heir!

Mary even started to talk to and argue with her man. James, still shocked after his son's death, had no heart to dominate her. Encouraged and emboldened Mary meticulously planned and schemed.

James had always planned and ordered. It was her husband who had seen to John's education and life. She had never once been consulted.

'But things will be different, this time!' Mary promised herself firmly.

Gradually she was getting her husband under her thumb. James was the type of person who respected someone strong enough to stand up to him. Anyone who gave in was despised and brow-beaten.

'I've been a fool. A muddle-headed idiot. I've wasted many years of life but I'll make up for them now. I'll bring this boy up. I'll decide his education and just let James argue!' she told herself grimly.

It never occurred to her she might have a daughter.

What did present itself to her though was

the fact that she was hopelessly ignorant of everyday matters. After her education as a girl she had learned nothing about world affairs. So now she started to pay very close attention to what went on in the world. Regularly James attended the market at Chipping Sodbury. He usually brought home a newspaper, always grumbling though about the stamp tax on them but nevertheless glad to devour the news. He was also an avid listener at the inns and taverns which he visited on Market Days with other farmers and even the gentry.

When Mary gently and cunningly started questioning her husband she found that he was a mine of general and fascinating information.

They started to hold animated evenings together, sitting up late by their country standards. James holding forth on some particular subject; Mary listening intently and storing all her newly-acquired information away to turn over and devour again the next day.

It was this that puzzled and, to some extent, alarmed James Mayo. This need of Mary's for talk and news was so out of character that he worried about her mind.

She was big and clumsy with the child now. So different to the past that, more than once, he found he was a tiny bit in awe of her. Such an alien feeling shocked him.

'What has come over Mary?' he asked himself for the hundredth time. 'Why this thirst for information? A woman's place is running the home. Men decide world affairs,' he told himself, frowning, trying to understand and being too masculine and obtuse to realise that his strong spirit had a rival now.

Mary thought about many things apart from what James told her. She considered the Howards. As she pondered about this family and past events she started to change. A latent fire fanned into flame. She learned how to hate.

Quiet, gentle, spiritless Mary Mayo grew up but with her sudden maturity her character altered—for the worse.

'It's all their fault. That girl led John on. She killed him as much as his father. They're rotten, all of them. I'll make sure this son learns who to trust and who to fight!' she stormed silently.

Even patient Martha puzzled over her mistress but, being female, and also very logical, she came to understand and accept that John's death had a far deeper mental affect on Mary than any of them had considered possible. Not that Martha minded some of the changes. She was glad to see the mistress standing up to her husband now. She liked the spirit and fire which the big-bellied woman could produce.

'It's long overdue that. It's high time someone stood up to you, Master. You're a good man, but a hard one. You've had your own way for too long in this life,' she thought in ironical amusement.

Outside the house their master's change was not so obvious. Only Barker, close and faithful, had some inkling of events in the big house. He was friendly with Martha. They exchanged many views and secrets but their loyalty to the family made their lips seal elsewhere. James Mayo did not realize how lucky he was with his workers.

All he now thought and sweated about was the birth to be. Boy or girl? Live or die? Healthy or abnormal? Dear God, what if Mayo's were left without an heir? So worked up did he become about this major event that he never once considered Betty Howard and his grandchild.

The weeks seemed to pass so slowly. The winter was of extreme severity and food became scarce. Already the potato crop had been lost in the wet autumn and thousands of sheep died from rot. Corn was scarce and if they suffered another bad summer heaven knew what would happen to the country James had told Mary during one of their evening talks.

'Things are worse in the towns. There's thousands out of work with no food or money. They should bring out the troops. I don't know what we pay our taxes for,' he grumbled.

'Is this what you call a depression?' Mary had asked him, knowing perfectly well that it was but wanting to keep James talking on this theme so that she could learn more.

'It was the war that did it. Most expensive we've ever had! And where's it got us?'

'But what about rioters? Will they come here?'

James snorted. 'If they do they die! They've hanged five and transported others for life. They should hang them all. Men should know their place in life. All this complaining because the common land has gone. Saying they can't gather traditional fuels—that's no reason to rampage through the land.'

In the spring it rained again, repeating the devastation of the terrible autumn. Floods developed and summer threatened even more bad weather.

Mary went into labour so suddenly that everyone was taken by surprise. Her pains started in the middle of one appalling stormy night and there was no time for outside assistance to be fetched. James Mayo was thrown into a sweat of panic, stomping backward and forward in the kitchen while Martha attended to her mistress.

It was a quick, almost effortless birth, the healthy boy being born with almost indecent haste and the farmer's relief knew no bounds. Mayo's had its heir again. A fine, strapping boy with well-developed lungs.

He felt great tenderness and affection to his wife as he sat with her all of the next day. Mary marvelled at her baby. So perfect and healthy. If only dear John could see him.

'Shall we call him George?' she asked the equally proud father. 'George John?'

James nodded as he smiled down at her. He was almost happy again, at last. John would never be forgotten, but once again he had an heir. He also had this wonderful refound feeling for his wife.

James thought about the other child, also very newly born. Barker had kept him informed in the last month of events in that direction.

'The other was a boy, too,' he told Mary.

She stiffened as she thought about this. So she had a grandson, did she, but she had no feeling for this other child. That slut of a girl. Iron entered Mary's heart again. It was a cold feeling which would have astonished James if he had known. Mary of old had been so pliant that, even now, James could not accept her complete alteration.

'George will know what those Howards are like. I'll teach him. I'll warn him, right from the start!' she vowed to herself. Mary would never rant or rave. Her gentle methods though would be far more insidious and effective than Sarah's tempestuous outbursts.

'The girl died,' he told Mary one evening.

Mary sniffed. A sniff which was more eloquent than words. 'And Sarah is going to bring the boy up,' James continued, watching his wife for some reaction.

'She's welcome!'

James considered his next words carefully before uttering them.

'The boy is our grandson.'

'He's a bastard and nothing to do with us!' Mary snapped. 'And who says he's any connection with the Mayos? That slut would go with anyone wearing breeches. I don't want to hear anything about that brat!'

James was staggered at the venom in her tone. Shocked, he regarded her, mouth slightly agape.

'But he must be John's child!'

'Rot! Prove it?' Mary challenged him.

'But!'

'No buts, James. John is dead and gone forever. George is our son. There is no other child in our family now, or at any time!' she said ferociously, daring him to rise and fight her back.

The old James would have done this. The old Mary would not have provoked such action in the first place.

He stood up and looked out into the black of the night before drawing the curtain.

'She's right, really. George comes first,' he muttered to himself.

Yet even then he decided to try and keep an eye on this boy. He must know whether John was the father. Every thought, on that line, would have to be discretion itself. Barker must do the necessary. James Mayo must *know*.

The next morning he was out early to catch his headman.

'Barker, I want to know everything possible about the Howard child, but you must be discreet. Never let old Sarah know that you are enquiring for me. Do you understand?'

Barker eyed his master and frowned. This he did not like at all. He had a sneaking feeling that he was doing the master's dirty work. For what reason? Martha and he had been making a few guesses along certain directions but they too lacked proof.

He liked old Sarah. She'd had a raw deal in life. What right had the master to snoop? He made up his mind. Cost him what it might, he had to speak. He lifted his grizzled head, faced up to the farmer and stared deep into his eyes.

'No, master, I don't understand,' he said flatly.

Mayo's brows lifted with astonishment. He had given an order—and were his commands being questioned? What the devil was coming over everyone?

He scowled in anger. 'Are you going to disobey me?'

Barker stuck out his jaw. 'No, master! You know better than that but I reckon I've a right to know why you're so interested in a bastard. What you're asking me to do is spy on the Howards. I'll not do that for you, master, begging your pardon.'

James was speechless at this. His brows

came together and he glared at his man. It wouldn't take much to get rid of him and get a more subservient hand. But James knew he could never do this. Also, his conscience had been bothering him about this quest, too.

'I think that bastard is dead John's boy but I don't know for sure; that's why I'm interested.'

Barker nodded his head slowly. So he and Martha had been right! Well, this was a nice kettle of fish!

'So now you know why you must be discreet. Don't whatever you do, let the mistress know but I must find out whether that child is my grandson or not. Do you understand?'

'Yes, master. I do indeed. Don't you worry. I'll find out what I can though it might take a while. Old Sarah's tongue is pretty rough nowadays.'

Barker took his time. Asked careful questions. Suitably admired the new baby and thus slowly acquired the information Mayo wanted.

'Sarah's called the boy Joseph, but he'll be known as Jos. She says your John was the father—and I believe her, master. She'd have no reason to lie, would she?'

The talks Sarah held with Barker though were not all one-sided. For all his loyalty Barker was not a very quick-thinking man. Sarah also wanted information and she played Barker with the skill of a fisherman after trout.

Often Sarah puzzled the not so sharp witted

Barker. He would be happily chatting to her when she would frown and withdraw into herself. When this happened, Barker had soon learned to leave, shaking his head in mystification. It never occurred to him that Sarah's mood only ever changed when the Mayo baby was mentioned.

Sarah bitterly resented this new Mayo heir. Why had Betty died? Why did everything happen to the Howards? It was all so grossly unfair!

She made a vow. This child, her Jos, must learn in great detail exactly who he was and his position in life. He must grow up strong and hard to be able to deal with the Mayos. He must develop into a man with a will of iron so that none might trample him underfoot. He must grow up to claim his birthright. His mission must be to win back the Howard land and to damn the Mayos for all eternity.

With her age, responsibilities and worry, Sarah also changed. She became bitter and twisted. At night, when the child slept, Sarah sat in a chair thinking deep thoughts always about the land which should belong to the Howards. The land and the power which always went with land.

And so young Johnnie Mayo's action, even though his intentions may have been the best, had started something when he rode out on his grey mare. Something which would be implacable in its age and intensity.

BOOK TWO

Jos Howard

CHAPTER ONE

When Jos looked back on his life from the lofty pinnacle of eighteen years he understood many things which had puzzled him for so long. His childhood had been a queer one. Pains and pleasures had been equally mixed. There were certain landmarks though which stood out with startling clarity even though he might not wish to remember them.

His very early memories were confused. His grandma Sarah was the dominating star of his life. As indeed she still was. He smiled as he thought about her, a frank smile coming from an open, honest face. Its most outstanding feature were two bright blue eyes. He was a tall, gangly youth with arms and legs which seemed to sprout in all directions. Already he topped the six-foot mark and threatened to pass this. Sarah said she did not know where he got it from. Certainly none of 'them' were tall and neither were the Howards. He frowned suddenly, thinking about 'them'. It seemed ridiculous to lump a family under such a word but it was this odd word which prodded his first specific memory.

The tiny village school was only two miles from his cottage home—no distance to a healthy country boy. He had loved school even though the discipline was severe. Reading came easily to him and he adopted a good script. Arithmetic was harder but he had a quiet, dogged persistence which produced its own rewards. He vividly remembered the first morning in the little playground. A small gathering of boys and girls had started playing games as soon as released. He stood aside, watching in curiosity, wanting to join in but a little shy.

He saw one boy staring at him. A boy of his own age. He had a square jaw and bold eyes. Jos heard him called George and, feeling friendly, he walked over and spoke.

'Hello! My name is Jos, what's yours?'

The other boy had regarded him thoughtfully for a moment. 'Mine's George Mayo. What's your other name?'

'Oh, it's Howard,' he said, eager to establish a friendship.

The boy George's eyes had taken on a different expression. They narrowed and before Jos could do anything, one small fist had smacked him on the nose. Taken unawares he fell down on his seat and, putting his hand to his nose, was astonished to find it pouring with blood. He stared up at George, unable to comprehend.

'What did you do that for?' he asked in bewilderment.

'Because you're a Howard!' George had snapped and walked away.

Later on he told his Grandma. Sarah had

listened, drawing in her breath with a hiss and thrusting out her chest. Her eyes snapped with anger as she comforted him.

'But why did he hit me, Gran? I only wanted to make friends,' he told her unhappily.

'He hit you because you are his enemy!'

Jos turned this over in his young mind. What exactly was an enemy? At six years of age there was much he failed to understand. It was then Sarah gave him his first lesson in hate. Carefully she told him how the Howards had been robbed and his grandfather had died because of the Mayos. She explained about the mother he had never known and how the Mayos had indirectly killed her.

'Everything bad is in this Mayo family. If you want to grow up you must always hate the Mayos and hit them first. They stole from us, cheated you of your birthright. Always remember that, Jos.'

Sarah had noted his puzzled expression.

'How do you get to school?' she asked next.

What a silly question thought Jos. 'I walk, Gran, you know that!'

'And that other boy?'

Jos considered. 'Oh, he rides a lovely pony with a groom.'

'Exactly! He is rich. You are poor. That pony should really belong to you!' Sarah had snorted. 'When he gets older he will go to a big school. You are lucky to go to school at all. I can't afford it, it's the Squire who has arranged for you to go to school. And look at this cottage! Go on, look at it, Jos. We should really be living in a big house with lots of servants.'

Jos had dutifully looked and thought, once again, what a wonderful place his home was. The tiny cottage was always snug. He knew nothing else. This was his home. Sarah was his complete life. What more could any boy want?

'Yes, Gran, but why am I his enemy?' he had asked again after listening with the painful concentration of the six-year-old.

Sarah had sighed with utter exasperation and started the whole rigmarole again.

Later, Jos had gone out into the fields to think. He dimly gathered what his Gran had been telling him but the actual reason was still not clear, puzzle as he might. So he just accepted the fact. Whenever he saw George Mayo he walked up and attempted to hit him on the nose. Sometimes he succeeded, other times George hit him first. At this stage there was no real animosity in either boy. They were both reacting to the doctrine which had been instilled into them. They must dislike each other. They were enemies.

Their fights became frequent despite constant canings. The teacher dreaded the sight of the two boys together in the same area. To the rest of the children George and Jos provided excellent entertainment. They could take sides without dire repercussions to their own anatomies.

As the two boys went up in the little church school so the fights continued. They were evenly matched and neither boy took an advantage for long. When George left to go for a better and more polished education at a famous public school, Jos quite missed the fights with him.

The next milestone had been one fine spring day when he first saw the horse. Jos loved horses. When he first saw the grey he stopped and stared in amazement. He had never dreamed such a beautiful creature existed. He was standing at the top of the lane, near to the Squire's house, when the horseman came into view, approaching at a controlled canter.

The grey was stupendous. It was a stallion, full of fire and presence. He had a beautiful arrogant head, long flowing mane and tail and a compact, muscular body. The feet were tiny, seeming to float over the lane. The animal's movements were smooth, like gently flowing liquid.

Jos watched, mouth agape. He drank in this gorgeous creature. The rider had stopped, an amused smile on his face as he became aware of the boy's frank fascination.

The stallion half-reared in protest then dropped down to the ground, one hoof restlessly pawing, tail switching. With proud head bent at the poll, he stared at the boy. The eyes were big, bold, bright and full of intelligence; the wide nostrils flared showing the red membranes as they drank in the boy's scent.

The rider watched the boy's pleasure, then spoke. 'You like my horse, boy?'

Jos nodded, blushing furiously. 'Oh yes, sir! I think he's wonderful!'

'What's your name?'

'Jos, sir, Jos Howard!'

The smile vanished from James Mayo's face. He regarded the boy carefully, eyes narrowed in concentration. If there had ever been doubt about this boy's paternity it had gone in James Mayo's eyes. Why—this handsome lad was the spitting image of John at his age. Dear God—what a resemblance! It was uncanny!

The boy, unaware of the man's change, had eyes only for the stallion.

'So here he is, after all these years. John's by-blow!' mused James. 'And what a fine boy, too. Tall, good limbs, sharp eyes and an intelligent face. I like his open eyes. They're honest ones. Sarah's looked after him well,' he reflected, and a short pain touched him again after all these years.

As James Mayo was a fine judge of horse flesh, he also prided himself on his ability to weigh up a human being. He studied Jos more thoroughly. He liked what he saw. As he admitted this to himself a frown snaked over his forehead.

'If only George had such open looks. There's something about George that worries me,' he thought unhappily. 'George has been spoilt, that's his trouble. I've let Mary have her own way with him too much. All this nonsense of a public school, apeing the gentry. I don't know what's come over Mary. She gets more difficult as the years pass!' and he sighed to himself.

'Do you know anything about horses, Jos?' he asked.

The boy looked up at him. 'Only a little, sir, but I want to learn. I want to work with horses when I'm grown up.'

'What kind? Coach horses?'

'Oh no, sir! Fast riding horses or hunters. Perhaps even racehorses!' Jos added hopefully.

'Do you know who I am?' James asked him.

Jos looked up, drawing his gaze away from the stallion. For the first time he took a good look at the rider. He saw a broad-shouldered man with grey hair and a square, red face with stern eyes.

'No, sir!'

'My name is James Mayo.'

'Oh! I know a boy called George Mayo.'

'My son!'

'We fight!' Jos told him proudly.

'So I've heard,' James remarked drily. 'Why do you fight?'

'Because we are enemies!' Jos replied.

James lifted an eyebrow. 'And why are you enemies?'

'Because my Gran says so,' Jos replied.

'But *why* are you enemies?' James persisted.

Jos was puzzled. If this man was George's father he must know.

'Because the Mayos stole our land and killed my Grandpa and made my Ma die,' he said, faithfully echoing Sarah's teachings.

James snorted angrily and bent from the saddle.

'That is not so! There's far more to it than that! When you are bigger you'll learn the whole story. Your Grandma is wrong to tell you things like that. There are two sides to every story. You remember that, Jos—will you?'

Jos nodded doubtfully. He was not quite clear why there should be any fuss over so simple a fact. He and George were enemies. They fought each other and that was that. Grown-ups did fuss so!

'Do you know who your father was?'

Jos considered this carefully. Sarah had never told him much about his father. All her talks had been about his mother and Grandpa. He shook his head.

'Your father was called John. He was my son.'

Jos was puzzled then. Relationships were still a bit hazy to him but this was something he did manage to understand. He put his head aside, thinking quickly.

'Does that make you a Grandpa then?'

James smiled slowly. This boy was sharp! 'I am your Grandpa, Jos!'

Jos's lips formed an Ooh! of amazement. Here was a treasure indeed. He had a real, live Grandpa. Then his boy's practical mind turned on another track.

'Then can I have a ride on your horse, Grandpa?' he asked excitedly.

James laughed. He was very taken with this fine grandson of his. Damn Sarah! To blazes with Mary! He bent lower and gave the boy his hand, hoisting him up on the front of the saddle.

'Hang on!' he warned.

'Can we go fast?' Jos called, curling his fingers in the grey mane as the stallion bounced in excitement.

James swung the horse about, touched with his heels and pushed into a rapid canter. Reins in one hand, he clasped the boy around the waist with the other.

For Jos it was a dream. He never forgot that first ride on a blood horse. It mesmerized him and charged him with excitement of the highest order.

As they sped between the hedgerows there was something quite exhilarating about the stallion's speed and power. The smoothness of the grey's paces, the rush of the wind on his cheeks, the way his hair whipped across his forehead—this was freedom! He released his grip and yelled with wonder, forgetting the man whose hand clutched his middle.

James stopped at the lane end, turned and galloped wildly back, as excited himself as the boy.

It ended too soon. The stallion slithered to a halt at a touch of the bit. Rearing high on hindlegs, he threw Jos back against his grandfather's chest. A thrilling fear coursed through the boy and he laughed wildly again. This was life! He knew then, that no matter what, he wanted to spend his life with horses like this magnificent creature.

Reluctantly he slid from the saddle, turned and looked up at his grandfather. James saw eyes sparkling with fun, red-tinged cheeks and a boy bursting with wonder.

'Why doesn't George look like that?' he asked himself uneasily. 'Why does my heir shout with fear if I go out of a trot even? What's gone wrong with the Mayo bloodlines? My son is spiteful, and a rank coward. This bastard is a true Mayo to his finger tips and will make a splendid man!'

James glowered. It was so unfair and for a few moments he wallowed in self-pity. Even Mary had gone so far as to admit that George was not made on the same lines as John had been.

'What on earth would she say if she saw

John's son?' James asked himself. 'There would be all hell let loose!'

He sighed unhappily again. Because this boy was nothing but a by-blow he would never amount to anything in life—and it wasn't his fault.

Jos stood, eyes unwaveringly looking at the rider and then the stallion. He wondered what the rider was thinking. He wanted to go now and tell Sarah about the wonderful horse. He knew it would be considered rude to run away until the grown-up had dismissed him.

James came back to the present, saw the boy's impatience and smiled at him.

'Here!' he said, fishing in his breeches pocket, finding a small gold coin.

Jos took the half-sovereign, his eyes opening wide with astonishment and pleasure.

'Oh, thank you!'

'Now that's a lot of money, Jos. What are you going to do with it?'

Jos thought. It was more money than he knew existed in the whole world. His first thought was to show it to Sarah, then some nudge of caution restrained him. Gran did not like the Mayos at all. She was forever telling him they were enemies. And how could a grandpa be an enemy? He suddenly experienced a wary suspicion that this morning's adventures might be better kept to himself.

He smiled up at James. 'I'm going to keep it

97

a secret and save it. Then one day I'm going to buy myself a horse like yours,' he said proudly. 'That is, when I'm grown up,' he added, acutely aware of a small boy's limited power.

'You do just that, Jos, you also remember what I told you!'

With a last, long look at his grandson he rode off.

Jos remembered now how he had kept his secret. Sarah had looked up when he returned. She noted his colour and barely contained excitement but asked no questions. She always had other more important things to think about. Like the sheer economics of living.

He had to work on the land. The hours were long, six full days a week; the work desperately hard, the pay pitifully small.

It had been a fine Autumn day when he again saw George Mayo home from his expensive school on holiday. The two boys had not met each other for a number of years. Both were surprised when they came face to face one warm evening.

Jos had gone for a walk in the direction of Mayo's. It was a path he often took, unbeknown to Sarah, for the sheer pleasure and excitement of perhaps seeing his grandpa ride one of the greys. On the other hand, George had seized his walk as a means of putting a safe distance between him and his father. Another poor school report had sent the old man into a cold frustrated rage. Even his mother had been against him. So George was deep in a fit of the sulks.

Both boys rounded a hedge and stopped abruptly, eyeing each other in amazement. Jos was much the taller, but still thin, while George had started to fill out. Physically he would resemble his father where sheer strength and muscle power were concerned. Both boys had the pugnacious Mayo jaw which immediately jutted out as they recognized each other.

Jos stood still, fists clenched. A bubble of excitement caught at his throat. It was a long time since he had enjoyed a good fight and George Mayo made a fine opponent.

George glared at the Howard brat. Mary's insidious talks had been far more effective than Sarah's out and out lessons of hate. Perhaps it was because George was better material to work on. Perhaps, also, he subconsciously resented this close blood relation. Could there be a threat when he came to inherit?

Jos's nose twitched as he stared at George. He was not in the least bothered by the other's obvious hate. Neither was he too worried over past history. Jos was ever easy-going, quite happy to live just for the day and take things as they came. In a way, he was sorry that he and George could never be friends. He had often wondered whether a friendship overture might produce something positive. But one look at

99

George's scowling face squashed those ideas flat. Jos shrugged amicably. He didn't mind having an enemy. In a way it was a distinct badge; it gave them both a certain air of notoriety and fame amongst their contemporaries in the village and surrounding countryside.

'Bastard!' spat George, squaring his shoulders and lifting his arms in the best prize fighter's style.

Jos lifted an eyebrow, grinned and copied.

'Murderer's family!' jeered George, intending to rile Jos and make him blind with temper. Jos was a fighter to be respected.

Murderer's family? Jos puzzled over it for a second. By now, he knew all the facts of that historic day—from Sarah's point of view. Yet this was the first time in his life that the word "murderer" had been thrown at him.

The smile vanished from his face as he eyed George coldly. Jos never wasted time on words when actions would suffice. He stepped forward leading with a left. George blocked, danced sideways and feinted. Seeing the opening Jos let fly with his right. It caught George fair and square on the jaw. He went flying backwards, fell and rolled over, eyes glazing. He sat, shaking his head, looking up at Jos. There was venom in his eyes.

He scrambled to his feet, seething with rage and humiliation. Jos waited calmly. They sparred warily for a minute, each respecting the other, seeking an opening, feinting with both fists. Then George charged. Jos blocked the blows but allowed his enemy to get in close. George's fists hammered home to the body, making him wince and grunt with pain. It suddenly dawned on Jos that he had the reach. He must fight from a distance.

They fought for ten minutes, dancing around, breathing hard. Blood flowed from George's face. Jos felt pain stab in his chest muscles. George fought in savage little bursts, trying to get in under Jos's longer arms. Jos calmly ducked, weaved and kept his distance. He planted odd blows on George's face. It was bleeding freely though he looked far worse than he was. Jos was unmarked but his ribs were paining him especially over the heart where George had landed two vicious blows.

As they tired they lost their little science and started brawling. They were anxious only to hurt each other. Fists and now feet flew out in all directions. They closed and grappled like wrestlers. Both boys' arms too tired now to be kept up. George banged with his bullet head, cracking Jos unexpectedly. He was dizzy. He clung on to George wildly for support. George, sensing victory, smashed heads again. Jos went hurtling on to his back. George leapt on him. One hand seized Jos's throat, and Jos felt fear. He suddenly realized this was not just another boyhood fight. This had far more depth; George was ugly now. With this realization

Jos's own temper flared sky-high. He twisted his face and sank his teeth into George's fingers, making him release his grip. George yelped with pain. Jos brought his knee up to unsuccessfully hammer a blow into George's groin. The two boys rolled apart, both paused for breath and eyed each other angrily.

They would have liked to stop now. The fight had gone further than either had thought possible. Secretly, they wished a grown-up would come along and separate them.

George felt blood in his mouth and spat to clear it. Jos took the gesture as further insult and fell forward again, fists ineffectually hitting George's bloody face. George hit back weakly. Both stood a foot from each other, tired arms lifting and red-stained fists tapping at each other's face. George felt his strength completely going and he staggered back a step and dropped his arms. Jos was far too tired to go forward and he too paused. He gasped for breath, feeling blood trickling down his cheek from a cut over one eye caused by George's head.

There was a moment of sobbing breath, twitching arms and trembling legs. Then without a word George turned on his heel and staggered away. Thankfully Jos heaved a sigh and also turned for home.

When both boys had returned to their respective homes there had been an uproar. Sarah stormed, raged and threatened all manner of impossible evils upon George Mayo.

Mary had spat out that dear John's boy was nothing but an evil viper caused by the tainted Howard blood.

'Go over there and thrash that bastard!' she had screamed at her husband while she fondled and pacified the bloody George.

'I'll do no such thing!' James had snapped back. 'And you'll keep out of this affair, wife!' he had warned her.

Mary had suddenly sensed that, in this, she would not dominate her man.

'Those Mayos!' Sarah had hissed as she bathed Jos's face. 'They want hanging. All of them. They're rotten!'

James Mayo, being male, had fully understood and said nothing further. A little sadly, he acknowledged that this had been bound to happen. The two boys were destined to be enemies.

'But why, why, *why*, do I like my bastard grandson better than my true heir? What's wrong with me? Am I going senile?' James Mayo asked himself for the hundredth time. But he knew there was nothing wrong with his mind just as he knew his instinct about the two boys was correct. The bastard one was of good stuff, the rightful heir was rotten to the core.

Why?

CHAPTER TWO

Sarah decided that she definitely felt her age. Her joints were very rheumaticky and it took her a long time to throw off a cold.

She seemed to keep a cough for weeks and she supposed that the bad years living in the hovel had done the mischief. Her face was old and well wrinkled but her eyes still shone, bright and very alert with often a twinkle in them as she watched her beloved Jos.

She was too old to work now. Too tired and worn out. Jos was the breadwinner and the Squire was generous. He charged them no rent and many a tit-bit came down from the big house as well as clothing and furniture.

Sarah looked around at the small cottage. It was now a snug home, tiny, but just right for her and Jos. She would be forever grateful to the Squire. Of course, this cottage would never be like the old Ferndale house, long since destroyed by fire and storm when empty.

Dear Joseph had been dead these 19 years now. At times, she had trouble in picturing his face. The same occurred with Betty. It didn't seem possible she'd ever had a daughter! Her whole life had always been bound up in Jos.

She smiled affectionately as she thought of him. He was such a dear boy but what a dreamer! She wondered, for the hundredth time, who he took after. None of her family had ever been anything but quick and practical . . . Certainly no Howard had ever grown to Jos's height.

Sarah sighed. Sometimes when she talked to Jos she knew she was not getting through to him. Uneasily she wondered just how deep were the teachings she had tried to instill in him. She knew he walked a lot on Mayo's land. She did not know that it was because he sought a chance to see the grey horses, or talk to his grandfather or have a ride with him. She thought he was studying the land which had once been theirs.

She knew all about George Mayo too and the animosity which existed between the two boys. She suspected this feeling was deeper on George Mayo's part. Jos was so quiet and easy-going.

'I do wish he had a bit more spark and go in him. I've never once heard him talk about a plan for getting our land back. I must have a set-to with him one day. Make him think up some plan of action. We can't, we just can't go on like this, year after year, doing nothing. I'm old. I'll soon be *very* old. I must get Jos moving before I die!' she vowed to herself.

The trouble was, Sarah admitted to herself, the horse. Jos was quite horse mad. He seemed to think and dream of nothing but horses. Sarah snorted. Fat lot of good horses were to them.

'We are farmers. It's the land that matters. Land, machines, and the ability to grow more crops with bigger yield.'

Sarah had heard about James Mayo's switch from plain crops to intensive horse breeding.

'I don't care if "They" do make horses pay,' Sarah muttered to herself more than once. 'We must have our land back.'

James Mayo was said to have hundreds of horses now and sold direct to the main coaching firms in Bristol, Bath and London. At the same time, the gentry had discovered the famous grey horses. They were in high demand as riding animals not only for the ladies but also for the men who now followed the favourite winter pastime of fox-hunting. They said that a good Mayo's grey fetched a fortune in the Shires.

She hadn't seen one of the Mayos since that terrible day. She knew that James kept well out of her way. Mary Mayo she thoroughly despised. Was it possible they had once been friends? She knew that Mary had changed and it was her teachings which had instilled such vitriolic hatred in her son. What a rotten breed they were, she thought, completely forgetting Jos had their blood.

'The only semi-decent one is old James,' she conceded. 'At least he speaks his mind. You know where you stand with him and what to expect. That boy of his though, is sneaky and bent. There might be some trouble with him but Jos will manage.'

Jos! Her life!

'*He* must marry and have a son!'

She suddenly realized the time. Jos was late again. Now where was he? Standing looking over some gate dreaming about horses most likely. What a boy!

Jos was not dreaming about horses. They had a rival now. An opponent who astonished Jos himself. That some other object could fill his waking mind was astounding, but then, Maud Gordon was no ordinary female.

The Howards' benefactor had managed to produce exactly one living child—unusual for those prolific days. She had been nurtured to adulthood like a treasured gem. The Squire adored her.

Big, bluff and a little foolishly short-sighted, he thrust even more worship on his daughter after his wife's death. He sometimes wondered uneasily what would happen to his Maud if he died with her unwed. Although he had position and class in the area the Squire was acutely aware of the precarious state of his finances.

He must find a suitable match for his girl. A title was out of the question. One had to be real gentry for that. Time and time again his quest drove him up against the Mayos. Young George was the same age as his girl though whether George and Maud liked each other he had no idea; not that this factor mattered, of course. They seemed friendly enough the rare times they met socially, but the Squire knew the power behind George was his father. Here the Squire always smiled to himself. His land bounded on to Mayo's. Whosoever married Maud would eventually inherit his land.

He knew James Mayo was still land-greedy. A marriage between George and Maud would be eminently satisfactory from the farmer's point of view. The idea did not displease the Squire. With such a match Maud and her children would never want.

That Maud might have her own ideas never occurred to her father. Squire Gordon knew that Mayo's was entailed. No Mayo, for three generations to come, could sell any land without the consent of his heir. Mayo's was safe for a long time.

Mayo and Gordon had a strange relationship. On the one hand contempt for obvious weakness. On the other, tolerance of an avaricious nature. They met once a month alternately at their respective homes suffering each other. They played chess, a game at which, to the Squire's surprised pleasure, he was better than James Mayo.

The Squire knew that Jos liked his girl, which was only natural. They had grown up together since that dreadful day when Jos had been born and his mother died. The Squire knew the whole story. That was all long ago now. The Squire had never regretted helping the woman and the boy. He reckoned they had gone through more than enough. He showed a regular interest in both of them at all times and was happy to allow Jos to work for him as soon as he could leave school. He had approved of Jos going to school but not of stopping there too long. After all, too much education could be dangerous to the lower classes. It was quite sufficient that he could read, write and do some figuring. Anything more than that would be ridiculous for a common labourer which was all Jos was.

*   *   *

Jos could see the major part of the Squire's acres from where he stood. Like so many of the upper classes properties it was a solid affair of white stone with a large rambling orchard and extensive stabling.

Jos and Maud had played in the orchard from the days when they first toddled out for adventure.

When Sarah had worked regularly in the kitchen at the big house Jos had spent hours there. He and Maud had taken to each other from the start. She had been an ideal playmate, always ready to follow his masculine lead.

After she too had gone away to her better school for young ladies of good family, Jos had missed her sadly. When she came home on holidays they had always picked up the threads of their friendship. At one stage George Mayo had started to come over but he had desisted. The boys did not dare to fight on the Squire's property. Nevertheless, they managed to strut around like cocks, taunting each other. Sarah had rushed out one day and boxed George's ears with more venom than the startled boy deserved. It was the first time she had seen him. It was also the last. George never came again.

Jos really opened his eyes when Maud came home from school for the last time. He could not remove his gaze from her. Where was the gangling girl with gigglish tendencies who had been his playmate? How was it he had not noticed this lovely creature before?

Maud was not really beautiful but she did have a prettiness. Combined with a happy, effervescent nature this made her startlingly attractive.

She was a tall girl, though nowhere near Joe's great height. Her skin was creamy with rich lips, high cheekbones and pale blue eyes. She had hair the colour of ripe wheat. She was full of kindness to animals and people, not yet having met the cruelty of the world in general. She was also conscious of her power over the male and her position in the county as the Squire's single daughter.

Jos fell wildly in love. Maud was the most gorgeous creature in the world. She was even better than the grey horses. His entire day, and half of his waking night, was spent thinking about her.

For the first time Jos thought seriously about marriage. To wed meant having money. Jos had precious little of that with no chance of getting any more. He still had his grandpa's half-sovereign but he had only been able to increase this sum with a few carefully saved shillings.

He was practical enough to realize that, with Maud, he was aiming high. Her station in life was far superior to Jos's. He always started sweating when he came to this part in his mental dreams. How could he improve his position and ask the Squire for Maud's hand?

Maud, acute and perceptive, her female instincts fully developed knew exactly what Jos was going through. She thrived on it.

It was a wonderful, tantalizing game she played. She was quite sure that she was in love with Jos. During the spring and summer of 1835 Maud led Jos a merry dance.

A horrific thought dawned on Jos one day. He did not know how Maud felt about him! Perhaps she didn't even like him! He was galvanized into action. He had to see her. He must ask her. Now!

Jos knew Maud's actions and he waited for her in the orchard. She always came out on a summer evening for a stroll. Sometimes with her father, often alone. He waited in a fever of impatience hoping the Squire had other things to do.

As soon as she stepped from the door Maud spotted him. She had enjoyed her fun that year but she now knew there was a time for the teasing to stop. She walked slowly towards the orchard, stopping now and again, caught as always by the view.

She did some rapid thinking. A few weeks ago she had told herself that she was seriously in love with Jos. Many things though had happened since then. The most notable being a talk she'd held with her father.

They had finished their dinner and were sitting in front of the open windows, relaxing in the evening air. Maud had felt her father's gaze. Smiling, she lifted an eyebrow in question. The Squire had cleared his throat, studied his hands, and taken the plunge.

'My dear, you are eighteen now. It's time you were thinking of getting married. I am getting on in years and I would like to see you settled,' he began.

Maud touched his hand lovingly. She did not like to hear him talk in this vein but he was, she admitted, starting to age rapidly now. She felt tender towards him. Since her mother's early death they had been very close.

'I have thought about it,' she replied gently.

He eyed her carefully. 'George Mayo would make a good match, my dear.'

'George Mayo! But!'

'No! Hear me out first. You know we are not in the financial position we were years ago. I would like to think that when you marry it will be to a man who has plenty of money so that you and your children will never want. You know the position of the Mayos as well as me. They could buy me out six times over with their loose change! George isn't a bad young man. Perhaps he's a bit thoughtless—but young men often are. He'd settle down with a good wife. You must admit, there's nothing wrong with his looks. He's a fine young man, the very best for miles around!'

Mrs George Mayo—mistress of the mighty Mayo's! Maud rolled the sentence backward and forward. Why, it sounded very impressive indeed. It was certainly very true that, as mistress of Mayo's, she would never want. She would have position, influence and extreme comfort. She realized that times were still difficult. Only a family like Mayos could offer her financial security.

She thought seriously about Jos while her father watched keenly, not wanting to interrupt her thought-line.

'Jos loves me, I do know that,' she told herself, 'but do I really love him. What is love?'

She lived in a day and age of arranged marriages where parental obedience was expected without question. Maud felt deep tenderness towards Jos but what kind of life

113

could he give her? He was nothing but a low farm worker without talent of any kind. Even though he came from good stock he was, after all, only a bastard living in a cottage. There was never a hope of his getting enough money to keep her as she liked to be kept right now.

With practical issues brought out into the open she was able to look at the situation from every angle. She considered George. As a girl she had disliked him for his sneaky ways. As a young man she had to admit she did not really know him. Jos had always usurped the field. George had never been given a chance to compete for her favours. George was most distinctly presentable, there was no denying that. George or Jos? Money or poverty? Comfort or misery?

She shuddered suddenly. Her life, to date, had been too easy. She knew, in her heart, that no matter how she cared for Jos right now, if she wed him her love might easily die when poverty knocked at their door. Maud Gordon was not too bad a snob for those times. She *was* extremely practical. Perfectly able to view matters with a realistic dispassion.

'Has Mr Mayo spoken of this?'

Her father nodded.

'He spoke long ago.' Then he grinned at her. 'Don't forget, our land runs alongside his. When I'm gone you inherit the land. Whosoever weds you does the same. If you marry George Mayo your son would be the biggest landowner for miles around.'

She had great, natural ambitions. She knew, only too well, the value placed upon the acquisition of land. She was also acutely aware of the power that went with the land. A large land-holder was somebody indeed.

'Jos cares for me,' she said, speaking slowly.

The Squire shook his head. 'That's only because he's been almost brought up with you. He's a nice enough lad but he's still only a bastard. He's not a penny piece to his name and absolutely no chance of getting money. He can't even talk correctly. Listen to that thick Gloucestershire accent of his! Sometimes I have a job to make out what he means! He is just a low youth, way below our class in life. I would never let you marry, Jos, my dear,' he told her firmly, adding, 'And even though you might think a lot about him now, that wouldn't last when you became cold and hungry.'

'But it would hurt him terribly!' had been her reply. 'Affianced to a Mayo too!'

The Squire had snorted then. 'I can't help how Jos feels. I've done my best for him and the old woman. I'm thinking about us now—and you mostly. He'll get over it and find some wench in his own class. Will you marry George Mayo?'

Maud sat up straight. She could still back out and fight her father, though such action would be contrary to her nature and stern upbringing. In her heart, though, she knew she did not want to. Everything would be so safe with the Mayos. The more she considered the idea the more she found it to her liking.

Dear Jos, she thought, and waited for a stab of remorse to come. Nothing happened. Instead she pictured handsome George. She wondered a little at the excitement tugging at her. Life with him would be so exciting. Why— they would make a splendid couple.

She nodded, the decision made. 'I'll wed George Mayo. What shall I do about Jos?'

'I'll tell him, if you like?' her father had offered.

Maud shook her head. 'No, I must at least tell him myself. I expect he'll be waiting for me one evening. I'll stop teasing and tell him.'

'And I'll ride over to Mayo's. You and George can get engaged shortly. I expect we will all arrange something very special for you my dear. You have made me very happy and stilled a lot of worries. The wedding can be next year. The sooner the better I think,' the Squire finished in a thoughtful voice.

Maud went to meet Jos, feeling guilt stab beneath pretended indifference. With increasing unease, the Squire watched from the window. There were strong blood lines in young Jos. A rejected young man either sank into the trough of human despondancy or rose to the heights of a fighting madman. Which way would Jos go?

Maud watched him step from behind the

tree to greet her, his blue eyes sparkling with happiness. She suddenly realized this was not going to be easy. Bitterly now she regretted the way she had dallied with his affections. All along, Jos had remained true. How could she tell him her decision without causing acute heartbreak? She hesitated, her feet turning to lead. She hated her past actions and herself even more. She stopped and Jos looked down at her, beaming his wide smile. His hand touched her gently.

'Let's walk,' he suggested happily.

Unhappily, she complied, head low, heart thudding with worry. It flashed through her mind she should stop, go back to the house and leave this to her father, but Maud was no coward. She set her jaw and started thinking suitable words. How would he react? When should she speak? Now or later?

Jos saw there was something amiss. He was too pleased to be with the girl of his choice to wonder at the reason for her unusual silence. It was enough that she was not in one of her teasing moods.

He was bubbling over with feeling, exhilarated beyond relief. He burst to tell of his love but he wanted a good setting. He chose the brookside at the edge of the orchard. He sat her on a log, looked down at her face then knelt. Firmly he held her hands in his, as if to will her to him.

'Maud! Maud!'

She forced her gaze up, feeling a prickling behind her eyes as she saw his expression.

'Maud, I've something to tell you. I've been thinking about it all Summer. I should have spoken before, but—!'

'And I've something to tell you,' she replied quietly.

'You listen to me first! Maud, I know I'm no great catch right now because I've very little money. Nothing much to offer a girl really except myself. I love you deeply. I think I must always have felt this way but I didn't realize until spring. More fool me for not speaking sooner! Maud, will you marry me? Not right now, of course. Perhaps in a year or two when I've something behind me. I'll work hard and save hard to make you a home. I'll look after you well, Maud—and—you're crying! What's wrong?' A worried note entered his voice. Then his arms went around her.

He felt her relax against him, then suddenly she went stiff. Her arms pushed against his broad chest. Baffled, he released her.

'What's wrong, darling?' he whispered anxiously.

Maud sighed. She bit her lips and looked at him. A tightness caught her throat.

'Oh, Jos! This is all my fault! No! You must listen to me now. I don't know how to begin. How to tell you! Jos, it can never be. I like you Jos, I've always liked you but I don't love you. I'm promised to someone else. My engagement will be announced soon. I can never marry you, Jos. I'm going to marry George Mayo. It's all arranged,' she announced flatly.

Jos said nothing. He was shocked and stupefied beyond belief. He had been quite prepared for her to say she didn't love him yet. That he would not have minded; he would have had the pleasure of seriously courting her but the idea that she was already promised to another had shaken his foundations. Had he heard her correctly?

One look at her serious, wan face convinced him. She was going to marry someone else— and George Mayo of all men. This was the bitterest blow of all. He tried to rationalize his thoughts into a logical argument in his own favour but speech now failed him. He was too mentally shocked and just knelt there, frozen, bleak-faced and wide-eyed.

'Maud!' he begged, then speech failed him again. His mind had stopped. Life had ended. What was there for him now?

'Jos! Don't take on! It was never meant to be—you and me!' she pleaded, standing up and facing him.

Sullenly he averted his gaze. A scowl on his face. His bottom lip trembling a little.

'Jos, look at me! Jos!'

He stared, seeing something new and alien in her eyes. It dawned on him that she was not averse to this distasteful match.

'Why?' he asked her bluntly.

Maud floundered. 'Because it's well—'

'Do you love him?' he asked coldly, gripping her white arm.

Maud hesitated unhappily.

'Answer me!'

'You're hurting! Let go!' she protested.

'Do you love George Mayo?' he barked at her, seeming to grow to a giant's size before her startled eyes. She shook her arm free and backed a step, watching him warily now. This was not going right, somehow. Jos looked ugly. She had never seen him like this before.

'Do you love him?' he roared at her.

'Don't shout at me like that! Yes, I do!' she snapped back at him in a wild lie. She was furious with herself but even angrier with him for making her say things which weren't true. 'Yes, I do, I do! I *do!'*

Suddenly she saw Jos sag. His shoulders slumped, his head bowed and he turned away.

Jos faced her again. 'You meant what you've said? You're not just teasing?' he asked hopefully. The look in her eyes squashed this final hope.

'Jos, I'm sorry, I'm so sorry—'

'You're sorry!' he said scornfully. 'George Mayo! Why pick on him or—!' and he paused, thinking quickly.

'There's more to this than you've told me. Since when have Mayo and the Squire been all that friendly? I know they meet once a month but there is something else, isn't there?' he bullied her, his voice loud and rough.

Maud flinched at his tone and her own anger rose. Her father was right! He was an uncouth labourer. Listen to that dreadful accent!

'Yes, there is if you want to know. When I marry George Mayo all the land that counts will belong to one family. My son will be *the* power around these parts when he's grown up. What can you offer to equal that?' she snapped.

Jos's face was bleak and cold. He drew himself to his full height and regarded her stonily.

'If that's the case, then I guess I've made a fool of myself. I hope you don't live to regret your action. You know what the Mayos are!'

Maud flared up again. 'And what are they then? Shrewd, clever and sound, which is more than can be said for the Howards! What can you give me but a dab of a cottage? There's no future in that for me, thank you. I'm used to better things. Just you remember *who* I am, if you don't mind! You talk about the Mayos as if they're poison. Just you remember Jos Howard, that one of your grandfathers is a Mayo and the other a common felon!'

As soon as the words were out of her mouth Maud regretted them. She would have given ten years of her life to recall them. The damage was done. Jos's expression changed.

121

An alien and revengeful look flashed through his eyes. His nostrils flared and his jaw shot out.

'Heavens!' thought Maud frantically, 'he looks like old Mr Mayo himself!'

'I'm a double fool then—and old Sarah's been right all along!'

Jos turned on his heels and strode away. His blood bubbled with anger, resentment and humiliation. He had come to see her as a laughing, happy boy. He left her every bit as bitter a man as old Joseph Howard had been that dreadful day 19 years ago.

Maud lifted a hand, opened her mouth to call after him and thought better of it. She walked back to the house. Slowly she began to look into the future, to feel the first tremor of sheer excitement. Why, she was going to be wed to the most handsome man in the county! Life was simply grand!

CHAPTER THREE

Where Jos walked that evening was always afterwards a complete blank. He was mentally shattered. He had been cruelly hurt not just by Maud's rejection but by what she had said at the end. For the first time he was acutely aware of his murky past. He wondered about his father. What might not have happened if he had lived. Would he have married his mother? If so, he would now be a Mayo. Maud would marry him then!

'But I am a bastard!' he shouted, 'a dog without a proper name!'

For the first time he was also acutely aware of Joseph Howard, his other grandfather. Now he knew exactly what he had felt. Sarah, too, what she had been telling him for years about the Mayos, was so very right. They took all if and when it suited their plans. No one could stand up to them. The debt owing the Howards was incalculable.

'I'm a Howard, through and through,' he thought, 'a dash of Mayo blood in me has done me no good.'

He lingered as he thought about James Mayo. His living grandfather. An old man who had showed him some affection. He had casually tossed him a gold coin.

'Patronizing me,' he thought bitterly. 'The gold coins he has should be mine my rights. My father was the first son. All Mayo's should belong to me!'

He pictured George Mayo's handsome face and cunning eyes. In the past he had fought him with happy indifference. Now he loomed as a spectre demolishing his life. Jos ground his teeth together in frustration. There would be a reckoning for all this.

In the morning he came down, limp, wan and quiet. Sarah looked at him, lifted her eyebrows and said nothing. Something was up. That much was obvious but, for once, she held her tongue and waited patiently. Jos was in an ugly mood. He sat on the stool regarding his hands, the fingers curled into hard fists, his eyes were narrow spots of flint. He made no attempt to get ready for work. He just sat, hour after hour, until noon. Even Sarah began to feel alarm.

She stirred the iron pot from which wafted the smell of soup and hesitantly she poured some. She held it to him and looked steadily at his face.

Jos came back to the present. The soup stirred his gastric juices. Slowly he took the bowl and wooden spoon and began to sip. Then he paused, and looked at Sarah with a smile. A wicked smile which twisted his lips into a leer.

'I've been and made a fool of myself,' he told her quietly. 'I fell in love with Maud Gordon. Last night she threw me over. I wasn't good enough for her. She's going to wed George Mayo. It will unite the land into one big tract. Her son will be just about the biggest landowner in this area!'

Sarah nodded to herself. The news did not surprise her too much. In a way, she was pleased that he had lost to a Mayo.

'Now you can see the Mayos for what they really are,' she said.

Perhaps Jos would stir himself at last and do

something. What this something could be she had no idea. Her only pleasure was that, at long last, Jos must surely follow her reasoning. He *must* hate with a venom of the deepest destruction.

*   *   *

It was a miserable morning for Jos and a happy day for Sarah.

'What are you going to do?' she asked him quietly.

Jos shrugged. 'I don't know. What can I do? I can't make her marry me, can I?' and he sighed deeply.

'But George Mayo!' Sarah said cunningly, bringing his name into the open.

Jos stiffened. Yes, George Mayo indeed. He suddenly realized he loathed the name of Mayo. As he thought a hardness entered his heart. He knew that he must do something physical. He felt ready to burst with frustrated anger.

Jos stood up slowly, unaware of Sarah watching him with bated breath. Like a robot he walked from the cottage, over their patch of garden and across the field. He must find George Mayo. He would never rest again until he had things out with him.

He was unaware of the Squire riding back from Mayo's, where he had just drunk a glass of port. The Squire felt mightily pleased with himself. He knew both Mayos were. The younger had unbent to show his most charming side. He had listened respectfully to all the Squire had said, called him 'Sir!' and generally made himself agreeable. The Squire had been happy to give official permission for George to call. The engagement date would be announced in a month's time with the wedding next year. Old James Mayo had not said much. Indeed, at one stage, he appeared to have been thinking about something else.

The Squire would not have been unduly perturbed even had he known what was in James Mayo's mind. James was pleased for his son. The girl was a suitable match. He was highly delighted that, at long last, the final parcel of land should come into their family. No! James was thinking uneasily about Jos. He too had not failed to hear of his grandson's crazy infatuation for the Squire's daughter. In the country there are few, if any, secrets, and James was worried.

Jos was, after all, half a Mayo. James knew what *his* reactions would have been had someone taken *his* girl. Blood would have flowed. He eyed George who seemed blissfully ignorant of possible repercussions.

Long ago James had thought there might be bad blood between George and Jos. Long ago he had envisaged this when he had entailed Mayo's for his heirs and successors. On that day he had carefully set aside a small plot of land for young Jos. Twenty acres of grazing and two Mayo's greys, a filly and colt. That was the very least he could do for poor John's boy.

He had kept this from George and his solicitor had tied up the bequest so securely that George would never be able to touch or break it.

Life held so many complications. He also felt old when faced with problems. He stole a quick glance at George, noted his almost subservient attitude to the Squire and frowned. If only George was frank and open—like Jos! He turned and looked out of the window. All of a sudden, the room stank of trouble. He was frightened.

The Squire had sensed none of this. It would have taken a far more astute man than Philip Gordon to guess another's worries. On his ride back he was too happy for himself to bother over old Mayo's queer silences.

He was sufficiently in touch with reality however to slow his horse to a halt as he came upon Jos. He watched the young man, puzzled, realizing Jos did not see him. He turned in the saddle and watched the lad walk past without even batting an eyelid.

'Well!' he thought, 'old Sarah always said he day-dreamed. Now I believe her!' He shook his head whimsically. 'I don't believe he had the faintest idea I was sitting here!'

Jos strode on, remorselessly hunting George Mayo. Jos *had* seen the Squire.

'Obviously riding back from Mayo's,' he thought bitterly, 'no doubt there's been celebrations!'

It stood to reason that George would shortly be taking himself out to call formally on his future bride. There was only one way to do that. Mounted, over the fields, then turn to ride up the narrow lane which led to the manor house.

Jos set his jaw. He would wait for George. He would wait all day if necessary. He lounged against a gate, eyes staring down the lane in sombre mood. It occurred to him that old Joseph Howard had also waited for a Mayo to come riding. It was an eerie thought. A repetition of history.

The horse's head bobbed into view as it cantered easily over the field, then up the long lane. It was a Mayo's grey. Jos recognized George's stance in the saddle.

His heart started to beat more easily. He shook the tingles from his fingers and, throwing a quick glance around, was relieved to see they would be alone. The fields were deserted. The Squire had vanished. It would be just him and a Mayo all over again.

As George neared he saw the waiting figure and instinctively drew rein, slowing his horse back to a trot and then a walk while he stared frowning. As he recognized Jos he glowered, then grinned maliciously. His first impulse was to heel into a canter and ride past. He laughed as he approached the waiting figure. He knew what was affecting that bastard. Jealousy! This was too good to be true. He halted his horse six yards away and stared down, supercilious, arrogant and reeking with triumph.

Jos moved and walked into the lane's centre, blocking it unless George chose to ride him down. Jos stared up at the rider, eyes small and hard, jaw set, fists clenched, silent and waiting.

The rider eyed his stance. He was dressed in his best breeches and coat as befitted a man going to call on a lady. He did not really want to fight and get his clothes messed up, but he knew he could not ride away without a coward's label being applied.

George respected Jos as a fighter. Though, in the past they had neither of them decisively beaten the other. George now reckoned he should definitely have the edge. He had the weight and the strength. His morale was peak high. Nothing could topple him today!

He dismounted slowly and tied the reins to a tree.

'I'm ready when you are,' George told him proudly. He squared up, fists raised, feet apart, knees bent. Jos copied and slowly advanced. The horse snorted and backed to the extremity of the reins.

They sparred for a minute, beginning to get each other's reach. George danced forward, fists whipping in and out in a rapid blur of speed. Two red welts were left on Jos's face. Jos ignored them, fascinated by the good looks facing him.

'I wonder what Maud would think of her prince if he was cut up?' he asked himself.

Not that Jos wanted her now. His pride had been hurt far too badly.

He stepped forward, long arms flailing, fists cracking down on George's face. Frantically George tried to cover and duck but Jos was everywhere at once. Jos was beside himself. A savage exultation filled his soul as he rained merciless blows down on his opponent's face. The blood spurted from a fractured nose, slit lip and cut eye. Jos hammered on.

Frantically George ducked, twisted and weaved to no avail. His feet moved to right and left but no matter where he turned the fists still kept hitting. All the time blows smashed down on his face, cutting between his shielding arms and fists. He tried to punch in return. He landed some blows but they had no power behind them. His eyes swelled and filled with blood. He only knew Jos was still there by hearing his heavy breathing and feeling the welter of pain crash down. It was a never-ending curtain of agony. His feet slipped and he fell. He rolled on the ground and instinctively tried to scramble erect again. One leg braced, his muscles heaved and he stood, swaying gently.

Jos eyed him, drew back his right and let it

fly straight for George's unprotected jaw. It connected square and true. George's eyes glazed and he crumpled into an unconscious heap while the horse half-reared in fright, tugged at the reins and endeavoured to free itself.

Jos stood, feet apart, looking down at George. He tried to understand how he felt now his urge was satisfied. George's face was quite unrecognizable. Blood streamed from forehead to neck in tiny rivulets. More than one tooth had gone. A great flap of skin hung down from one eyebrow. He breathed through his mouth, the nasal cartilages horribly mangled.

Jos was satisfied. George Mayo would never look the same again. He did not yet know enough about females to realize that, ever contrariwise, Maud would become even more tender to her injured fiancé.

What would George do now? It had been a mutual fight. Jos had lost his girl; George had lost his looks. All things were equal again.

He turned and walked slowly back to Sarah. Apart from two red welts on his cheeks he was unmarked, though the skin was split and bloody around the knuckles of both hands and one thumb had started to swell in a strain.

'George's blood!' Jos said aloud in satisfaction as he studied his great hands.

Sarah raised her eyebrows as he entered the cottage. She took one quick look at him and stood, hands clasped together, waiting.

'I've just carved George Mayo up so that his own mother won't know him!'

Sarah's eyes burned with pride. She took his hands and, fetching water, bathed them while he sat wearily.

'You've really hurt him?' she asked.

Jos nodded. 'I have!' he told her grimly.

'And now what, Jos?'

He thought for a minute. 'I think I'll now have to go.'

'But where will you go?'

'I'll go to the Midlands. To Leicestershire. That's where the good hunting is. I've always wanted to work with horses.'

'When?'

'Not yet. Not for a few days. I don't want people to think I'm running away. If I could get work here Gran I'd stay with you but we both know that's out of the question now.'

'But the land, Jos! Our land!'

Jos shook his head impatiently. 'I know Gran, but what can I *do* about it? Land costs money. We don't have any and, if we had, do you think the Mayos would sell to us now? They'd see us in hell first! God knows what things will be like here when George inherits too! No, Gran! Everything you've said over the years has been right. The Mayos are rotten. I'll never forget and neither will those who come after me—but right now, there's not a thing I can do about getting our land back. I've got to

132

get money. Get good work. I can do that in the Shires.'

'But Jos, oh, how I'll miss you! We've always been together! You're all I have!' she told him wistfully, and for the first time in Jos's memory tears trickled down Sarah's withered old cheeks.

'Gran! Gran! Don't take on so. I have to go. You must understand!' he told her urgently.

Sarah acknowledged his wisdom but sorrow swept over her. She was to be left alone without even a chance of seeing the Howard land returned in her lifetime.

'You'll come back—someday?' she asked him hesitantly.

Jos nodded firmly. 'I'll be back—and I'll take what's ours!'

*   *   *

Jos hung around the cottage for two days, not attempting to hide. He knew who would come eventually. He kept taking little walks away from the cottage and Sarah's sad eyes.

On the second day the stallion appeared cantering over the fields in the exact place he had first seen a grey horse as a boy. He watched James Mayo ride up, slumped in the saddle. Jos's feelings were mixed. He loathed the Mayos yet he did not dislike this old man.

Jos stood, legs astride, firm as a young oak, face expressionless as James rode up and slowly dismounted.

'Well, Jos, I must say you don't do things by half measures, do you?'

Jos said nothing.

'You know that you've marked my son for life. You've branded him!'

'Just as your first son branded *me* for life— as a bastard!' Jos retorted coldly.

Old James flinched at this harsh truth. His shoulders slumped wearily. Mary had thrown a fit of wild hysterics when they brought George home. Even the doctor had been sufficiently shocked to bite his lips with worry. The Squire had been too appalled to do anything but freeze while Maud had done what any well-bred young lady did in such circumstances. She had calmly fainted with the shock.

'By God!' James Mayo told himself. 'He *is* a man!' as he looked up at Jos. 'But what's going to happen when I'm gone and George runs Mayo's?'

Jos read him. 'I'll be going soon,' he said flatly, 'but don't think I'm running away from you or anyone. I'm only going because I know there'll be no work for me from now on.'

'Where?'

'Leicestershire.'

'Have you any money?'

Jos grinned ruefully. 'The half-sovereign you gave me as a lad and a few shillings I've managed to save.'

Old James felt in his breeches pocket,

fingering the coins there. He only had a few sovereigns with him. Small change to him. A fortune to Jos. He took them out and handed them over.

'Take them! Go on! This is nothing to do with anyone but me and you. Whatever has happened in the past and no matter what comes in the future, you are my blood grandson, Jos Howard. Just you remember that!' he told him firmly.

Jos looked down into tired eyes. He saw genuine warmth. Quite suddenly, he felt for this old man. Instinctively he understood that the man did not care for his own heir.

'Things won't be easy for you when I'm gone, boy. No harm will come to old Sarah. I'll see to that,' James promised Jos, 'but when George inherits things might be bad for you around here.'

Jos frowned. What was coming now?

'I've left you some land, Jos. Not much. Twenty acres. It's rough but you could lick it into shape if you'd a mind to. I've tied it up so George can't touch it. There'll also be two Mayo's greys for you. I'd like to have done more but George—and my wife—,' he ended lamely, shrugging his shoulders while his eyes appealed to Jos for commiseration.

'That's all right, Grandpa! I didn't expect anything at all!' Jos replied softly.

The old man was all right when you got to know him! It wasn't his fault that things had turned out the way they had. At least, he had thought enough to *try* and make reparation. Twenty acres was little enough compared to the mighty Mayo's but it *was* land. Twenty acres! Land of his own one day! Now he had a real incentive to go and try to acquire capital. And two Mayo's greys!

Jos's heart swelled. Surely this would please old Sarah? Old James warmed at Jos's term. Stepping forward he gave his hand which Jos took in a firm grip.

'Look after yourself, my boy. When you return, and especially if I'm gone, watch George. Don't trust him. He's a bad one,' he warned his grandson carefully. 'You'll want some clothes and travelling money. I'm going to send these to you. Barker can bring them over. Old Sarah doesn't mind him. They're both so old now they can natter over the past. God go with you, Jos!'

Turning, he quickly mounted and, without a backward glance, rode away.

Jos watched him disappear, a choking feeling catching his throat. His grandfather really cared for him. He preferred him to his own son! The knowledge hit Joe like a hammer blow.

He chinked the gold coins in his hand. He had some money. He would travel in style now. He would coach up like the gentry and eat well at the overnight taverns. No cheap rushes for lights. He would have an expensive candle.

'I've always been poor. Now I'll just see what the gentry's life is like,' he told himself. 'I'll try it and if I like it—which I think I will— then I'll make sure I get enough money to live like them always. I've had enough of being poor. I'm well-bred even though a bastard. I'll be a landowner one day *and* I'll have more than twenty acres too. I'm going to be a man of means.'

CHAPTER FOUR

Jos felt the horse hump its back and he swayed. The stallion ducked his head. Thrusting with his hocks, he snapped a wicked fly-jump, back arched like an arrow, hooves drumming the ground in anger. Feeling his rider's solidity the horse changed tactics. He bored with open mouth, oblivious to the snaffle bit, the animal shot forward in a wild gallop and hurtled down the grass.

Jos swore angrily, aware he was the subject of many interested and highly amused looks. He pulled on the reins, dropped a hand and tried to turn the horse. Mulishly the animal ignored the pain in his mouth. He charged straight for the fence. Jos felt the sweat break out on his forehead. He gripped tightly, held his breath, then the horse was lifting. Great muscular quarters and powerful hocks drove man and beast through the air. Jos caught a glimpse of the thick hedge underneath then the ground came up, hard and fast, for a drop landing.

Jos swung his weight backwards. The horse pecked a little at the landing and, quickly working both hands, Jos pulled the black's head up, rammed with his heels and regained control. The black snorted wildly, bounced in a ragged canter then sullenly stopped.

He turned the animal and drove him back at the fence. With pricked ears the stallion hesitated a second, felt the ram of spurred boots in his flank and took off again. They jumped back into the field where the hounds and people had paused.

Two black-habited ladies, riding side-saddle, nodded to each other in approval. As rider and black horse passaged through them there was admiration in the eyes of the top-hatted, long-coated men. Joe Howard deserved his name with horses. A name legion among many great ones in Leicestershire.

Deciding he'd had enough for one day, and with nods to people he knew, Jos turned.

It seemed so long ago since he had stepped off the Leicester coach. He had then been a green, gangling youth without much future and no home. Now he was a man of 23 years with an established reputation. He earned very good money—and all because of horses.

From talking himself into a job as a humble

stable boy Jos had soon graduated to nagsman. His ability to ride a rough horse had spread. He was in great demand from the gentry whenever they had a horse beyond their control or when the ladies' mounts wanted gentling.

Jos thought back as he rode. He now had a nice cottage, two rooms downstairs and two good bedrooms above. A change from the crowded bothy where he had first been thankful to lodge and eat. His stomach was always full and his purse never empty. The gentry could be generous and Jos was canny with his money.

His only grave mistake had been with Ann.

'If ever a marriage is a disaster, then mine is,' Jos thought ruefully, 'but what can I do about it?'

He was a married man with a son to show for the alliance too. A fine healthy boy of a year who took after his father more than any child had a right to. As for Ann—his heart quailed as he thought of his wife.

Jos was honest enough to admit that he was more than half to blame. He had married Ann Tate on a complete rebound. He had been infatuated with a pair of wild, black eyes, black hair and a lush figure—now he was suffering the consequences of utter foolishness. He had jumped into her bed with the wild abandon of blighted youth. He had washed the self-pity from his system with the fullness of a young male's lust. Now he was both wed and a father. He was still not quite sure how it had all happened, and he was thoroughly miserable.

What could he do? Ann was a shrew of the highest order and, Jos suspected, she had a different side for other men. What she denied to him she was not impartial about distributing elsewhere. As time had passed Jos had realized he couldn't care less. He had considered leaving her more than once but had always hesitated at the irrevocable final step.

'What came over me? Just what did I see in her?' he asked again and again.

In his eyes she had become coarse and abandoned in both speech and gesture whereas Jos had changed in the opposite direction. He had watched the gentry, listened to them, noted how they acted towards each other and those in the lower classes. He had painfully schooled himself in both manners and speech until he knew he could pass as real gentry if he wished.

It was good that he had such wild and dangerous work. Jos was the type of man to vegetate under a woman's scorn and biting tongue. Though he might be a genius with horses where women were concerned he was a helpless fool. He admitted this.

'If only I could take Peter and go back to Sarah's!' he mused. He could then be happy again but who would welcome him there? And

140

what could he do to earn his living with his reputation in Mayo's territory? And Ann was the child's mother! She certainly wouldn't allow herself to go to the wilds of Gloucestershire when here, in Leicestershire, she was meshed in the activity of a big stable with its attendant comings and goings of notables.

He received snatches of news from home. Verbal messages were passed to him from coachmen. Rarely he received a note written in Sarah's shaky hand. She was still well, though crippled with rheumatism and inclined to be bad-tempered in her old age. She was living out of her old age under the Squire's wing and watched over, at a discreet distance, by his grandfather.

Maud had married her George. They had managed to produce a son called Jon. A boy the same age as Peter.

'It's odd that me and my enemy should both have boys in the same year. Is this an ominous sign?' he asked himself. How did the feud stand now?

George had changed, his gossips told him. Deprived of his good looks from their last encounter so had also disappeared any good nature he might have had. George drank heavily, was obese, foul-mouthed and, so 'twas said, was the disgust of old James Mayo.

The old man, now feeble, was ready to die at any time. Jos didn't know whom he pitied the most. His disappointed grandfather or one-time girl. What a bed Maud had made for herself. She had the land and riches but what she must be suffering for them!

As he rode into the yard he sighed to himself, squared his shoulders and slowly dismounted. He gave the black's reins to a groom.

Jos looked round the busy stable yard. It was owned by a group of London business men. Regular toffs who knew how to invest their money for a quick and sound return. It housed various types of animals from hunters and ladies' hacks to coach horses. It catered for both private and commercial use.

The head stableman eyed Jos and hurried past with a brief nod. Jos was a little surprised. He suddenly became aware that the other boys and men were whispering surreptitiously. For a moment he wondered what was attracting their attention, then he shrugged and turned towards his home.

His cottage stood on its own as befitted a top rough rider earning big money. He immediately became conscious of two things. All the men and boys stared after him and there was no smoke from the chimney. Unease started to fill him. He hurried his steps. Now what was wrong?

He opened the door with a bang and clumped over the stone floor into the downstairs room which doubled as living-room and kitchen. As soon as he entered he sensed the cottage was empty. It was so still and cold. Last night's ashes lay in the black-leaded grate. No smell of hot food touched his nostrils. He stopped, trying to puzzle it out.

'Ann! Ann?'

'It's not a bit of good you calling for her, she's gone!' the voice told him calmly.

Jos whipped round in alarm. The woman in the door was holding his son in her plump arms. She was Jenny. The stud groom's wife, a buxom female with a large brood of forever squabbling children.

'She went off early this morning. Left the child with me,' explained Jenny, watching Jos's reactions with interest.

'Gone off! Where? Why?'

Jenny shrugged eloquently. 'That's her secret, but she didn't go alone,' and she paused, eyeing Jos carefully. What would his reaction be?

'Happen you know that Ann Tate, as I think of her, had an eye for the men? You weren't the first—but you'll be knowing that fact—and after the young 'un was born you weren't the last by a long chalk! Common lot! Always has been. Anyhow, she's gone off with a soldier. Him and her went on the first coach to London. My guess is you'll not be seeing the likes of her back here again and good riddance!'

Jos leaned against the wall, staggered with

this information. He knew things were bad between him and Ann but for her to prefer a common foot soldier—his pride was shattered. His lips tightened. He quickly debated what to do. He could go after her, thrash her and the man and bring her back, but then what? Did he *want* her back? And wouldn't she do the same again as soon as his back was turned? He was honest enough to understand his feelings: In a way he was glad to see the back of her—it was just that he should have taken the step. Not his wife!

The child whimpered and the woman lifted her eyebrows.

'Fine type to run off and leave her young 'un,' she added caustically. A man with a toddler and no woman could get himself in a mess, though she knew, as did everyone, that Jos Howard was not short of money. He'd not have trouble in finding a wench to warm his bed for him either. This giant of a man had a quiet magnetism about him which brought out the mothering instinct in most females.

'If I'd been a bit younger I wouldn't have minded jumping into bed with you, Jos Howard,' Jenny told herself. 'You're all man!'

Jos reached out and took his son in his arms. He felt great tenderness towards the small child, now so utterly dependent upon him. He smiled down, watching the tiny hands form fists while big blue eyes looked up at him trustingly.

'He's been fed and changed,' Jenny informed him. 'I've had him in with my lot.'

'Thank you, Jenny. You've been kind,' he told her sincerely.

'What'll you do now, Jos?'

'Do? I don't quite know. Have a good think, I guess.'

'You'll be staying on here then?'

Jos considered. 'I don't know, Jenny.'

So many implications were hitting him. He was free! At last! No longer did he have to ponder the means to obtain his freedom. Ann had given it to him. His relief was overwhelming. He knew he would never marry again. Once bitten had made him more than twice shy.

Slowly he showed her to the door, making small talk, assuring her he would call if he needed help. He latched the thick wooden door to and leaned back against it. This was all his now to do exactly as he liked. He lifted the boy high in the air, laughed up at him and the child gurgled back.

The knock at the door was both loud and unexpected. Jos jumped with shock, then swore in annoyance. Jenny back to peep and pry! He opened the door, ready to be brusque, but choked the words back. He looked at the stout middle-aged man dressed in sombre black from his top hat, coat and trousers down to expensive boots.

'Jos Howard? Ah! At last! I've had a long

journey. May I come in?'

Jos stood aside, wondering, 'What now?'

'You'll be wondering who I am, no doubt? Let me introduce myself. My name is Cleeg, and I'm from the Bristol firm of solicitors Frewster and Frewster. I regret to inform you that Mr James Mayo died very suddenly last week. The will was read after the funeral and you are a beneficiary. Perhaps you knew?'

Jos stared in surprise. So old James was dead. His grandfather for whom he had always had more than a sneaking regard. A great, true yeoman gone forever; they didn't breed them like old James nowadays. Jos felt pain clutch at his heart. He was surprised to realize how grieved he was.

'I did understand there would be twenty acres of land for me and two Mayo's greys,' he replied, bringing forward two stout chairs.

'Mr Mayo deeded you twenty acres of land a number of years ago. However, two years last March he added another codicil to his will. You now inherit fifty acres of very prime land indeed, all of which abounds a small cottage where your grandmother lived. The original twenty acres stays with Mayo's. You have also been left a filly and colt of the breed now known as Mayo's greys. You know them?'

Jos nodded. His two Mayo's greys and fifty acres of best land. This was news indeed. The old man had done him proud in the end. Good old Grandpa. You tried to atone—and you have, Jos thought quietly.

'I was also instructed to give you this letter when my client was deceased.'

Jos took the heavy letter in his hand and looked down at it. Apart from Sarah's scribbled notes this was the first real letter he had ever received. Instinctively he knew the hand which had penned this had put very private thoughts to paper.

Something prodded at him—a word the clerk had used. His excitement waned. The man had referred to his grandmother—in the past tense! That could only mean—and Jos turned to stare at the wall. He averted his gaze, not wanting a stranger to read the emotion on his face.

Sarah must be dead. Dear, tough old Sarah. Gone forever. The aggressive little old lady who had been mother and father to him; who had poured over him enough love and kindness for six boys. Tiny Sarah of the fighting heart who had been ready to take on the mighty Mayos!

Jos swallowed. Grief stormed through his body. His Gran had gone. He would never see her again. She had died without him at her side, her life's dream unfulfilled. He knew he was very near to tears. He fought for self-control. He set his face in a bleak mask impossible for anyone to read.

'Goodbye, Gran! I'm so sorry you had to go without me there—but I'll do it. By God I will!

I'll get all our land back somehow. And I'll see that my boy receives the lessons you gave me!'

He turned back to the man. Face white. Emotions under tight control.

'I regret I have further sad news for you,' the messenger continued, 'your grandmother, Sarah Howard, died the same day as Mr Mayo. She went very peacefully. There was no pain at all. The vicar and the Squire were with her at the end.'

'Squire Gordon requests that you make arrangements to remove your grandmother's possessions as soon as possible. He wishes to sell the cottage. I realize this must all be a big shock to you, Mr. Howard. I can stay overnight at the Bell Inn, but I must chaise back to Bristol no later than tomorrow. Perhaps if I call in the morning you can give me your instructions then?'

Jos's brain had been working rapidly. His decision was already made.

'There's no need to wait until then. I can tell you my plans right now. I will return with you if you care to share your chaise with me? Myself and my son,' Jos said, pointing to the child lying quietly watching the stranger with fascinated eyes.

'And your good wife?'

'My good wife has run off with a soldier. I'm glad to see the back of her. The child is mine and comes with me,' Jos told him.

The clerk coloured and cleared his throat

uneasily. For once he was at a loss for words to utter. This young man was unnaturally blunt. He sniffed uncomfortably.

'And about—er—funds?' he asked hesitantly.

'I'm a man of means,' Jos told him. 'I've over £400 in a Leicester bank which I'll want transferring to a good bank in Bristol. Oh, you needn't look like that! It's money I've earned!'

The clerk coloured as he pricked up his ears. A young man living in a place like this with so much money was unusual and the unusual was always worth cultivating. He eyed Jos shrewdly, wondering his mental strength.

'And it's money put by for a purpose, not to be thrown away!' Jos warned him firmly.

The clerk wondered curiously why the mighty James Mayo had taken so much interest in this young man as to leave him good land? There was much more to this than met the eye!

'I'm pleased to be of assistance to you, Mr Howard. You know that if we can be of any help to you, Frewster and Frewster are always the first to act.'

The clerk watched Jos carefully and noted the wary look.

'I think, sir, if we were good enough to act for Mr Mayo we could also prove satisfactory to your good self,' he pointed out.

Jos nodded. That was a good point well made. I'm going to need legal protection for Peter. If I know George Mayo there was all hell let loose when that Will was read. I wouldn't put it past him trying something in the future. I must think of Peter.

The clerk sensed Jos was making an important decision. 'Naturally, anything we do for a client is held in the highest confidence,' he said suggestively.

Jos, looking speculatively at the door, nodded.

'Very well! Now listen carefully. I'm James Mayo's bastard grandson. George Mayo hates my guts because I beat him up—perhaps you knew that—and I hate his! He took my girl. I suspect he wasn't pleased to say the least, when his father's Will was read. I want my land and horses protecting legally, you understand? I also want my grandmother's cottage. I want you to go back and negotiate with the Squire. Keep it quiet that it's for me or that I'm coming back into the area again. I'll lodge in Bristol for the time being. Once the cottage is mine and the land is secure no one can touch me.'

'I quite understand, sir. I'll see that immediate action is taken. If I might offer a word of advice? George Mayo is, I regret to say, going from bad to worse. He's full of hatred for you. You are womanless with a small child. Might I not arrange the hire of a suitable housekeeper—I think the knowledge of your home always being occupied might stop George Mayo from doing anything rash on those lines. But I cannot guarantee your own person!' he warned carefully.

'I can look after myself,' grinned Jos, a wicked look in his eyes. 'I've beaten George Mayo up once. I'll do it again if he crosses me!'

The clerk nodded silent agreement. This young giant would be hell to cross. He suddenly decided he would rather have Jos Howard on his side than against him. He was also astute enough to realize that this young man was bursting to read the letter in private. He stood, stretching and, offering a farewell, left Jos to his thoughts.

They were very confused thoughts. Too much had been sprung on him in too short a space of time. Ann gone. His freedom given to him. Old James and Sarah both dead. And himself the owner of fifty acres of good Glos. land. He looked at the child then moved and slowly attended to him. His fingers fumbled with unaccustomed garments. Only when his son slept peacefully did he break the letter's wax seal.

The paper was nearly as thick as parchment. The words were written with a bold, flowing script. Jos settled down, head bent near the candle.

'My Dear Grandson,
When you receive this Jos I will be dead, and because of the past I feel I must write and tell you my feelings. You

151

know, Jos, you think of yourself as a Howard, but you are far more Mayo than you realize. You are certainly more Mayo than my son George will ever be. You're exactly like your father, my long-dead John. Somewhere Jos the blood-lines have gone wrong. George is bad, through and through. I worry for Mayo's when I'm gone. I've entailed everything, he cannot touch or sell it without his heir's consent and, you may know, he has a son called Jon. But he's a waster, Jos. A drinker, cheat and liar. I'm frightened what he will do to Mayo's when I'm not there to control him. I suspected him as a child. I feared more as he grew to manhood but that beating you gave him finally showed my son in his true colours. It's hard for a father to despise his heir but I despise mine. He disgusts me. How I wish things had turned out differently. Jos, you should be my heir. You are the only true Mayo. You would be kind to the land, cherish it for what it is, nurture it and make it produce. George, I fear, will let it backslide. I can only hope that Jon will not follow his suit.

I'm a tired old man, Jos. I wish I could see you again. I would even go and talk to Sarah if she would allow it but I know better than to try. She has carried her hate far too long—like Mary. Try and

152

end all this Jos. What happened, happened so very long ago. I hear tell you too have a son. I hope to God he doesn't cross with Jon when they both grow up.

Take care of the horses which I leave you. Breed true and well. Always keep two of them. They will never let you down. Take care of your fifty acres. Feed it, guard it and it will reward you well.

Watch George. He is wicked and mean. He is afraid of you. When he strikes it will be in the dark or behind your back. I put nothing past my rotten son. Maud is a weak fool. You don't realize how well rid of her you were. She's afraid of me and even more terrified of her husband. You certainly gained when you lost her, Jos.

I only hope that this weak strain does not come out in Jon. *You* will only ever breed true, Jos. I feel so old and weary. I look forward to the peace of death. I will never see you again, dear Grandson. Think of me—will you? May God be with you and yours always—remember— cherish the land!

James Mayo.'

Jos sat for a long time, his head bowed, reading and re-reading his letter. Memories flooded through him.

He sighed, and looked at his child. How

would Peter turn out? Would he be a Mayo or a Howard, or an equal mixture of both? What lay ahead for his son? How would he fare when faced with his distant relation. Jon Mayo, a lad the same age as Peter, would, no doubt, be brought up to hate as he himself had been.

He thought for hours into that night, reflecting about the two people who had most influenced his character. That old Sarah and James were no more was tragic news. He was acutely aware that now he stood alone. He had no true friend to whom he could turn and talk. He was solitary by nature. He had been hurt too much in the past. When friendship had been offered his wariness had made him decline. He knew that his future could be very bleak indeed. To claim his own he had to step back into the area of a man who seethed with hatred for him.

If anything happened to him—Peter must know their story. Jos had a good if slow script. He resolved, when settled, to spend his evenings writing down his history as a legacy for his son and his son's sons.

They had a right to know who they were and from whence they came. Sarah had been so right. She had only ever thought of him.

'Now I must think only of my son!' Jos vowed. 'Peter should be the heir to Mayo's. Not this boy Jon!'

'What Peter does when a man is up to him,

but I must mould him as Sarah moulded me.'

What he would think about his turbulent past Jos could not imagine. He did not want a spineless son. Neither did he want an evil one. He did want a son who understood his place in life. A son who would be ambitious for his children in turn. Most of all, he wanted to rear his son to have the same love for the land which was, he admitted, the true legacy of both Mayo and Howard.

CHAPTER FIVE

Jos sat his grey overlooking the expanse of Mayo's. From the top of the hill he had a splendid view as the countryside rolled away to right and left. He shook his head in amazement. It was incredible how a bungling fool could so start a ruination. It was impossible to believe that it was only a year since James Mayo's death. How could land go back so in such a short space of time?

Jos had been deeply shocked when he first heard about George. That drink could damn a man he knew only too well. He had not allowed for the fact that it could also muddle his senses and addle his wits. Only the entailment had saved the property and kept it intact at least. The horses—the proud Mayo's greys—had all been sold long ago to pay for drink.

Jos shook his head again unhappily. It grieved him to see the proud Mayos reduced to this, though how Sarah would have chortled. At this rate there would be precious little left for Jon to inherit but a mass of debts.

He had not learned this all at once upon his return. For many weeks he had been too busy seeing his solicitor and making legal arrangements to safeguard his property for his son. It had taken time but after three months he had considered himself established as a man of property should be.

Jos had been surprised at the old Squire's attitude when they first met. Particularly, he felt, after the Squire having sold old Sarah's cottage should learn its new owner.

The old gentleman had ridden over one day and Jos had been more than prepared for a shouting match. The man on the brown hack was weary. Some of the spark had left him. He seemed but a bag of bones which moved automatically.

Jos had invited him into his cottage, proud to show off what he had already achieved. With a careful loan through his solicitors he had extended the original structure and it now boasted two large downstairs rooms with three big bedrooms. One of these doubled as a living-room for his housekeeper, an amiable widow from the village. She was thankful to keep his house, feed him and not have to offer anything else.

The furniture was solid yet graceful. The rugs scattered over the stone floors were thick and warm to the booted feet. A cheery log fire burned in the hearth. From the kitchen wafted smells of soups and meats. Copper pans, burnished like gold, hung like soldiers from pegs on one wall while jars of preserves and spices marched cheek by jowl with bacon flitches, hanging from ceiling hooks. The whole building had not just an air of prosperity and solidity, it extended the warm welcome of a real home.

The Squire had a fleeting thought for his own stark house and the even more dismal welcome he could only ever expect at Mayo's. He eyed Jos thoughtfully, sipping the hot toddy offered to him by the housekeeper.

'You've come up in the world, Jos!' he said, nodding at the room in general.

Jos smiled quietly and said nothing. He watched his son crawling over a clip rug intent on some involved game of his own making.

'I made a bad deal for my gal. I should have let you wed her when she wanted,' the Squire admitted slowly.

'Maybe it was all for the best. For myself I can say a wife isn't everything. What wife could give me more than I have now? I would never allow myself to be tied to a woman again!' Jos replied firmly.

'Mayo's has come down in the world. That

would have pleased old Sarah!'

Jos snorted. 'It pleases me too! It'll come down even further while that fool George lives with the port bottle at his elbow!'

'But you just go up and up!' the Squire stated in admiration.

Where had the old Jos gone? This man sitting opposite him was an assured gentleman of the world. Jos's prowess as a horseman had preceded his return to the county. He was affluent. That was the only way to describe him.

He even had these new-fangled loose boxes erected for his best horses, those two Mayo's greys. While twelve stalls at the back of the cottage were regularly filled with animals he was breaking and schooling for the gentry.

The Squire knew that James Mayo had left Jos the land. He guessed that Jos had done well in the Midlands but to have the solidity to acquire a loan to found his horse stud—the Squire's mind boggled. Who would have thought it? Certainly not him!

'Why, look at his workers!' mused the Squire. 'He employs six stable lads and pays them twenty pounds a year and their keep! I've heard tell the stud groom gets double that too! Fancy being able to afford such fantastic wages to common workers. It's bad though. All the men want to work for him and everyone else can go to hell. He's not liked for it—and I don't believe he gives a damn either about public feeling among the landowners. How does he do it? What is there about him?'

The Squire knew that Jos had obtained a row of cottages in the village where he housed his married workers. The single lads lived and fed in a bothy, their creature comforts attended to by a female cook and two serving wenches.

Jos watched the old man and read his obvious thoughts. They gave him immense satisfaction. He felt pity for the Squire. An old man, with an empty title, worth precious little and having no one really to care for him in his old age. Above all, he knew the sad man had made a terrible mistake.

Jos saw him often after than day. The Squire developed the habit of riding past often. Between the two men an odd friendship grew. It amused Jos and warmed the Squire's heart.

As yet Jos had not met either of the Mayos. That interesting event took place shortly before the harvest. It had been a splendid summer. With his new machines Jos had succeeded in making two hay crops and history at the same time. The hay now stood, neatly stacked, in three large ricks at the rear of the stables. Jos's oats promised to yield just as well. He saw that with satisfaction and all things being equal, his property would be self-sufficient throughout the winter.

Jos had named his property Ferndale after

the old Howard house which had been destroyed in Sarah's days. His stallion he called Mayho, combining the first letters of both Mayo and Howard. His in-foal mare he called Grace. She had been served with a thoroughbred from Somerset and Jos had great hopes of the foal. Whether it be filly or colt it would be a foundation animal for the Ferndale Stud with the famous grey bloodline. Mayho he used as a travelling stallion during the breeding season as well as on four mares which he had carefully purchased.

Jos loved Mayho and so did Peter. Already the boy showed no fear when the stallion danced and squealed with pride. Jos knew that the blood had run as true in his son as in the grey. Peter would be a horseman. His father would teach him everything he knew.

On the momentous day of the Mayo-Howard meeting Jos was riding Mayho around his fifty acres.

Jos rode out into the long lane which communicated between Mayo's and the Squire's. There, so long ago, he had seen his first Mayo's grey.

From the opposite end of the lane he spotted two riders approaching at a slow walk. To his rear he heard the clop of more hooves. He turned in the saddle, saw the Squire coming up at the trot and waved, waiting for him. At the same time, he watched the riders approaching from his front.

He saw one was a woman sitting side-saddle, her long brown habit waving in the breeze. The other he recognized as George Mayo. A nerve fluttered in his throat. They had to meet sometime. It was amazing that during the time he had been back, they had not met before this. He wondered idly if this was George's doing.

'Daughter and son-in-law,' Jos said, nodding to the Squire in the riders' direction.

He watched the old man pull a face, his eyes grew sad as he watched his daughter ride towards him.

Jos stared in horrified amazement. This was never his Maud. Not this tired, beaten woman with a lock of grey hair showing under her bonnet. Her face was a mixture of the young and old. Lines creased her forehead yet the cheeks still held the pink flush of youth. She sat her saddle as if worn-out. Even so her eyes still held fire. Jos felt them burning into his with an expression he could not name but which made him recoil uneasily.

He switched his gaze to his enemy. His interest was cool and dispassionate. George's face was a mess. Jos supposed he should have felt pride at what his fists had done but only a deep pity stirred in him. This man, his own age, looked forty. A horribly broken nose sat slantwise, there was a thick coarse red scar above one eyebrow and the once slender lips were thick and ugly. The drink had left its

161

indelible mark. His complexion displayed that over-ruddy alcoholic glow and the eyes were distant.

Jos slowly shook his head. Perhaps it was this movement which attracted George's attention. No one quite knew what happened to him. Events moved with a speed almost beyond the eye's ability to register. Wagging tongues over tankards of ale all said afterwards that George Mayo had a brain storm.

The truth of the matter was that George had the biggest shock of his whole life. He knew Jos Howard was back. He had heard he was even doing well but port and bad living do not give a man sharp wits. He had never forgotten the beating from Jos's fists. It was a recurring nightmare of magnific horror which always left him dripping sweat and crying aloud with moans.

To be confronted suddenly with the man who had ruined his face, the man who had given him such terrible dreams, shocked George Mayo back into the present with an explosion. Jos Howard represented everything bad to which George was now heir. Before the astonished eyes of them all he dug sharp spurs into the chestnut's flanks and charged at Jos's stallion. They were all taken by surprise, Jos most of all.

What George thought he could actually do was never clear. It was conceded that his brain was too befuddled for logical thought. For this one instance, though, George *was* thinking like any sane man. The bloodlust swept through him and his hands itched to fasten themselves around Jos's throat.

The terrified chestnut crashed into Jos's stallion, throwing the shocked animal back on its hindlegs, hooves slithering to retain a footing. The chestnut half reared and George leaned out of the saddle, slashing with his switch.

Jos felt sharp pain across his cheeks. He ducked frantically, at the same time trying to control his stallion. The grey's temper flared and he attacked the chestnut in rage. For two seconds Jos stared into George's eyes. They mirrored a life-time's hate. They discharged a loathing so deep and venomous that inwardly Jos shuddered.

He heard Maud scream frantically. He also heard the Squire shouting wildly, then George was at him again, taking advantage of his surprise attack. The switch flailed down, again and again. It cut the skin of Jos's face, giving him blinding pain. With this pain his own temper flared like a winter gale.

He fought the stallion, bringing him down on all four legs, driving with his heels, parrying the blows with his right hand. Now the chestnut backed away, ignoring the spurs. Blood streamed down its red coat.

It panicked, it reared high, going up and up into the sky, teetering on its hocks and George was finished. He had little real skill as a horseman. He had none when frightened and George Mayo was a frightened man now. He had regained his true sanity, realized what he had done and knew, instinctively, he could never best Jos Howard.

He grabbed frantically at the reins to keep his balance and signed his own death sentence. The cruel curb bit, with its painfully high port, crashed up against the tender bars of the chestnut's mouth in a sheet of pain.

The chestnut flung its head back to dodge the pain and, already standing nearly vertical, went too far and lost his balance. The hind hooves scrambled wildly backwards but slowly, almost beautifully, the horse fell over, the man underneath.

An experienced horseman might possibly have lived. He could have twisted his body sideways and saved part of himself. George was frozen into stillness. The ground came up, hard and fast. The last picture his eyes ever filmed were of tangled red hairs from the chestnut's mane hurtling towards him.

There was a dull thud. A second's silence then his back and neck snapped. George Mayo died. The horse fell better, partly protected by the man as a cushion. The animal, frightened out of its wits, panicked, thrashing around with its hooves, struggling to regain its footing. Its off-fore reached out, and found a hold. The chestnut heaved and started rising. He slipped and with an ugly crack the cannon bone snapped. The chestnut opened his mouth and screamed in sheer agony.

It was bedlam, Jos realized afterwards. His own stallion was screeching with boiling anger. Maud was screaming her head off like a demented soul. The Squire was roaring and futilely waving his crop about in the air.

Jos drove with his heels, used wrists and hands and brought the stallion back under disciplined control. He flung himself out of the saddle, jerking the pistol he always carried from its saddle holster.

Jos sprang over the still suffering chestnut. One look was enough to show him George was dead. He grabbed Maud, brought his hand round and slapped her hard across the face. She flinched and looked up at him in horror. Jos grabbed her arm and pulled her away. He thrust her into the arms of the Squire who, like Maud, had dismounted and was standing dithering from one foot to another.

'Hold her! Keep her looking the other way!' Jos snapped at the bewildered old man.

Jos approached the chestnut warily but the animal was far too concerned with its own pain to snap at a mere man. Jos saw the dangling foreleg. Sparks of pain were shooting from bewildered brown eyes. Lifting his pistol, taking aim, he destroyed the horse. The animal stilled, hovered, then lost its balance and crashed down on the dry earth.

Everywhere was silent again, except for a gentle whimpering which seeped into Jos's ears. He realized it came from Maud, held tightly in her father's arms.

Jos rubbed his hand over his burning face. He felt the salty taste of blood on a lip and wondered if George had marked him for life. It was an interesting question which he would have to answer later.

He pulled the man's body from under the horse's hindlegs. Removing his coat he covered the hideous face then slowly stood and looked at Maud and the Squire.

Maud turned and stared back at him. Her eyes were needle points of hatred. They scorched Jos's soul.

'Maud! Maud!' he said gently, walking towards her.

'Keep away from me!' she hissed back and he halted in shock.

'But Maud!' the Squire started to remonstrate gently.

Maud Mayo jerked herself away from her father's arms and stared up at Jos, lips drawn back showing bared teeth.

'It's all your doing!' she spat accusingly.

Jos was too stunned to reply at first. 'What do you mean, my doing? I didn't attack him!' he protested wildly.

'Everything's your fault, Jos Howard! And to think I once nearly married you!' Scorn whipped through her voice.

Jos stood frozen, utterly bewildered. The Squire's mouth gaped and the two men looked at each other, stupefied by her words.

'I'm now a widow—at my age—and have a son to bring up and not a penny piece to my name!'

'Well, that's not my fault!' Jos retorted quietly.

'Of course it's your fault!' she snapped at him. 'It's you who ruined my husband's looks and drove him to the drink in the first place! It's you who terrified him so much that he never once, in our married life, slept the whole night through without screaming your name! You're bad, Jos Howard. Bad through and through! Oh, my word, George was so right when he said he hated you more than anything else in this world. That old fool his father couldn't or wouldn't see it but George's mother could! And so could George! And where is he now? Lying there dead—to prove it!'

'Maud, my dear!' the Squire began again unhappily.

'Oh, don't you start doddering around me. I've enough on now to rear a son on money I don't have!'

'But you have the land, daughter!'

'Fat lot of good that is; it's entailed, it's not mine. I can't sell it to get some money!'

'You can use it!' Jos told her coldly.

Jos looked at Maud steadily. He had been told that the true person only came to the surface in times of crisis. It occurred to him that he had, perhaps, been lucky. Perhaps saved something quite appalling. Right now, Maud Mayo acted and spoke like a mad woman. She was beyond reason. Words flowed from her mouth which she had never learned from her gentle father. Only from drunken George could she have learned these foul obscenities. Jos was sickened.

'Use it? Use it? With what?' Maud screamed at him.

'There's bad blood in you, Jos Howard!' she raved on. Saliva trickled from her lips. Her eyes became bold and glassy as she worked herself into a rage. 'But what can you expect from a bastard? A beggar whose mother was a kitchen slut, and whose Grandpa a murderer!'

Jos went white. His fists clenched and he stepped towards her. He swelled, the muscles of his neck standing out like steel cords. Maud was stilled into silence, dwarfed by this now angry giant. One hand flew to her mouth. Her eyes opened wide, showing whites tinged with yellow. She caught her breath, fear and reason stilled her tongue.

'I've never struck a woman in my life yet,' Jos told her quietly. 'But there's always a first time and I swear by God, Maud Mayo, you let any more filth like that out of your mouth either before me or anyone else and this will take every tooth from your gums!'

His giant fist emphasized the threat,

brandished within an inch of her lips.

'Your mouth will stay shut, once and for all!'

Maud cringed like a whipped cur. Her arms covered her breast in an instinctive female gesture. Her head bent aside, eyes slit, watching him in apprehension.

The Squire stood in horror. This frozen tableau of fear before his eyes was unreal. It had to be.

A bird flew over and the scene altered. The man moved, lowering his hand, loosening his thick fingers, stretching his biceps. His face was sculptured in lines of scorn and disgust as if looking at a diseased foulness which had crept from some horrible hole in the ground.

An honest face now marred by two crimson weals which would become permanent scars.

This isn't Jos, the Squire told himself. This was some devil sent to haunt him. As the devil stepped back, lowered his head and half-turned, he became young Jos again.

And the harridan, where had he seen her before? He had once had a daughter. A charming, gentle girl. Was that slavering hag with the half-crazed eyes and dribbling lips all that was left? For the remainder of his life the tableau would haunt him.

Jos turned. With slow, measured steps he gathered up the reins and swung into the saddle. He sat a minute looking down. He spoke to the old man.

'Take care of her. I'll go for help!' He was

gone in a clatter of noise and sparks where iron-shod hooves struck flintstones.

The Squire, feeling like a man of a hundred, approached his daughter with some trepidation. Gingerly he touched her arm and she turned to him. Her eyes were brimming with tears of self-pity and highly-charged emotion.

'My dear Maud? What has happened to us all?' he asked plaintively.

A wan smile touched her lips. For a brief while, Maud Mayo became the Maud Gordon of old. One hand came up and touched the grey hair exposed when the old man's hat had fallen off.

'I don't know, father. All I know is that everything goes wrong in my life and everything goes back to Jos Howard.'

'But, dear child, you can't blame Jos for what has just happened,' he protested mildly.

Maud stiffened. 'I can and I do! There's a devil watching over him, guarding his every move, saving him! Look at him! Secure, rich almost, the talk of the county and what was he as a boy? Nothing! How is it he's gone up so while me and mine have come down? It's not fair!' she cried petulantly.

The Squire sighed. His shoulders sagged wearily, as he shook his head.

'I don't know what's happened, child. We must do the best we can now. That's all we can do.'

'And what's that? I'm poor, father! Poor! And I've a son to raise. All that he has right now is worthless land. I've no money to work it. I'm going to be as poor as a farm worker!'

'It's not as bad as all that, child. Be fair! George did not have to drink!'

'What else could you expect him to do after Jos Howard nearly killed him? He was ugly, father! Ugly—and he knew it! People laughed at him behind his back; sneered at him too and he knew that as well! His own father despised him. All he ever thought of was that by-blow of dead John's! Never a real thought for George. His son and heir!'

CHAPTER SIX

'Poor old devil!' Jos thought as he rode back from the funeral. 'I guess in a way I'm slightly responsible for his death too. Is there a spell on me? Is there?'

His thoughts were a web of logical reasoning and suspicious invention. After all, he told himself, the Squire was an old man and it was obvious that George's death had just precipitated a natural end. The old man had died peacefully in bed which Jos considered a fine way to go. What worried and upset Jos was the fact that people, and especially Mayos and their kin, seemed to die where he went.

171

'Did old Joseph put a spell on all of us Howards that day? He killed John. I've killed George—what comes next? Does Peter kill Jon? God forbid!'

The Mayos were just too big to forget. Even in their poverty they were still the largest landowners around. Why is it land gives power, he wondered.

'I've only fifty acres. I could do with more land but where can I get it? Certainly never from Mayo's and now the Squire's dead all that land goes to Mayo's too!'

What would Sarah have advised? How Jos wished he could talk to her. At times, he was acutely lonely. He had no spiritual friend to consult or who could console him. If Peter were bigger—he sighed to himself.

Just where did he go from here? Business was going to boom. He knew that. The demand for good horses was fantastic and here he had vision and skill. He knew he could make money. Lots of money to hand down to Peter and that was the only thing to count now. Peter! He must settle down, erase these weird thoughts and bring up a fine son to make a splendid man.

*   *   *

Which is exactly what he did. Even Jos had to admit to himself that he had done a splendid job. At twenty Peter Howard was Jos all over

172

again. A great, upstanding man with a gentle nature, honest face and popular with everyone. Especially the girls.

But Peter had no intention of being hurried into anything. He went out with the girls. Called on them and danced attendance enough to satisfy any girl's heart but no further would he go.

Jos watched in amusement. Peter was the catch of the county. He had been given a fine education at one of the lesser public schools and his schooling had been finished off with dancing, fencing and shooting. Peter could hold his own anywhere, Jos thought with pride. He wondered idly what Ann would have thought about their son.

What had happened to her he never knew and cared less. Peter was his product. Often he forgot that a woman had been involved in the boy's creation.

'What are you going to do now, son?' he asked one evening after dinner.

'Do? Why, work here with you and breed even better horses!' Peter replied in surprise. He had an excellent relationship with his father.

'And marriage?'

Peter grinned. 'Plenty of time for that. When I marry it'll be to the best only!'

With that, Jos had to be content, but even he began to feel some alarm as the years passed and Peter still lived a single life. Wasn't he ever going to settle down? Ferndale must have an heir apparent.

So when Peter brought his Jane home Jos was almost speechless with surprise and delight. She was a pretty, vivacious girl full of mischief and Jos could see the couple were head over heels in love with each other.

At twenty-six Peter had kept his word and chosen only the best. Jane Evans came from a respectable family in the Midlands and was the only daughter among a brood of boisterous boys. Jos gathered that his son had met his fiancée on one of his frequent journeys around the country delivering the valuable greys for sale.

Peter married his Jane in a burst of celebration which had the house thronged with friends and family. Ferndale exploded into new life.

Jane was a small, dark-haired girl with thin, delicately chiselled bones which gave her face an elfish look. She had deep brown eyes which twinkled and her lips seemed to twitch constantly with joy at life itself.

She had a mischievous nature and, at times, was just a little girl as she sped through the house like a miniature and likeable storm. She was not above playing tricks on her two men as she called them and she so bubbled with vivacious life that from dawn until bedtime her chuckling laugh echoed around Ferndale.

Peter adored her. She was his jewel of life.

174

She could do no wrong and Jos was perfectly well aware that this imp of a girl could twist him around her little finger with consummate ease. Once he tried to act the crusty father-in-law but she saw through him in a flash, ruffled his hair and ran away entirely unimpressed with his mock sternness.

It was a happy year. The family was small but Jane's spirit welded them into a tight-knit little group and it was a debatable point who was more excited when she became pregnant.

To Peter his jewel of a wife became even more precious and, given the chance, he would have coddled her in a cocoon of absolute safety but Jane laughed at him. She had no fears about her condition. With a commonsense unusual for those days she told her worrying Peter that such an event was normal. She was well: she brimmed with life and health. If she did not worry—why should he?

For men who bred animals it was somewhat astonishing that they did not appreciate the smallness of Jane's pelvis. The danger to her in childbirth was something that neither man perceived. Perhaps they were too happy, their joy blinding them to danger.

When the tragedy came it was sudden in its onslaught. Her pregnancy had been normal but when she went into labour Jos had his first presentiment of danger. He sent for a doctor from Bristol. One of the grooms being despatched at top speed and told to ride the horse into the ground if necessary but to get a doctor back quickly.

When a hot, tired doctor finally arrived Jos told him his new fears. After an examination the doctor rejoined the older man and confirmed what Jos had expected.

'She's very small and it's going to be a big child. She's strong but not that strong.'

'Do something! Anything, but save her!' Jos told him knowing as he uttered the words what would happen. The doom-feeling was so strong in the house that he shivered as if it were mid-winter.

When Jane eventually died, worn out after an appallingly long labour, Jos and Peter were shattered. They were unable to comfort each other but just sat in opposite chairs each man deep in his own thoughts.

Jos thought his heart must break now. He had lost the sweet girl he loved so much. His friend was gone forever—but what was his grief compared to Peter's? Peter had never dreamed this would happen. Right to the very end he had hoped and prayed to no avail. Even the birth, at last, of a fine son had failed to touch him. All he wanted was his Jane. His tears of anguish had driven Jos to leave the room and stagger downstairs.

Peter Howard never did wholly recover from the loss of his beloved Jane. Very slowly he changed to a sombre man who rarely smiled. He hardly ever mixed now and he never again showed a lot of interest in another female.

With the passing of the years Jos had hoped that he might marry again. Peter was a fine catch. Many a girl rolled her eyes invitingly at him. To be Mrs Howard was something indeed. Ferndale was a very prosperous stud but Peter was disinterested in marriage again. A vital spark had left him. His only interest was in tending to the property and rearing his son Robert.

'It's queer, thinking back. Our family only ever seem to produce the one living child. I wonder why?' Jos asked himself one fine evening on his sixtieth birthday.

As usual he was working on his diary. He peered again at the last page, covered with his sloping handwriting. Every night, since just after Jane's death, he had written down the day's events. As he had vowed so many years ago, his son Peter should know his full history and so must Robert. It was only right and proper.

Jos had started his diary with the events of his father's death. The young John Mayo in 1816. Often he thought about the early days. Of old James and Sarah. Everything he had been told had been faithfully recorded. The pile of papers was thick and kept in a leather box whose cover Jos had skilfully carved himself many winters ago.

Jos leaned back in his chair. Slowly he let his eyes roam around the room he loved so deeply. Over the years the cottage had changed drastically. It was a comfortable, warm and cosy home, strictly masculine in appearance despite his housekeeper's attempts to instal items of femininity. Both Peter and Jos scorned frilly cushions and fancy curtains. It might have been different if Jane had lived.

Jos knew that the men looked a trifle askance at him. They respected him. They admired him but they did not like him. There was about Jos the aura of tragedy and death. To be friendly with Jos Howard was not easy and with Jos's life story common knowledge men were inclined to be wary with him.

They sympathized with Peter Howard. He treated them well. Their wages were above average and he had the men's loyalty and affection. Something Jos knew would never be his. Not that he minded. Ferndale was Peter's now in everything but name. Jos did not care a damn whether men liked him or not. At sixty years he was extremely fatalistic.

His great joy was Robert. What a boy! He was eleven now. A bright, mischievous imp of a lad with laughing eyes and cheeky grin. He was worshipped by the men and utterly spoiled by their wives. Already he could ride a straight line over country on his pony and Jos had promised him a grey for his next birthday.

'The future rests with Robert and it seems

bright,' Jos told himself thankfully.

Robert was quite horse mad and vowed, when he grew up, he was going to be a rough rider like his Grandpa had been.

Sometimes the boy's questions had hurt as he probed back into the past.

'But Grandpa, if my great-great-grandfather was James Mayo doesn't that mean we are all relations to the Mayo family?' he had once asked.

Jos had nodded slowly, wondering what was coming now. 'Well, in that case, why don't they like us then?'

Jos had sighed wearily. 'I've told you, Rob,' he started patiently, 'There's been lots of trouble between the two families long ago. They sort of blame me for all of it.'

The boy had puzzled about this. 'But why?'

'Look, Rob! It's all written down in my diary. You've looked at it before!'

'But I don't understand all of it,' the boy had said slowly.

'Well, in that case, leave it until you're grown up and then you'll understand. This will all be yours one day and Rob, look after it!'

The boy's mind had changed direction. 'I know they don't like me but I like them—or at least—one of them. I like Giles very much,' he had confided.

Jos smiled at this. It really was a wonder any Mayo liked a Howard after the past years of Maud's bitter teachings. Jon had been brought

179

up under a rigid hate-Howard-code. Even old Sarah would have admired it.

For years Mayo's had been a mess. When Maud finally died, worn out with her vituperation, Jon had quickly and quietly married Julie Coleman, a very distant cousin. She brought with her a substantial dowry which Jon put to immediate use. Slowly, over the long years, Mayo's had started to better itself and become a productive farm once again.

Julie gave Jon three children in quick succession then, after two miscarriages, decided enough was enough and produced nothing further. James was born in 1863 followed by Mary in 1864 and Giles in 1865. The three Mayo children were incredibly different almost as if they had been bred from alien stock.

James was a firebrand and, Jos suspected, inclined to be rather spiteful if he couldn't have his own way. Mary had a sweet and pensive nature. Giles was a rock. Solid, determined and reliable. Jos approved Robert's selection. Giles was the best of the Mayo bunch though, being the younger son, what good that would do he had no idea. The odd thing though was the resemblance that Robert and Giles had for each other. Facially they could have passed as brothers.

Jos knew that Jon hated him every bit as much as had George which, after growing up under Maud, did not surprise or worry Jos in the least. What did concern him though was the future behaviour and relationship of the next generation.

Robert seemed without hate for anything at all. Peter had been so engrossed in Ferndale since Jane's death that to a large extent Jos himself had brought Robert up. Of the Mayo children Mary was too sweet a child to harm or hate any living thing. Giles, tough, square and solid, was a boy not given to making any hasty decisions but whatever he did finally decide would be final. James though was a different kettle of fish entirely. Already James was aware of his position in life and inclined to be cocky and play the young master. There was just a little too much of George in James.

Jos did not learn this all at once. Gossip was natural in the country and took the place of newspapers in an age when many still could only read a little. Although he did not fraternize a lot Jos was able to acquire any information he wanted when in Chipping Sodbury taverns and indeed even in Bristol.

With the growth of Bristol itself the surrounding Gloucestershire villages had also developed. More schools sprang up and thus Robert and the Mayos had little to do with each other to Jos's thankfulness. He suspected that, once or twice, Robert and Giles had met and even fought though nothing was ever said outright.

Ferndale thrived. Sarah would have been so proud, Jos acknowledged, though even then he guessed she would still have been crying out for the return of their land. The property was a shade small for the amount of business the Howards now did.

Long ago Jos had foreseen the danger of steam. He had sold all his carriage horses and concentrated instead upon fine riding animals. Others less astute had clung on to the glory of the coach and lost everything.

'If only we had a bit more land,' Jos had said one evening to no one in particular. 'Ferndale is too small for us now.'

'But what chance have we of getting land around here?' Peter had asked him while Robert watched both adults. Saying nothing yet missing nothing either.

'That's the trouble. No Mayo will ever sell us land. James can break the entail when he comes of age, if he wants, but he'd die before he sold to us.' Jos had explained slowly. All the Mayos had been brought up to the creed never to part with one square foot of valuable land especially to a Howard. Jon had seen to that.

This all made Jos more than a little uneasy for the future. How long could Ferndale run and support itself on its present lines? The thought of horses having to be sold because of lack of land, appalled him. He knew, though, this might happen in the future. He had often thought that if machines could be invented to

182

cut corn and transport people on rails might not the day come when horses were not required—it was a horrific thought.

'At least I've lived in the heyday of the horse,' Jos told himself thankfully. 'And it's been a grand life too—even with the bad times.'

Jos realized he had been musing back over the past for nearly an hour. Robert was long in bed while Peter was out doing evening stables with their stud groom.

He stood after adjusting the flame of the oil lamp. Jos's hair was quite grey now. His once straight back had the stoop of age. Even now though, on this his sixtieth birthday, he was still a giant of a man.

Jos sat down in his chair. At times he did feel his age and lately there'd been a pain in his chest and left arm which he had kept to himself. He closed his eyes and started daydreaming. As always his mind went right back to those very early days. To wonderful, little old Sarah. To hard, ruthless James. They had been good days, in a way but the best, the most wonderful day of them all, had been when he first rode a Mayo's grey with his Grandfather's arm around his waist.

'All right now, hang on!' said old James touching with his heels.

Jos yelled as the stallion burst into a gallop, straining against the bit, wanting to go faster. This was incredible, this speed and power.

Great shoulders slid under a satin skin; strong, clean legs whipped backwards and forwards, tendrils of white mane flowing before his eyes. He could feel the almost awful power from the hocks as they drove the grey body into even faster propulsion.

Jos roared with excitement, waved his hand—and fell out of the chair, dead from a heart attack. On his old face was a peaceful smile. His outstretched arm, with the fingers tightly curled together, meshed in a thick white mane was rigid.

Peter found him when he returned from the stables. He bent over and gently hunted for a heartbeat then stood and looked down at his dead father. He noted the peace and joy on the lined face; he studied the arm and hand.

'God bless you old man! You've been a grand father. I'm only hoping I can do the job as well now you're gone. You've gone as you'd want to go. Riding a grey in a wild gallop!'

Peter saw the diary, read the last entry and carefully placed the pages back into the box. He sat and wrote the last entry in his own bold script.

'There, that's finished it. If you want to know your heritage, young Robert, it's here ready for your eyes. Until that day comes, this diary can be put safely away.'

Jos Howard's only true friend had been a grey horse and only he could contrive to die in such a satisfactory way.

BOOK THREE

Giles Mayo

CHAPTER ONE

Giles Mayo stared glumly at his brother James. Giles was pure Mayo. At eighteen years he had attained his full height. He was built on square lines, already very muscular and would, later on, have powerful strength whereas James, his senior by two years was tall, leggy and almost lean.

There was little facial resemblance between the brothers and little love either. Temperamentally they were poles apart. James had, up to now, always been the dominant brother. He had quick fists and a raging temper. He thought Giles an inquisitive fool, always wanting to know everything going on. His younger brother was always asking questions about their family's past. It irritated James enormously. James lived for the present only. The past bored him. Frequently his temper flared with impatience, yet more and more he was forced to acknowledge Giles's strength as a power to be reckoned with.

Mary watched them both, deeply worried. She knew the signs of old. They were getting ready to square up to each other. When that happened trouble came next.

Mary, the middle child, was the peacemaker. She was not beautiful and acknowledged this fact frankly. Like her brothers, she had inherited the stolid, square features of the Mayos which, though they suited the males, did not become a female.

Her one valuable asset was an incomparable sweetness, so genuine and sincere, that it shone from her steady eyes and transformed the heavy Mayo features into an acceptable female charm which few could resist. Mary was also placid. It took a mighty upheaval for her temper to show let alone rise but, when it did, she was able to demonstrate that peculiar Mayo trait of stubborn hardness and implacable determination which none could brook. This iron streak hidden in her was something which quite a few people did not suspect.

Giles had more understanding than his brother and he was also partially responsible for the situation which had developed. Mary was in love.

As befitted a farmer's daughter, Mary helped her mother around the house and met other people of her own age group only under escort. Both her parents conceded that Giles was a better escort for his sister than the heir to the farm. James, though he did have affection for his sister, was inclined to think just a little too much about himself and not bother with others. James was all self.

It became customary for Giles to take his sister for a pony and trap drive in the good weather and what was more natural than that

Giles should introduce her to an old school mate one day when they met accidentally.

Giles had been unprepared for what had happened but sufficiently of age to understand what he witnessed. Robert Howard and Mary Mayo had met, looked at each other, said 'Hello!' and known in that one still minute of time that they were meant for each other.

Their eyes had held in a gaze which excluded the world and time. A spark, an emotional feeling, had travelled backward and forward, which became a revelation to them both. In a few mere seconds they were the only two people alive on the earth as they stared at each other. The young, hard male on his big horse and the frank-eyed girl sitting in the trap.

Mary stopped breathing. She knew, quite definitely, that her heart had missed a number of beats as she continued to stare in the most unladylike manner. Giles was forgotten. The trap had gone. She had risen onto some mystic cloud and was alone in infinity. They did not speak. They did not have to. Their eyes said all. They were a pair apart who were born to be together as one.

Giles was speechless. Even a fool could not have helped but notice the instantaneous reaction and Giles was anything but a fool. He was appalled at the situation which he had innocently contrived just as he was suddenly aware that many girls of his sister's age were already married.

But for his sister Mary to fall in love with a Howard—his mind whirled.

Later, when they were alone, he spoke choosing his words with care and delicacy.

'Mary, when you and Robert met there seemed to be something—well—what I mean is, you went very quiet,' he said tentatively.

For a few seconds Mary was silent before she turned to him. 'That's the man I'm going to marry. Him and no one else.'

'But Mary, the trouble there's been—and you know how our father feels about—' and Giles halted uncertainly.

'I don't care. I have my own life to lead. Giles, I want to see him again, I must. You'll take me, won't you?' she pleaded grasping his arm.

At first Giles had firmly refused but Mary had wheedled him round. With extreme reluctance and considerable foreboding Giles had, finally, assented. It became customary for the brother and sister to go driving that summer. Long drives when they were away for hours and in areas at which, seemingly astonishingly, they always seemed to meet Robert Howard riding one of his fine horses.

To start with there was little but general conversation until Giles took pity on the pair. He would help Mary out of the trap and tie Robert's horse to a wheel and watch while the couple strolled together. His nerves became so strained with tension that Giles took to the foul habit of smoking.

This situation went on for many weeks and Giles knew something must happen. One day he was fortunate enough to catch Robert alone and tackle him.

'You and my sister?'

Robert sighed and smiled slowly. 'We are in love. There's no two ways about it. When she's of age I'll be asking for her hand formally. I'll be coming to see your father. I'd have come before now but Mary stopped me. She said there might be some difficulty.'

'Difficulty! That's the understatement of the year!' Giles echoed in horror. 'My father hates you. He'll never give his consent for you to call on my sister and marry her—' The thought made Giles shake his head vehemently.

'When she's of age she can marry who she likes and your father can do nothing about it!' Robert replied flatly. Then his voice softened. 'We love each other. Deeply and sincerely. What does the past matter? It's over and done with. It's history. We're what we are now. We love each other. There's nothing amiss at Ferndale. I can give Mary anything she wants and I'd be a good husband to her. I want her. No one else. Ever!'

'But!' Giles began helplessly.

'There are no buts,' Robert told him with quiet force. 'It's me and her and your family will have to lump it. Come to that, if there's

191

any bad blood around still between our two families it's us Howards that should be complaining. We're the ones who lost our land to you Mayos!'

Giles gritted his teeth trying to think of a logical objection. 'We're related!'

'Generations ago yes but what does it matter now? We're too far apart. We're not first cousins or anything and the Church wouldn't object!'

Giles would not concede defeat. He fell into the habit of seeing Robert regularly for the main purpose of arguing against the proposed marriage.

Mary blossomed. Her love was a secret known only to her brother. It was too precious to be broadcast as yet and it was delicious having such a wonderful secret. The touch of Robert's strong hand as it enfolded hers, the strength of his powerful body as they took their walks under Giles's watchful eyes; the long stares which probed out all secrets and fears. The complete understanding and utter trust were so deep and mutual that they both knew they had found something precious and rare, shared with only a few lucky ones.

Both Julie and Jon had learned long ago that Mary had far more authority over her brothers than their parents. Jon was secretly glad of this. He had all the problems he wanted in just living and making a decent sum of money out of land which had been neglected so long.

Julie loved all her children but for James she had more affection. She knew she was wrong to have a favourite but she couldn't help herself. Apart from the fact that James was her first-born there was something about his nature which told her he needed more affection. He could be moody, surly and hot-tempered. She knew he was unsure of himself; lacking natural self-confidence.

Giles of course was a rock of dependability. No harm would ever come to him. He would always be able to look after himself and so too would Mary with her innate commonsense. But James—a doubt always arose in Julie's mind when she thought about her favourite. If only she could take some of Giles's assurance and give it to James. She was sure that he would be a better tempered person. She sighed, children were queer. These of hers were so different and Jon didn't really help matters. He didn't understand his children.

'It's not that he's thoughtless or doesn't care, I know that,' she often told herself. 'It's this farm. He's so engrossed in making it pay its way he has no time for anyone else. Hardly any time for me but I understand, the children don't—especially poor dear James.'

Sometimes she thought of their neighbours, the Howards with whom, of course, no social intercourse was allowed. Ferndale was a much smaller property but the house must be easier to run. From what she had heard it also had charm and was spoken of by people as a happy home now that Jos Howard had died.

Peter Howard had seemingly altered now that fatherhood had been thrust upon him with Jos's death. Not that he would ever be a gay man but he was approachable which she knew her Jon wasn't.

'I like that boy Robert. He's a fine looking boy and how like Giles he is! It's almost uncanny!' she thought as she surveyed her shopping list for the next trip to market.

She had once mentioned this to Jon. He had snorted angrily at her.

'It's that bastard's blood coming out again!'

Julie had gasped with both shock and astonishment.

'But this bastard, as you so politely call him, was surely a close relative of your family too? Now let me think. Yes! This bastard's father was in fact your uncle and you can't get away from it!'

'They're a bad lot those Howards. I'll not have anything to do with them. Julie, I forbid you and the children even to talk to them!'

Julie had tightened her lips in annoyance at this.

'The fact that I am your wife gives you no right to run my life! I might point out I brought the dowry which enabled you to put some new life back into this place which you think so much of. Often more than me and the children I'd like to point out!' Julie had retorted acidly. 'You didn't buy me, Jon Mayo, and just you remember that!' The words dripped with ice. Her backbone was rigid, her eyes frosty with anger.

She had frightened Jon, though he had tried to hide the fact. Julie aroused was more devil than he had anticipated. He had blustered, shouted, then let the matter drop.

'It's all so ridiculous, this family feud just because of something which happened so long ago,' Julie muttered to herself. 'But how similar those boys are!'

Both Giles and Robert were built on the same solid, square lines with jutting jaws, open—almost hard eyes, and thin, compressed lips. The resemblance carried on details like brown hair parted on the same side and ending in the exact spot at a point just above the collar.

She stared from the sitting-room window.

'Now what's going on?' she asked herself. She could see both of her sons standing on the gravel driveway scowling at each other. Mary was getting ready to put on her peace-making act. Julie had no intention of stepping outside to stop a row.

Mary was far more efficient at that. She turned back from the window and wandered into the dining-room where Jon was standing over an account book.

But for once, Julie was sadly wrong. This

row between the boys had deeper roots. Instinctively Mary knew that no helpless act on her part could stop them. They were getting really angry and all over such a stupid thing as a horse.

'Well, it's true!' James again challenged his brother to deny the fact which was so obvious.

'All right! So it's true! What do you think you can do about it? Just because you're the bloody heir to the place. Who the hell do you think you are?' snarled Giles.

'When I do run this place you'll mind your manners and your tongue too!' retorted James. Instantly he regretted the words.

'Or you'll do what?' Giles asked quietly, eyes dancing with fire. 'The trouble with you, dear brother, is you're all talk and noise. You've never done anything sensible in your whole life and I don't think you ever will. When it comes to talking you're the king of them all but I notice you don't push so far ahead when action is required!'

'Well, after all, they *were* ours in the first place,' mumbled James petulantly. 'They were called Mayo's greys after our great-grandfather James Mayo.'

'So?' asked Giles irritatingly.

'Well, they're now called Howard's greys and that's wrong! Look what they've done too! One's come third in the Grand National and two have come second in Classic races. There they all are, those wonderful horses which

196

should belong to us. What do we have here to ride? Not one of *our* greys!'

Here it comes, Giles thought sardonically. I know he wants me to do something he daren't do himself, the miserable worm.

'Well, we should have some here or at least one. Look at us! All this land and only two miserable halfbred riding hacks. A fellow can't get a decent day's hunting on those bone-bags!'

'Of course he can't when he can't ride properly in the first place!' Giles jeered, thoroughly enjoying himself now. 'You always were a lousy horseman and let me tell you James, if a Howard's grey were here right now you'd be too scared to climb on his back let alone stay there for five minutes!'

'That's not true!' stormed James. He wanted to hit Giles but could not muster the courage.

'Of course it's true! You can hardly ride mother's clothes horse let alone a fiery Howard's grey. Those animals have power. Some even come out of their stables on hindlegs!'

James eyed Giles, a crafty look crossing his face.

'Just how do you know that?' he snapped quickly.

'I went over and had a look!' Giles replied calmly.

'Well!' said James. Now *he* had the whip
197

hand again and about time too. 'Father told us we were not to have anything to do with those rotten Howards. You know what they've done to our family in the past—and you actually went over there?' this last incredulously.

'Yes, why not? They're distant relatives. Anyhow, Robert's not too bad when you get to know him. At least you can have a fight with him and he doesn't bear malice for months afterwards if he loses!'

'I like Robert too!' Mary said gently, breathing more easily now as the tension seemed to be relaxing a little.

'What do *you* know about him. You've been there too—you sneaky little bitch!' James snapped suddenly.

'Don't you shout at her, you—you—cowardly lout!'

His blood boiling now, Giles shot forward his right fist. He caught James unexpectedly on the jaw and sent him flying backwards.

'No! Don't fight! Please don't fight!' Mary shouted. They were going at it hammer and tongs. Mary's shoulders drooped. She was helpless once they really started. Miserably she looked around for help. There was none.

Turning back to the boys she knew, with sudden instinct, that this was not another ordinary fight. Both brothers were fighting with a silence that terrified her. It was as if they were seeking to maim each other for life. She stood appalled, for once at a loss as to how to pacify them.

Mary gasped, both hands to her mouth, then her common-sense returned. She turned to the house.

'Mama! Papa! Oh, come quickly!' she shrieked.

The boys were oblivious to her shriek. They were intent on hammering the living daylights out of each other. In a panic Mary rushed forward. She reached out to grab Giles's arm. At that identical moment James let fly. His fist connected with Mary's face just below her left eye.

She screamed and fell awkwardly. The boys halted in horror.

'You bloody swine!' roared Giles, bending over his sister. Mary looked up at him. Both her eyes were watering with shock. A small deep gash started to bleed freely below the left one. Giles dabbed frantically with his handkerchief. His face was white with shock and remorse. James stood aside. Silent and morose, his eyes mirrored his guilt.

Mary clutched Giles's hand. 'Oh, please stop!' she begged.

'It's all right!' Giles soothed her. 'We've stopped—but this cut! Here's Mama!'

Thankfully Giles stood back as Julie rushed up with Jon at her heels. Jon's face was a picture of rage. His daughter lay bloody and limp on the ground. His two sons stood like defiant cocks despite their guilt.

199

With a foul oath Jon sprang forward and cracked Giles across the head, sending him flying. He repeated the blow across James's white face.

'I've just about had enough of you two! Get back into the house, go to your room and stay there until I give you permission to come down. Go on! Get in that house!' he bellowed.

*　　　*　　　*

Later, much later, Jon called the boys down. He stood facing them in the large sitting-room. Julie sat watching uneasily. 'What exactly was all that about?' he asked coldly. James flushed and scowled. Giles shot his brother a look. 'It was about horses,' Giles explained.

'Horses!' Jon snapped. 'Explain!'

'Well, it's true! We've no decent riding horses. In fact, we've hardly any horses on this place. We should at least have some of those greys. It was our great-grandfather who bred them. Other fellows can hunt on decent animals. What's the good of having all this land if we can't have a decent horse?' James grumbled.

'Horses, horses, horses! That's all you think about!' Jon snapped at his scowling heir. 'It's about time you gave as much thought to running this farm as to dreaming about horses. What the Howards do with their damned grey horses is their business. They can rot in hell as far as I'm concerned! It's taking me all my time to run this farm and unless things improve we'll have to go.'

'When did you last ride out and examine the land, James? Fine heir you are! At least Giles here shows some interest in what's going on. Look at last week when we discussed this new method of fertilizing with artificial manures. What attention did you pay?'

'If we had more horses we could use horse manure,' James replied.

'Horse manure my eye! And just how much horse manure do you think you'd need for a place this size? Rubbish, boy, a farmer must move with the times. This is 1883 not 1783. I know there are still some old fools who think the horse is the be-all and end-all of existence but I'm not one, thank God! Look what happened in '65! Look at all the head of cattle that died through rinderpest! Farmers relying entirely on cattle were wiped out overnight!'

'But they got compensation. We learned that at school,' James argued indignantly.

'Not at first they didn't and how do you think they managed to live while they waited? Ever thought of that? Not you, the food is put on the table before you; clothes on your back—you never give a thought to how they came. Why do you think we were not affected with the rinderpest epidemic? Because we are mixed farmers. We do not depend entirely on just one thing. We grow corn and crops and we

201

run cattle. No boy, the farmer must look ahead. Horses! Let me tell you, James, times are altering rapidly. It won't be so very long, certainly in your time if not in mine, when horses are not used on the land at all!'

'Rubbish!' James snorted rudely.

'It's not rubbish, James,' Giles told him. 'I know what you're getting at, sir. Mechanization!'

'Exactly!' Jon said. 'Machines! You don't have to feed them three times a day for seven days a week. Look, we've had steam omnibuses for a while already!'

'But they don't work all the time!' James protested.

'Maybe not, but they will. Heavens almighty, boy, look how things have changed on the land in this century alone! We can cut the hay and corn with a machine now. We don't need to employ so much labour, we needn't keep so much capital back for wages. We are not so dependent upon the weather. We're much better off!'

'Yes, we are. The workers aren't!' Julie added drily.

'Well, that's not our fault!' Jon said, turning to his wife. 'I've got my work cut out here looking after my own. Let them go to the towns. There's plenty of work in the factories for those who will work.'

Mary came into the room and stood listening intently. Her face was swollen, the eye already black with bruising. It gave her face a lop-sided appearance.

Giles anxiously helped her to the most comfortable chair in the room. James threw his sister a beseeching look.

Then all their attention riveted back to Julie and what she was saying.

'I still don't think they have a fair deal,' Julie persisted. 'I read that 59 per cent of men earn less than 25/- per week and it's not long since poor women and children were hired out like animals!'

'And another thing you all want to remember—the farmer is competing with corn grown abroad,' Jon pointed out.

'Well, see that some of the land is sold if you are so short of money,' Julie said.

'Never!' Jon told her. 'I'll see none of this land is sold. It's a sacred trust!'

'But James can if he wants to,' Julie pointed out shrewdly. 'The entail is broken entirely when he inherits. He can do exactly as he likes and he might have different values to you!'

Jon paled and turned to his heir. 'And will you sell, James?'

James flushed. 'I don't see the point in hanging on to land which doesn't bring in plenty of profit!'

'But you can't sell!' Giles cried, horrified.

'I can if I want to when it's mine and there's nothing you can do about it either. I'm the heir—not you! What's the point of having all this work and worry when a chap can't have a decent hunter?'

Jon was speechless.

Back to square one, Julie thought in amusement and affection. He really does have a one-track mind, this boy of mine.

'Look at the Howards,' James continued, oblivious to the effect upon his father. 'They're doing all right and they have all the horses they want!'

'You bloody young fool!' roared Jon in exasperation. 'I am sick and tired of hearing nothing but horses coming from your mouth day after day! The Howards are heading for a fall and serve 'em right! I hope they fall long and hard. All their money is tied up in breeding horses. They've so many on the place now they are having to buy corn and hay. Horses take up room! They are wasteful on land! For God's sake start to act your age and use your brains!'

'But I still don't see why I can't have a decent hunter!' James muttered mulishly.

'If he had a Howard's grey he wouldn't be able to ride it,' Giles said sarcastically.

'Giles!' warned Julie, but she was too late.

James spun round and faced his brother. 'I can ride anything you can!'

Giles grinned. 'Prove it!'

'Right!'

The brothers had forgotten everyone else now.

'If I can arrange a hunt on a Howard's grey, you'll do it?' Giles challenged.

'What do you mean?' his father asked suddenly, glowering at his younger son.

'I know Robert Howard. I bet I could talk him into lending us a grey for one day.'

'I thought I'd told you boys to have nothing to do with that family! How dare you disobey me!' Jon stormed.

Julie stood up. This had gone far enough. 'Jon, stop it! What harm is there in Giles speaking to a distant relation of his own age? I think this family feud is too stupid for words! Heavens almighty, do you intend to carry it on for another generation? What do you hope to gain? I've never heard anything so ridiculous in all my life!'

'They're a murdering breed,' Jon told her sullenly.

'What arrant nonsense! The Mayos are not all angels, I can assure you!' Julie snapped back at him.

'Well, I don't like it!' Jon yelled at her.

Suddenly Jon wilted. Julie had the stronger character by far. She didn't respect his position as a wife should. He stuck out his bottom lip in a sulk.

'Well, I'll have nothing to do with them,' James said, siding with his father. Here was a way he could get round the old man and have the horse he so badly wanted. After all, he was a potential land-owner. He should have only the best.

Giles watched his brother, a frown creasing his forehead. Long ago he had realized that James did not share his love for their land. If only he were the heir—what would he not do for Mayo's. Machinery fascinated Giles. Like his father, he thought that the day of the horse was receding fast. Why, who used coaches now with the modern trains?

He had heard that over in France someone was experimenting with something called the horseless carriage! He supposed there were men in England making machines which would never require a horse. He did not know their names but he did know, in his bones, that machines had come to stay.

Giles also suspected that Howards were heading for an almighty cropper. Peter Howard knew one thing only. Breeding horses—and Robert took after him.

'Well,' he said, 'do you or don't you want to ride a Howard's grey?'

'I forbid it!' Jon shouted.

'Yes, I do!' cried James.

'All right, I'll fix it. Make sure you don't fall sick on the day!' he sneered softly.

James coloured and took a step forward.

'Giles! James! Don't you dare!' threatened Julie.

'James, get out and go and check all of our fences. That should keep you busy for a few days riding around the land. Giles, since you are so fond of machinery, go out to the barn and find out what's wrong with that binder!' Jon ordered his sons quickly.

When both boys had departed Jon turned to his wife, sighed and sat down heavily.

Although they quarrelled and even had verbal fights Jon was fond of his wife; more so than Julie realized. He was the type of man who always finds difficulty in showing true emotion.

'I just don't know what's wrong with those two,' he complained.

Julie shook her head. 'I'm afraid they just don't like each other. It does sometimes happen between brothers and sisters and they are so very different.'

'Yes, it's all machines with Giles and confounded horses with James,' said Jon, taking Julie's hand and holding it in one of his rare affectionate gestures.

Mary came over to them and they both smiled at this dear child. She never gives us any trouble, they thought together. If only the boys could be like her.

Mary's mind was whirling but, long ago, she had learned to keep her thoughts hidden. The ferocious fight of the boys had frightened her but, more important, she was suddenly afraid for herself and Robert. Her father's venom for the name Howard had wounded her deeply. She loved both of her parents, not with the love she held for Robert, but with a fire from a different fuel.

She was realistic enough to know that marriage to Robert would cause trouble; what she had failed to calculate was the depth of Jon's venom. She knew with feminine instinct that her mother would be sympathetic to her cause but, when it came to the vital issue at stake—matrimony—where would her mother stand? Where can she stand but alongside her husband, she thought practically. And where does that leave me and Robert?

It was a horrible mess. She and Robert had talked about the family feud. Robert had told her frequently not to worry. He would take care of matters when the time was right, but would he—could he? Mary knew that she could not bear to be the cause of grief to her parents—but her love for Robert consumed her night and day.

And Giles—he had been seeing Robert! He had never taken her to the stable yard. He had not told her! Why? For a few seconds her faith in her brother was shattered, then her innate commonsense told her that Giles would never hurt her. Perhaps he had been trying to help. She must talk to him but now was neither the time nor the place.

She switched a smile on her face as Jon took his daughter's two hands in his own and smiled at her.

'And what do you think of your two brothers?'

Mary laughed back at him. 'I think they make a lot of noise and fuss about nothing. They both want to show off to each other. When they find a young lady they like they will then be on their best behaviour!' she replied, wise beyond her years.

'As long as they don't chase the same young lady!' Julie pointed out.

'God forbid!' groaned Jon. 'That would be the last straw!'

'Papa! Are we going to become poor?' Mary asked anxiously.

Jon smiled at her, shaking his head. 'Not if I can help it!' Mary looked a little dubious.

'Now don't you worry your pretty little head about things like that. There's enough with your mother trying to run the world. No, we must just be a bit more careful and farm in the modern way.'

After Mary had left the room to start getting the tea, Jon turned to Julie and said, 'Howards will crash!'

'And you'll be glad, won't you?'

He thought a moment. 'Yes, I will. I don't think I hate them quite as much as my father must have done but I don't like them and never will. I don't trust them and will never do business with them either. Really, if anyone is talking of buying land James should sit quietly, wait for the Howards to crash and buy them out cheaply. That way he would get those horses he makes such a fuss about, because the

Howards can't go on as they are!'

'But surely good horses will always be needed by the gentry?'

'Yes, I think they will but only for riding and hunting. How many gentry coach anywhere now? Coaching is dead! Everyone uses the railway—even the common people travel third class in open carriages. Look how life itself has changed in my day. Gas lights, the telegraph, steam trains and look at that ship they call the Orient. She is steam driven and even has something called an electric light, if you please. Now that is progress! No, Julie, we live in a wonderful age but if we are to survive we must move with the age.'

'I wonder where it will all end?' Julie said thoughtfully.

Jon looked at her. 'Unless we watch out it will end in war! Look at the troubles in South Africa. You mark my words, that's only the start of something. I don't like the way our world is moving politically. There's too much talk of freedom, suffrage and votes. I can't think what's come over the lower classes. In my father's day they knew their place and kept it!'

'Perhaps it's because it's such a bad place they want to leave it then!' Julie pointed out quickly.

CHAPTER TWO

'Well, there he is!' Giles said slowly, turning to his brother. 'Not getting cold feet!' he teased.

'I'll thump you when we get back!' James threatened.

'You can try!' Giles replied cheerfully. 'Hey, Robert!' and he stood in the saddle, waving to the youth who walked his grey stallion towards them.

James stared, eyes opening wide in amazement. He had been told this distant relative looked like his brother. He had no idea this resemblance was so startling! At close quarters Robert and Giles could have passed as twins. The thought sent a cold shudder down his spine. He scowled at the Howard boy who lifted frank, merry eyes and returned a steady gaze.

Robert respected Giles. They had fought quite often as boys, considering it the dutiful thing to do. Yet, not once, had vice come into their fights. Robert knew it would not take much for him and Giles to become good friends. Grandpa Jos had always liked this Mayo and that was good enough recommendation for Robert.

Robert eyed Giles carefully. He woud make a good friend and an even better brother-in-law. He grinned to himself. Thank God Giles had the guts and humanity to understand the love between Mary and himself. Thank God James had not been with Mary on that first meeting!

He wondered what Mary was doing right now. He wanted to ask Giles about her but had sense enough to know that it would not yet do for the Mayo's heir James to know their secret. There would be trouble in that direction but Robert was not unduly worried. He was sure that his ability was equal to any situation. He loved Mary. She returned his love. When of age they would marry and that was that. Simple, dry and quite clear-cut. Robert failed to realize that his presumption was dogmatic, arrogant and totally without understanding for Mary's feelings towards her family. It was, after all, nothing but a product of their similar blood. The dominant pre-supposing Mayo arrogance which the old James Mayo had bred into all his stock. Legitimate or otherwise.

'Hello! You've brought him then! You don't mind if my brother has a ride on him?' Giles asked.

Robert shook his head. 'He's on his toes though, so he'll have to sit tight,' he warned, turning and looking at James, noting his bad seat in the saddle.

'What do you call this one?' Giles asked, leaning out of the saddle of his gelded hack to rub the stallion's fiery face.

'He's descended from our great Mayho so we call him Mayson. We like to keep those first three letters on all the breed if we can.'

James eyed the stallion, a pulse starting to flutter in his throat. He had started to wish he was a thousand miles away now that his ride was being granted. What an utter fool he had been to allow Giles to goad him into it.

James slowly dismounted and Robert did likewise, each exchanging horses. Giles eyed his brother in amusement. He could read James like a book and he knew exactly how he felt right now. Serve him right for keeping on about horses so!

Robert flashed Giles a look, then turned to James. 'Keep his head down. He rears when excited. Don't let him get it too low or else he'll buck when hounds first run!' he warned carefully.

James swung into the saddle and glared down at him. 'I don't need advice from you!'

Robert again looked at Giles, who shrugged his shoulders and pursed his lips eloquently. Fair enough, Robert thought, he'll have to learn the hard way. He swung gracefully into the gelding's saddle, turned and watched the hounds restlessly roaming around the huntsman's horse. Giles let his eyes drift over the large gathering of riders. There were a number of ladies out on their side-saddles. They looked most elegant in black habits, boots and top hats with white gloves and stocks. Giles felt a stir of excitement. He loved a good day's galloping and jumping.

Giles grinned wryly at Robert. 'You're lucky you don't have a brother!'

Robert returned the stare, eyes soft and thoughtful. 'That's a matter of opinion!'

Giles suddenly thought why, he's lonely! 'But you've friends, from school days?'

Robert twisted his lips. 'Not a real one with my own interests. Even an arguing brother would be better than no one,' he pointed out.

Giles nodded silently, suddenly remembering that Robert lived in an almost all-masculine house. No mother, no sister, no real friend—it was a rotten shame. What had *he* to grumble about? He wondered why he liked Robert so much better than his own brother. It was all wrong somehow. If only there was not this rift and dislike between the two families. They are distant kin, he argued with himself, even though they do seem to bring nothing but trouble down on Mayos' heads. If only Robert were not a Howard!

James swore as the stallion started to act up. All animals have an inherent instinct where human emotions are concerned. In no animal are they more highly developed than in the horse.

The stallion felt his rider's fear and maliciously, as horses will, seized advantage of this. He half-reared, felt the check of the curb bit and bounced down again, dropping his head between his forelegs. He humped his back, clamped his tail against his quarters and bucked hard. His legs drummed the ground, tendons straining, muscles set. He bucked three times, each buck being higher and more vicious than its predecessor.

It would have taken a far better horseman than James Mayo to ride this storm. James felt his knees slipping. His head jolted back painfully and his breath came in gasps. He was going—he knew it—and in front of Robert Howard and that odious brother of his. He flung out one arm in a wild gesture to regain his balance but he was far too late. His body jerked from the saddle, rose up in the air gracefully, then fell back on to the grass, hard and fast. He hit with a crump, rolling over and over, having no control over himself until he slithered to an inelegant halt.

Highly delighted with himself, the stallion stopped his antics, lifted his head and with big, innocent eyes stared back in mock astonishment. Robert felt his lips twitching and he struggled to control himself. Giles threw back his head and roared with laughter, not so much at his unfortunate brother as at the expression on the stallion's face.

Regrettably, James failed to understand. The horse he had boasted he could ride had dropped him off, at a crowded meet, before his insufferable brother who was bellowing with malicious laughter.

He scrambled to his feet, cheeks flaming with mortification, lips quivering with humiliation, eyes burning hatred at Giles. He stood, trembling, struggling to control himself and regather his lost dignity. Slowly he walked back, gathered the stallion's reins and remounted. He hauled the horse's head up short and high. The stallion did not like this. His ears went back in annoyance. As the pressure on the bit failed to relax, he snorted and reared high, clawing for the sky.

James was nearly caught unawares again. Quickly, he thrust his weight forward and with his right hand smashed his whip down on the stallion's poll. Shocked and appalled with the pain, the animal dropped down to the ground, shaking his head, eyes rolling showing their whites.

Robert stiffened with anger. He hated a bad horseman who used punishment because he could not control with skill. He opened his mouth to snarl at James. Giles poised himself for trouble when the horn sounded.

James struggled to control the stallion. Anger chased away fear. He felt all eyes upon him and with his recent humiliation his temper had risen. He *would* ride this brute. He *would* show them!

Giles swore to himself. James had no more control of the horse than a baby. He felt sudden worry hit him. If anything happened— the thought was horrifying. He drove his horse forward, trying to intercept James and persuade him to dismount but the Field were in a close group now, all trotting briskly along the road towards the Cover.

Giles looked round for Robert, anxiety chasing over his features.

'What's to do?' Robert asked, riding level with him.

'It's James! That horse is beyond him!'

Robert snorted. 'What do you expect? Look how he's handling him! Holding his jaw back like that and yet heeling him on. It's a good job for him he's in the middle of the Field but wait until we get out in the open. Mayson will soon drop him off again and serve him right. Your brother isn't fit to ride a donkey!'

Robert was white with anger now at the way his beloved stallion was being treated and contemptuously unconcerned about James. That's all very well for you, thought Giles. If James gets hurt who's going to get the blame at home? Me! Yet privately he agreed with Robert. He had never seen James riding in such a ham-fisted manner. He guessed it was because his brother was both frightened and humiliated.

'As soon as we get to the Cover, change horses again, Robert, will you?' he asked.

'You just bet I will!' Robert replied grimly.

Giles saw the Cover come into view. He watched the hounds stream in at one side. The Field Master halted to allow them to work. It was now that Giles intended to get James to change horses. Ordinarily, this would have worked out fine, but the fox had different ideas.

Paramount amongst these was the safety of his brush. He shot out of the Cover like the devil possessed, the hounds running silently after him. The Field Master took one expert look at the situation. He knew instantly this was going to be a far and fast ride. With a nod from the Master he let the Field go.

They streamed forward with a clatter of hooves, jingling of bits and stirrups and wild, excited yelling. It took James unawares. He was swept forward.

The stallion felt the slackening of the reins. He twisted his tongue and with one convulsive movement pushed it over the port of the curb bit. Lowering his head, he bored forward in a flat-out gallop. Robert and Giles were left hopelessly behind.

James hauled frantically at the reins but the stallion now felt nothing. He jerked with his powerful neck muscles and nearly dragged the struggling rider out of the saddle. James grabbed the pommel with his right hand, gritted his teeth and gripped with his knees as he had never gripped before. This was pure, unadulterated hell. He realized he was riding a runaway. Sweat burst out on his face, streamed down his neck into his stock, soaking his shirt and breeches. He had never been so afraid in all his life.

Giles and Robert drove their horses frantically in chase. The grey was just a blur in the distance. How the devil is he staying on, Giles asked himself anxiously. If he comes off now—and the thought made him go cold. What a fool he had been in goading James into this.

Robert rode furiously, sw, aring gently to himself. What was that maniac doing riding .t that speed over such a country? If the horse came down he would break a leg at the very least. He had no thought for James and neither youth dreamed the stallion was bolting out of control.

'He's turning!' Giles shouted, pointing with his left hand.

Robert stared. 'He's crazy! What's he going that way for? Hounds are running in the other direction!'

A horrible thought entered Giles's mind. 'The horse is a runaway!'

Robert gasped, suddenly realizing this was the truth. 'Well, why doesn't he let himself go then? The horse would stop by himself!' he shouted back as they rode knee to knee. They swung their mounts to the left in a flat-out gallop.

He won't, because he's scared, Giles told himself grimly. Too bloody scared. And so am I!

'Look out! Here comes a blackthorn!'

Robert warned, easing back on the reins, collecting his horse under him. Giles followed his example, and they placed their mounts at the hedge, neck to neck. Both horses lifted at the same time, both landing clear and free.

'Which way now?' Giles called, pulling back to a canter, looking around quickly.

'Over there!' Robert shouted. 'My God! He's heading for the quarry!'

Giles felt saliva fill his mouth. His stomach heaved and nausea swept through him. In one prophetic moment he knew the ultimate. He stood in his stirrups and roared wildly.

'James! James! Fall off! You're heading for the quarry!'

Robert dug his heels into the gelding. The animal was not bred for speed and was already starting to slow. He looked helplessly at Giles's horse. It still had some running left.

'Go on after him! My horse is blown—but hurry man, hurry!'

Giles savagely rammed spurs into his horse's flanks. The animal winced with pain and tried to increase its pace. The fool, why doesn't he fall off now? Surely he must have heard me?

But James had not heard him. He was in such a state of fear that he was beyond coherent thought or action. He was a mesmerized passenger on a bullet of speed. He was utterly incapable of saving himself.

The stallion was losing interest. He was

starting to tire and getting ready to stop but he had one final burst of power to drive from his system. He pounded up the slope, straight, fast and powerful. He breasted the hill crest, saw the fence on top, caught a glimpse of something frightening way below and instinctively veered sharply to the left. It was a savage propping turn, his hooves slithering, ripping up the turf.

James had no chance at all. His body left the saddle like an arrow from a bow. He flew upwards, over the fence, then slowly descended into the nothingness way below. For two seconds James tried to understand what was happening. His bemused brain suddenly cleared; sanity returned and with it dreadful knowledge. He opened his mouth, emitted one, soul-searing scream of fright, then plunged to his death.

Giles and Robert struggled up the hill and heard that awful scream. Giles was out from the saddle before his horse had stopped.

'Watch out for that fence!' Robert warned.

Giles, already over, dropped flat on his stomach and gingerly peered over the edge. Down below, something grotesque and red sprawled still and silent. He stared, then withdrew his gaze. He stood up slowly, head bent, chest heaving, tears running down his cheeks. Robert stared at him in horror, mouth agape, eyes distended.

Giles climbed back over the fence and

looked into Robert's eyes. He was the colour of a snowdrift, trembling all over, crying like a girl. Robert felt like death himself. He wanted to touch Giles's arm, tell him he understood how he must be feeling but he was frozen inside like winter ice.

'I'll have to go home and tell them. My mother and father,' he whispered, his voice breaking.

Robert could not let him go alone. With a sudden flash of intuition he understood Giles was blaming himself for James's death. Robert was as much to blame by allowing it all. They had neither of them bargained for this.

He faced Giles squarely, head back, eyes steady. 'I'll come with you!'

Giles slowly shook his head.

'Yes, I will!' Robert insisted. 'I'm as much to blame as you!'

'But you are a Howard, and my father . . .' and Giles's voice trailed off miserably.

'I'm still coming with you!' Robert told him firmly. They turned to the horses.

'So once again Mayo's has lost another heir!' Giles said softly, more to himself than to Robert.

His companion paused, eyed him carefully and replied firmly. 'No! It's not lost its heir. It's just obtained a new one—and one I like very much. One who I think will be the best yet!'

Giles heard the sincerity in Robert's honest

voice.

'You really mean that, don't you?' Giles asked as the tears flooded down his face.

'Yes, I do!' and Robert slowly offered his open hand. 'Maybe this is neither the time nor the place but Giles Mayo, I've always liked you even when we fought as kids. I don't like your family or the way they've hurt us Howards in the past but I live for the present. Can't you and me start to put things right again?' he asked hopefully. 'I've never had a real friend. Will you be my friend. My father says every man must have one real friend in life!'

Giles slowly took the offered hand, enclosing his fingers with Robert's.

'I don't like your family either Robert for what they've done to us in the past but I'm willing to give it a try. I'd certainly like to call you my friend!'

They shook hands, firm and sure between themselves.

'It won't be easy,' Robert warned. 'It's all right with us but the old folks won't understand and when they know I want to marry Mary—' his voice tailed off as, for the first time, unease set in.

'There's that too! My God! What's my father going to say?' groaned Giles. 'I've helped to kill my brother and my sister wants to marry you—the enemy!'

'But this won't—it can't—' and Robert felt the first wild stir of fear tinged with panic. He

223

halted his weary horse and stared at Giles anxiously.

Robert's mind was also wildly swinging off its usual even plane. What had happened was partly his fault. It was a terrible disaster but—it had happened. It could not be undone. He and Mary still had their lives to lead. They had such strong love—and here Robert's thoughts shied nervously on to a different track. How would Mary view James' death? How close had she been to her elder brother? He did not know. He had never asked. All he had ever wanted to do was be with her, his chosen one. It suddenly hit him with a sledgehammer blow that there was much he did not know about Mary. Her feelings for her parents and brothers; her ability to deal with tragedy; the actual depth of her love for him when sudden and violent death appeared in which he was an indirect party.

They mounted, Robert leading the now quiet and tractable grey stallion. They slowly rode for Mayo's. With every step they took Giles felt cold fear sweep through him. How *could* he break such news?

He paused finally at their driveway and looked into Robert's eyes. Giving a sickly smile he rode up to the house.

Both Jon and Julie heard the horses and came out of the front door. Jon's facial expression changed as he recognized this alien who looked so much like his son. Julie felt fear stab at her heart. Something must be wrong! Where was James? What had happened—that look on Giles's face. James! What had happened to her dear James?

Giles and Robert looked at each other. The silence was awful.

'James is dead!' Giles said finally. 'He rode Robert's grey. It bolted with him and threw him over the top of the quarry!'

He was incapable of breaking such news with delicacy.

Julie doubted her ears. This was wrong. Horribly, cruelly wrong! She looked at the boys' white, drawn faces. At the red rings around Giles' eyes, evidence of tears. Giles— crying? No, she thought, one hand clasping her throat. James dead? James dead! Killed—over the quarry! Her favourite? She opened her mouth, screamed, screamed again, then one hand went to her head and she fainted at Jon's feet.

Giles sat frozen in the saddle. He could help no one. He was too weighed down with the most appalling guilt. He saw Jon turn and look up at him. A cold stare crossed his father's features then Jon's gaze moved on to Robert. The coldness became a mask of hatred. Loathing shone from two diamond-point eyes.

The cook came running out with Mary hastening after her.

'Mrs Dobson! Take the mistress into the house. Mary, go with your mother. Johnson, help. Lift her man, gently now!'

They slowly lifted Julie and took her back inside. Not until she had disappeared from sight did Jon Mayo turn and slowly stare again at the two frozen boys.

Slowly he walked over towards Robert. Giles felt his companion stiffen in the saddle. Nervously he threw him a glance. Robert sat as if carved from stone of the purest white. The only signs of life were the faintest flutter of a nerve twitching under his jaw and the delicate flaring of his nostrils.

Jon stepped to one side of the rider and gazed at him for nearly a minute. He took in every detail of his son's replica. Then he opened his mouth. In one supremely contemptuous gesture he spat at Robert's horse's hooves.

'So yet once again a member of my family is killed by a Howard!' he snarled, 'and unto the third generation indeed!' he said, his words so low that Giles had to strain to hear them. Robert sat unmoving, just his eyes flickering emotion, a thin bead of sweat appearing above his right eye.

'It wasn't his fault, Pa!' Giles said slowly.

Jon ignored him. 'And again another Mayo dies in the most foul manner. What is there about you Howards that you must kill the males of my family? From where do you get your tainted blood? First my uncle John. Then my father George and now—my son! My son,

James! My heir! I despise you Howards. Despise you! That's too weak a word. I don't think I know a word which so expresses my loathing for you and all of your bastard tribe. There's a curse on you. A hoodoo of death. Wherever you go, down through the generations you strike back at us. I wish I could kill you for this, Robert Howard.

'This I do tell you though. As long as I live, as long as there is breath in my body and strength in my brain I will fight you and cripple you and break you until I have ground you Howards into dust! Think about this Robert Howard! Think long and hard because if I don't my son will and my son's sons. What has passed between our families before is nothing to the feeling which is between us now. I curse you and yours. I wish death and misery upon you and yours. Now—get off my land! Now—and forever!'

If the man had raved or stormed or acted in a demented manner Robert could have stood it better. He averted his eyes, looked helplessly at Giles and asked aid from his new friend.

Giles returned his gaze sadly. He shivered uncontrollably. They were doomed, all of them damned to go down through the generations causing pain and misery. He stared at Robert, trying to put his helpless resignation into a message the other could understand.

What chance have we all, his eyes asked? We are all lost souls moving in a desert of misery. What chance was there for us to be friends—and you and Mary—marriage? Now? Don't you realize, it's hopeless. It's impossible. We are doomed for ever and ever. The three of us. Our ancestors damned us for all time. We diced with the devil. And now we pay. We should have known better. I want you for my friend Robert Howard. You want my sister to take to wife. It can never be now. The hate is too much. It is sweeping over me in an aura. We tried. We all three tried—God knows that but we come from the wrong bloodlines. We are doomed to a hell on earth.

Robert's eyes crinkled. He felt moisture and blinked hastily. He understood the hopeless misery in Giles' eyes. The telepathic message was so plain to read. Mary—dear God, life without Mary? He couldn't stand it. Death would be better. Why was it wrong to love so? What had they all done to deserve such eternal punishment?

Mary! Mary—my love. I want you! I need you! I must have you or die!

But he knew he would not die. Just as he now finally accepted that Mary he could never have. It had never been meant to be.

He gathered up his reins, touched with his heels, turned his horse very slowly and walked down the drive and off the Mayo property.

CHAPTER THREE

Although he was to live into his eighties Giles never forgot nor wholly recovered from that terrible event. His whole character was to change. The guilt he felt for the death of his brother weighed upon him like lead. If it had not been for the kindness and understanding he received from Mary he might even have lost his reason.

Once she had learned the full facts Mary turned to her brother. She understood, with a wisdom far beyond her years, and gave silent comfort.

It was not just James's death. That he might have overcome gradually. It was what happened to his mother. Kind, practical Julie who only ever wanted to make a happy home and, perhaps, just to change the world a little. She would do nothing further.

The shock had been too appallingly brutal. Her favourite had been snatched from her without any warning. Julie's mind closed. It refused to accept anything. She sank into a dream world where nothing was real any more.

Jon nearly went mad. His precious Julie ill? He stormed and raged. Sent for one doctor after another and neglected his own work. He spent hours hanging around her bed, hoping for a word or even a gesture from his wife. His whole world had turned topsy-turvy. He tried everything he knew to draw his wife back to him. The hard reserve which had always been the mask on his face was shattered.

Julie lived for months but never left her room again. She became a mental invalid. Exactly twelve months to the day she quietly died. The doctors could give no name to what had killed her.

Jon went frantic with grief. Coming on top of James's death he went to pieces. If it had not been for Mary there was no telling what might not have happened.

Mary became the king-pin. Upon her shoulders fell the business of managing the house and staff. Suddenly, it was she who had to order the meals, make all the domestic arrangements and see to the two men.

She had her own private misery. Her own deep guilt. She had to make peace with her own conscience. She had never cared for James as much as Giles and this troubled her deeply. She had never really given James a chance. He had his faults but hadn't he had his virtues also? What these were Mary would have been hard put to pin down if questioned. She side-stepped this though. Giles, dear Giles, what was he going through and it was all her fault. If she had not been so besotted with Robert, Giles would not have seen so much of him and the stupid ride would never have arisen. She was as much to blame as anyone.

Robert! Dear Robert! She would never marry. She knew that now. No other man would ever hold her hand, place his arm around her shoulder and murmur into her ear. No other man could ever match up to Robert's little finger and, anyhow, marriage was totally impossible now. Quite out of the question. There was too much to do. The men to look after. Her personal feelings were irrelevant. She had taken her fun; now she must pay. She would live and die an old maid. Giles and her father came first while the farm ran a close second.

Mary handled her father like porcelain and he, sunk in dreadful grief, was amenable, willing to do as his daughter bid him. He simply ate the meals, changed his clothes and slept. On Giles's shoulders lay the running of the farm. The hard work was exactly what he needed. He flung himself into it with every jot of energy, staggering home at night almost too exhausted to eat. He worked with the men, using his bare hands as they used theirs. He visited the markets, bought and sold the stock and produce. He attended to the machinery and at hay and harvest times he stood atop of the ricks, patting the sheaves into position, swinging his pitchfork with easy, rhythmic movements. He was up and about before the cows came in to be milked and he was still working, inspecting the stock and checking when the last hand left at night. He was everywhere and everything. The men who worked at Mayo's worshipped him. Nothing was too good for the young master.

Giles Mayo became the talk of the county and the idol of the working man. Men applied to work on the farm for no other reason than that the young master was there. He often conducted an all-male gathering when questions and suggestions were tossed back and forth in open discussion. A shockingly new state of affairs according to the old diehards in the county who still considered their cattle more important than their workers. With all this, Mayo's boomed.

Any newly invented machine which was capable of doing work better than muscles was acquired. Giles would first find out the cost, talk with his men, sell something of equal value and obtain the machine. No worker ever lost his job because of Mayo's mechanization. With the increase in machinery Giles was able to put more land down to the plough and increase the farm's yield.

The workers' cottages were also the talk of the county. Giles inspected them once a month and this was always an occasion. This was the women's day when they greeted their young master, took him around their small homes and gave him refreshment. Mary had learned, from experience, that Giles never wanted much to eat when he returned home on those days.

Giles divided the farm's profits into three scrupulously fair piles. One third was put straight back into the farm; one third was for the family and the other third was set aside to give his workers what Giles considered to be a decent standard of living.

He liked to see his workers' children tall, healthy and full of high spirits. Most of all he liked to see food about their cottages. During his visits a pot of bubbling stew topped with good dumplings always brought a word of praise from him. There was nothing that delighted him more than a tiny cottage filled with the sweet aroma of freshly baked bread.

Giles paid well above the rates. Most farm workers received 9/d a week with the shepherds and cowmen getting a little more. Rents averaged one shilling a week. Giles paid four shillings above the standard rate and took only two thirds of the normal rent. Consequently he never suffered from labour troubles.

The other farmers hated him for it. But Giles was a pure Mayo. He did not give a damn about what others thought or said. He went his own sweet way regardless. If anyone had told Giles that he was a Victorian reformer he would have laughed in their face. That was precisely what he was. In that day and age of sweated labour he was a hundred years ahead of his time and quite disinterested in politics as a whole.

He even introduced a system whereby all his workers contributed sixpence a month to a common fund. Out of this, they received instant medical attention for nothing. It was a daring scheme he innovated but was typical of the man. Giles had sought a suitable arrangement with his own doctor but he, a staunch Tory, had sneered at such goings-on for the common herd. Without more ado, Giles rode into Bristol and spent days hunting out newly qualified doctors. He sounded them out on their basic humane principles. When he had found a man who thought along his lines, he brought him back to Mayo's and established him in one of the better village houses.

Despite all his enthusiasm and hard work he still had time for his father. Jon had died spiritually when he lost his precious Julie.

Every evening, no matter how tired he might be, Giles always sat with his father and told him, in great detail, the day's events. Jon would nod or grunt. He never passed a comment or showed a jot of interest in the farm. Patiently Giles took him out on his rounds but soon realized that Jon was quite content to leave the running of the property in his son's very competent hands.

Mary slowly found that she could think about Robert without tearing her heart to shreds. It took time, considerable time, but as she fitted herself into her domestic role and kept herself so busy, the pain of lost love eased slightly. It would never fully go. She was too sensible to think it might but instead of that wild, tearing love of so long ago, it seemed, she could now think of Robert with a quiet gentleness which became a beautiful dream of a memory.

She never mentioned her feelings to Giles and he never thought to ask. He was not selfish. He knew his sister had suffered but, in his clumsy, masculine way, he avoided the subject for fearing of inflicting new wounds. It was a long time before he realized that Mary had accepted the situation with a fatalistic calm. Gradually, tentatively, Robert's name slipped into their conversations again but they discussed him calmly and as casually as the merits and demerits of a breeding cow.

No one ever saw Robert. Giles certainly never looked for him and he suspected that Robert avoided him deliberately. He heard tales of him and of Ferndale. Sometimes Giles talked to Mary.

'Things aren't good at Ferndale, I've heard.'
'Why?'
'It's the land. It's horse-sour and the horse market itself is dying. Father was right. I'm glad we got rid of the horses and concentrated on mixed farming instead.'

It never entered Giles's head to seek Robert out and offer land. He knew that Mayo's was a sacred trust handed to him to keep firmly united and to go down through the generations as it had already done for so many years. As his father had said, so long ago, what the Howards did was their affair.

'But it'd be nice to have a friend. I've never met anyone I liked as much as you, Robert Howard. Why did it have to be?' Giles asked himself often because he was a very lonely man. Guilt is a poor companion for any human being.

Even the workmen took sides. They all knew the history; it had been handed down from father to son and naturally, they sided with Giles. No Mayo's worker who wanted to see the dawn with sound limbs would dream of drinking with a Howard's man. And a Mayo's woman would studiously ignore a Howard's woman. If it had not been so tragic it might have been humorous.

*　　*　　*

When he was twenty-four years of age, Giles did some serious thinking in his position as nominal head of Mayo's. Mary would never marry. That much was obvious. Giles knew she wanted nothing from life now but to run the farm and spend her days on it. For Giles, it was very different. What was going to be the outcome of it all; this hard work and planning? Who would claim Mayo's if he died childless?

He sat one evening, considering the matter

seriously. He was the direct heir. Through the years the Mayos had only ever managed to produce one surviving son per generation. Pondering this all out it struck Giles with a distinct shock, that if he died childless the Howards might well inherit! They stemmed from the same stock. Would they, in law, have a legitimate claim to the land?

'I don't like that,' Giles told himself. 'I don't like it, Robert, and I can't help it either. But when all is said and done you *are* a Howard and I am a Mayo and never the twain shall meet!'

Mayo's must stay in the Mayo family. Giles did not need a Jon or George to tell him this fact. It had been instinctively bred into him.

He took a deep breath and sat back. 'Well, then, there's only one thing to do. I must marry and soon!' he declared to the empty room.

He ran his mind over the single eligible females of the county. He had no illusions that he was more than a good catch. If he had wanted, he could have married long ago.

The girl must come from good stock. That, of course, was obvious. She must be a good breeder from a line of good breeders. A barren wife was no good to him.

There was a branch of the Gordons, distant by two marriages. They had two marriageable girls ready for the market. Priscilla and Helen. He tried to remember what he knew about them. Helen was the elder and about his own age. Coming from the Gordon family she would obviously be adaptable for a country life. A town girl was no good at all.

Mary would still run the house he decided. Though he was contemplating matrimony in the most cold-blooded way, he had sense enough to realize that two women in a house could cause untold friction. Mary must like the girl and she like Mary. There was a Hunt Ball the next month. Not having attended for years Giles decided this would be a good time to view the matrimonial field.

He told Mary that same night. She listened to him thoughtfully. She noted his cold sentences and desire for marriage solely to produce an heir. It had obviously never entered his head that he might father a litter of daughters. Mary kept this interesting thought to herself.

'It is time you married, Giles,' she agreed, speaking softly. 'Have you told father?'

Giles shook his head. 'There's no point. He's not interested in anything I tell him. I think he's just patiently waiting to die and join mother.'

Mary nodded. The words sounded cold and harsh but she knew them to be true.

'I thought about Helen, the Gordon's cousin.'

Mary furrowed her brows. 'I remember her. She's quite pretty and used to laugh a lot at school—not giggling though!' she added hastily, seeing a frown cross Giles's face.

'Did you like her?'

Mary nodded. 'Yes, I did! Why?'

Giles stared at her. 'Because whoever comes here as my wife defers to you. You are mistress here, Mary,' he said firmly.

Mary pursed her lips uneasily. Being feminine she knew the danger of such a situation. Two women lording it over one kitchen! Why, such a situation could be explosive!

'Helen as a sister-in-law,' she mused to herself.

It would be fun to have another female about the house. One of her own age and station in life! Even though the worker-staff relations at Mayo's were good there was still the basic gulf of class distinction. Mary had found this to be far more rigidly upheld by the workers than themselves. It was as if they had pride in knowing their station in life and adhering to it. Sometimes they exasperated her.

She nodded at Giles. 'I think Helen would fit in well here—but Giles—she might be spoken for!' she pointed out.

'I've thought of that,' he replied. 'I'll take the carriage and look her over some time this week.'

Mary looked sharply at him.

'Dear Giles, don't be so cold-blooded about

this!' she thought to herself. 'You are not going to inspect a piece of machinery now. You're going to meet a woman. Someone living of flesh and bone and human emotion. A person who can laugh and cry and know fear!'

But she knew better than to say any of this aloud. Giles was sometimes quite unreachable. He must find out for himself.

True to his word, Giles surveyed the field. He went to the Hunt Ball, danced dutifully with the girls, flattered their mamas and was highly respectful to their bewhiskered papas. He compared all the marriageable daughters. He tabulated their good and bad points, discarding some instantly and putting others aside for further consideration. At the end of three months his first choice was still the best.

He drove over to see Helen's stuffy, old-fashioned parents, and stated his intentions. He asked permission to call and court their elder daughter. The Gordon-Smiths were delighted. Giles Mayo was the catch of the county. They had never dreamed that his eyes had alighted on their first born. There were, of course, others dancing attendance on Helen but both Papa and Mama Gordon-Smith decided that Giles Mayo must take priority. Firmly and quietly, the other suitors departed, leaving Helen rather mystified and more than a little hurt.

Helen Gordon-Smith was no raving beauty. Her attractions emanated from a cheerful nature, happy spirit and the sheer vivacious love of life.

At first, she eyed Giles Mayo askance. Who wouldn't? He had a reputation of being a determined man and who, horror of horrors, thought his workers human beings and treated them almost as equals! Helen unfortunately had been reared by a family who considered workers almost with revulsion.

But Giles, with his rugged good looks and virile masculine body, was magnetic. His personality was powerfully strong. Even though he was rather silent and aloof when he took her drives or escorted her a ride through the countryside. When he took her to a party it took him time to unbend.

Helen felt there was something about him which touched her. He aroused her dormant maternal instincts to a height which embarrassed her. She was left breathless and trembling though he never dreamed of going further than a respectful kiss. Fierce, inexplicable currents churned Helen's body, leaving her perplexed and utterly bewildered.

She had never known such emotions existed. She was the typical, narrow-minded ignorant girl of the times. From where babies came she had absolutely no idea and knew better than to ask. There were many subjects rigidly taboo in her stuffy Victorian home. She sensed her mother would have swooned if questioned upon some of them.

241

One day she sneaked into her father's library when the house was empty. She sought for the dictionary which, like certain other books, was considered unsuitable for young females. It was kept hidden in a locked cabinet. With the skill worthy of a burglar she unpicked the lock, selected the dictionary and started looking up words of interest. At first, she had a problem. She did not know the names of the objects she wished to study but eventually turned to 'organs', 'sex' and 'copulation'. By the time dusk fell Helen Gordon-Smith had acquired a major part of the purely technical detail necessary for her curiosity's satisfaction.

'Well!' she exclaimed to herself, 'who would have guessed babies came from doing that!'

She was still too prudish to actually utter the word 'sex'. Then something else struck her like a bomb.

'If I marry Giles Mayo does that mean *I'll* have to do that?'

This was entirely different. What other people did she could view dispassionately. That she too would have to get involved in such activities and positions was a staggering thought!

Was that what marriage really meant? She now knew it was!

'But could I let Giles Mayo do that—to *me?*' she asked herself nervously. No sooner had the question been asked than her body willingly answered. Electric tingles chased down her spine. Her breath came in sharp, little gasps. She certainly could, she told herself and, adding practically, the sooner the better too!

Unbeknown to himself, Giles Mayo could not have chosen a more suitable mate than the happy, laughing and very intelligent Helen Gordon-Smith.

The courtship proceeded along well-run lines. Giles took Helen to Mayo's to meet Mary. The two girls fell into each other's arms with genuine cries of pleasure. Mary promptly took Helen on a slowly conducted tour of the house while Giles sat smoking his pipe and waiting for their return.

He was very pleased with the way things had turned out and smugly satisfied with his choice of female.

As he waited, he attempted to analyse his actual feelings for Helen. She was tall. Not too tall but certainly above average. She had her curves well developed in all the correct places. Though not having what he considered to be a pretty face she did have charm. She had a button of a nose which tilted slightly at the end. Coupled with dancing brown eyes, it gave her a perpetual mischievous look. She had long brown hair which waved and fell on her shoulders in a gentle curl. Her teeth were white and sparkling with health. Her cheeks had that rose tint only found in British country girls. Perhaps her most outstanding feature was her hands. Her nails were long, the fingers thin-boned while the palms were well-developed showing unusual strength.

He told his father his intentions and afterwards wondered if Jon had understood. Did he understand anything nowadays? All Jon wanted to do was sit in the kitchen rocking chair, smoke a pipe and look blankly out of the window. He was no trouble to them, being as tractable as a well-fed baby. But Jon's passive disinterest in life upset Giles. It reminded him too vividly of that horrible day.

He was glad to think of other things. He flung himself into plans of matrimony. Helen was agreeable to an immediate wedding and they were married one sunny Saturday. All the village attended the nuptials of the young master and the feast afterwards was held in one of the Mayo's emptied barns.

The house staff spent the preceding week in an orgy of cooking. Mary was worked up to a state of frenzy and could only talk of hams and roasts and cakes. Giles wondered whether they had an army to feed. Precious home-brewed wines were brought up from the cellars. The village women produced their home-made ales. Such was the frantic activity that even Jon was stimulated enough to take an interest. He passed one or two scathing comments about 'clucking females' which delighted brother and sister.

They watched their father carefully and saw

244

a gleam of interest enter his blank eyes. Slowly, very gradually, the mentally dead man was drawn back into the emotional world of the living. With a start, Giles realized that nothing better could have happened.

He went to his nuptials feeling reborn. His father had returned to them. His guilt feeling began to diminish. Giles's feelings were humble with thanks. This humility increased when, standing at the altar watching Helen walk up the aisle on her father's arm, he was suddenly conscious of what the word love did mean after all.

This was *not* just a female capable of producing an heir for Mayo's. This delightful creature was flesh and blood like himself. For the rest of his life she would stand at his side. With overpowering emotion Giles Mayo became aware that he was, indeed, very much in love with this Helen.

As they walked back down through the crowded church, her arm on his, he paused and looked steadily into his father's eyes. Jon slowly smiled back at him. Stepping forward, one hand touching her pink cheek, Jon Mayo kissed his daughter-in-law.

'Welcome!' he said softly.

Tears ran unchecked down Mary's cheeks. She looked up at her brother through a downpour of salt droplets.

'Dear Giles! God bless you both. Look after Helen! Remember, I'll be watching to make sure you do. She's the dearest, sweetest friend to me and, Giles, our father, he's recovered at last. Thank you, Giles! All is right with us again!'

Giles took the unprecedented step of a week's honeymoon in London, that mysterious den of noise and iniquity. It was a week of bliss.

CHAPTER FOUR

Then came the good years thought Giles as he looked back later. Wonderful years full of joy and promise. Times when he learned to laugh and become really human again. At thirty-five years he was an outstanding figure of a man. He was the delight of Helen and the pleasure of Mary and Jon. The children adored their strong father who could pick two of them up together and hold them aloft, squealing and shouting with joy.

It was a happy house now, though tragedy laid her fingers upon it briefly. They called their firstborn John and he was quickly followed by Mike. Jane came a year after in 1892 and George completed their family in 1893. After George, the doctor took Giles aside and told him his brood was complete. There would be no further babies. The last birth had been difficult and prolonged. Only the use of chloroform and Lord Lister's teachings about antiseptics had saved Helen from a horrible death.

Giles did not mind and reassured Helen of this fact. His family was complete. He had three strong, healthy sons to inherit. He had done what he had set out to do, succeeding beyond his wildest dreams in more ways than one.

The black spot was baby Jane. She was the weak one of the litter. Despite the doctor's most strenuous efforts she died shortly after George's birth.

With the coming of the children Mayo's burst into noisy activity and Jon, even if he had wished, would have found it impossible to remain mentally aloof. He adored his grandsons and they delighted in him. Jon had a fund of fascinating stories to tell them and a myriad of small pockets where such objects as shiny stones, birds' eggs and other mysteries managed to appear.

Jon left Mayo's completely to Giles's management. After the wedding, when his wits had returned, he inspected the farm while Giles was away with Helen. He talked to the men, examined the machines and few carthorses still left. He crumbled the soil in his old hands, eyeing it knowingly. There was nothing left for him to teach Giles. A quick inspection of the accounts which Giles meticulously entered once a week showed him that he could never have put the property back on such sound legs again. Jon was immensely satisfied and resolved that for the rest of his life he was going to work at one thing only. He would be a Grandpa. In this he succeeded beyond his wildest dreams.

'You are the three most unholy terrors and the most un-Mayo like people I could imagine!' Mary exclaimed frequently.

The boys used to take this as a compliment, though the Mayo-like bit did puzzle them a little. Giles agreed with his sister. Not one of his sons showed physical Mayo features. They all took after their mother in looks far more than boys should, Giles told himself. They had her brown hair, brown eyes and small noses. Yet in temperament, they were Mayos to the fingertips. They were stubborn, tough and self-reliant. They worshipped the land and, copying their father, mixed freely with the workers' children. This disgusted Giles's contemporaries and bothered him not at all.

John, being the eldest, was the natural leader. Mike and George were his sworn followers though, at times, they were perfectly capable of thinking up their own peculiar brand of mischief. Then they would inveigle John into thinking the idea was his. They were so close and harmonious in their relations to each other that it was almost uncanny.

They really were good years, Giles told himself again. Good for us though pretty rotten for the Howards.

Giles never saw Robert. The gulf was immeasurably wide between them but news was still easy to come by. Robert had married. It was a sudden affair and took the area by surprise. One day Robert was single and the next married to a small, dark-haired girl from Gloucester called Eliza.

She was a darting minx of a female who, Giles guessed, would keep Robert on the hop. When Giles first heard the news he wondered uneasily how to tell Mary. Years had passed. Time had mellowed a situation but he knew only too well that the heart was a highly complicated organ. Mary had been so much in love.

He did not like Eliza. Her character appeared to be furtive and he wondered exactly how much happiness Robert had with his wife. There was something about Eliza which Giles did not trust. Other men ogled her too much and she was certainly not averse to masculine flattery. But he knew why Robert had married. Heirs! Ferndale too must have heirs. Eliza was going to be a breeding vessel. The Howard line had to be perpetuated just like that of the Mayos. It was basic logic where land and its power was concerned.

He mentioned Eliza's name to Mary one evening, watching carefully for his sister's reactions. Mary was sharp. She understood and although the news had sent a stab of jealousy searing her heart she had quickly banished it. She listened to Giles in seeming indifference.

'I don't care for her,' Giles told Mary one morning.

'But you don't know her!' and Mary thought what a typically arrogant statement Giles had just made. How very masculine!

'Can't help it. She's not the right girl for Robert!'

'How do you know?' Mary challenged him. 'When did you last speak to Robert?' and she could have bitten her tongue off.

Giles hesitated before he replied, 'You know the answer to that, sister!'

'I didn't mean—oh, Giles, I'm sorry. That was a tactless thing for me to say,' Mary stammered.

'It's all right. It all happened a long time ago. I don't think of it very often now. There's no point. Thinking doesn't bring people back. No, it's just that I know Robert. We were such kindred souls. If things had been different we would have been good friends to each other. Far better friends than James and I would ever have been. He was lonely, too, you know.'

'But things can't be all that bad. They do have three sons, you know!' Mary pointed out, then blushed a little. Some things were still unladylike to say even to a close brother.

Giles grinned at her embarrassment, reading her mind. 'You look most attractive sister when you do blush! You should do it more often—but I understand your meaning perfectly. The point is that still doesn't make a healthy marriage!'

Mary fell silent, not knowing what to say. Giles could be most perceptive at times. Was Robert unhappily married? She had never heard controversial gossip about them but, on the other hand, she didn't stray far from Mayo's.

'Does Helen know about what's happened in the past?' she asked, changing the subject on to safer ground.

Giles nodded slowly. 'I've told her some of it. I'll tell the boys some too when they get older but there's no point in thrashing over every little detail again. It's funny though, about Robert's boys. I saw them a couple of weeks ago with their parents in Bristol. No, they didn't see me. I kept well back but their three lads are roughly the same age as mine. Joseph is John's age, David and Mike were born within weeks of each other and Harry Howard was born just after Jane. There is one very weird thing. Our three don't look like Mayos at all. They take after their mother too much for that—but those Howard boys look just like Mayos!'

'Oh no!'

Giles nodded. 'You'd think we'd each bred the other's brood.'

'It's the old Mayo blood throwing back

again,' Mary said, speaking almost to herself. 'Because you can't get away from the fact that we do come from the one family.'

'At least, those three are going to a different school. That's Robert's doing, thank God. I don't fancy our three devils tangling with three Howards!'

'Especially as things don't seem to be going too well at Ferndale. Father was right, what he said years ago,' Mary added thoughtfully.

Giles nodded in agreement. At first the preparations leading up to the Boer War had boded well for the Ferndale Horse Stud. Horses were in tremendous demand and the special Howard's greys were much sought after by the officers. Robert made money hand over fist. What he did with it Giles did not know, though he suspected that what Robert earned Eliza quickly spent.

Tragedy struck Ferndale practically overnight. A wounded officer returned from the Cape with a favourite mare. He planned to have her bred by a Howard's stallion but the mare doomed nearly all the famous grey breed. In a few short weeks the great horse herds were decimated as the terrible and, to then, unknown Epizootic Lyphingitis swept through them. There was no cure, no answer to it all. A stricken Robert and unbelieving Peter watched their precious horses die under their very noses.

Hastily they isolated a stud stallion and six

mares, sending them to another part of the county. They waited, with bated breath, to see if the disease had been carried.

It was all just too much for Peter Howard. He lay down and died. Worn out and quite heart-broken before his time. Robert was harassed beyond endurance. Giles watched from a distance. He badly wanted to help but dared make no offer. While his father was alive his hands were tied.

Mayo's thrived and now Howards sank into the mire. It was not just the disease but also the state of the war. English horses were, it was admitted at last, quite useless for that type of mounted combat. They did not have the high training the Boer gave to his small, tough, veld-bred pony who could travel incredible distances. The pampered English horses had to be fed the best hay and corn, all of which was imported. Its Boer counterpart lived quite rough off the land and thought nothing of being ridden for 40 miles with a heavy man on its back and then charging at the gallop into attack. This small animal was carefully trained to stand while his rider dismounted and used his neck as a level for his rifle. An English horse in similar circumstances would rear up and take off at the first shot. One English fighting man in four was compelled to stand uselessly holding reins.

Many horses arrived in South Africa wearing their thick English winter coats. They were not acclimatized and horse losses grew alarmingly high. The men's morale was affected.

As the news filtered back to England it became obvious to Giles that this was more than the beginning of the end. Horse breeding, as now known, was obsolete.

The Howard greys had been bred, down the years, following the same faithful pattern laid down by Jos. They were very good horses. Supreme riding animals but out of date for professional competition or war. They had spirit, beauty and fire, but somewhere along the line, they had lost some speed. They failed hopelessly on the race track and were now unpopular as officers' chargers. Only the ladies liked them and this market was small.

'Bread and meat are aways wanted and never more so than when a country is at war,' Giles told himself. The population was booming, food demands were increasing but Robert had become dangerously conservative.

'Why can't he see what's happening?' Giles groaned to himself. 'He must plough up those horse pastures quickly. Unless he changes, he'll go bust!'

They met one momentous day in Chipping Sodbury market. It was a pure accident, surprising them both and leaving them in shocked and embarrassed silence.

Giles had turned rather sharply from the stall selling saddles and cannoned into his double.

'I beg your pardon—good God! Robert!' he exclaimed. Without thinking his hand shot out. Robert grasped it without hesitation, smiling gently with a queer expression in his eyes.

They fell silent then. Each waiting for the other to break the ice. Not knowing what to do or what to say. So many years had passed, yet looking at each other they were back again to their last parting. Memories flooded through both their minds. They remembered what they had both sweated to forget.

'It's been a long time, Giles!' Robert said slowly.

Giles nodded. 'A very long time, I . . .' and he had hesitated at a loss for suitable words. He didn't like what he was remembering. They were in the middle of a crowd yet alone again on two horses galloping wildly after a grey stallion and terrified boy.

Robert sensed his thoughts. 'It's not easy to talk—after—well, so much has happened and, oh damn it all, Giles! I am pleased to see you again!' he said sincerely.

A slow, tired smile crept over Giles's face as his heart warmed to this man so like himself. 'I'm glad to see you. Let's have a beer!'

They pushed their way into a tavern and a pint of ale in each hand, backs against a wall in a packed room, they drank and looked at each other. They had sworn friendship for each other. Where had it got them? What would happen if they dared to pick up those same reins again? And how could I, Giles asked himself, not while father is alive.

'How are things with you—now?' he asked Robert after a long pause.

Robert shook his head. 'Pretty bad but thank God we saved a breeding herd.'

'Are you going to keep on with horses?' Giles asked him casually.

Robert paused, chewed his bottom lip, then shot a frank look at Giles.

'Would you?'

'I'd stop concentrating on horses—but then you know me. I've never held much stock for them,' he prevaricated.

'But what would you do instead?' Robert persisted.

'Grow corn for bread. Rear pigs for meat with some cattle thrown in. That's what I'd do!'

Robert fell silent, chewing this over thoughtfully. 'I've been thinking that but it hurts to see so few horses on the land. The thought of ploughing up the pastures, well, it's like sacrilege. I think Grandpa Jos would turn in his grave!'

Giles shook his head. 'Not from what I've heard about him. He would say it was the practical thing to do. Let's face it, Rob. Ferndale is more than your home. It's your business. Don't forget, you can always go back to horse breeding—you say you've kept a stud nucleus!' Giles pointed out.

'I know, but it's alien to the way I was brought up! However, I guess we all have to move with the times or go under. You have done well at Mayo's! Look at you, the showpiece farm of this county. I'm glad for you, Giles!' Robert meant it.

He paused then and studied Giles's face carefully.

'How is Mary?' he asked quietly.

Giles returned the look and plumbed to the depths of Robert's heart. There was unhappiness in those eyes. There was also wistful longing for something precious and lost forever.

'She's well,' Giles told him.

'She never married?' Robert stated flatly.

Giles paused. This was dangerous ground. They should both get off it quickly.

'Why didn't she marry?' Robert persisted.

Giles had to give an answer. 'How could she? With father and after James—' then he fell silent.

'Such a waste—for both of us. We didn't deserve it because we were meant for each other. It's not fair. Nothing's fair. There's no justice in this life!'

Giles could think of nothing to say. He understood, in a clairvoyant flash of sympathetic knowledge that he had not been alone in his suffering. Bitterness rose in him too then. Robert was right. It had all been so grossly unfair. Mary and Robert had indeed been made for each other.

*   *   *

The Mayo boys grew and grew, their wild spirits seemingly uncheckable. With great reluctance Giles despatched them to a public school where discipline and manners were considered more important than book learning. They came home at frequent intervals and, Helen thought, they're just the same.

'Have I reared myself three tartars?' she asked Giles more than once. 'But they are lovable boys with all their devilry!' she weakened almost immediately.

Helen, like Julie, had been amazed when she had heard some of the details of the Mayo-Howard feud. When Giles described his family's turbulent history though she started to understand some of the deep passions involved. She never mentioned the past to Jon. Mary warned her early on when she first came to Mayo's that ground was too dangerous to tread.

To Jon, a Howard was still something lower than a rat. Only Giles and Mary could fully understand the deep current of hatred running through the old man's memory. Gradually, though, the boys began to grasp this too, though not without asking their Grandpa a multitude of questions. Jon eagerly answered their questions and the answers worried the adults, especially Giles. Because, quite naturally, Jon gave answers according to his gospel. Sometimes the boys didn't fully believe everything Jon told them, so they would come to Giles with their questions.

John, at eighteen, was the spokesman. 'We know we're vaguely related to the Howards, Pa. We know that Uncle James, great-Grandpa George and great-Uncle John all died because of them, but—' and here John paused hesitantly looking at his brothers.

'Oh Lord! What's he going to come out with now?' Giles asked himself anxiously.

'Well, spit it out, son!'

'Well, we heard that you and Robert Howard were once friends. Jim Charlton said so. I hit him on the nose for it because it was a lie, wasn't it?'

'Oh dear!' said Giles, shaking his head. 'Here we go again!'

Jim Charlton, who went to their public school, was a notoriously gossipy boy. He was supposed to be a friend of the Howards but Giles doubted whether he would ever have a true friend with his wicked tongue.

His three sons stood waiting for his answer. Giles knew they expected him to deny such treachery.

'Look boys! Once long ago when I was only your age I had a brother whom I didn't like—

and he didn't like me either.'

The three boys looked at each other in astonishment. Brothers disliking each other. This was not possible!

'We didn't like each other because we were so different. And because we didn't like each other we were both, in our way, very lonely. The only boy I ever spoke to at school was Robert Howard. Even in those days we fought more than we spoke!'

'But you always beat him?' George stated flatly.

Giles grinned. 'Sometimes and sometimes not! One day Robert and I met and we talked instead of fighting for a change. He was as lonely as me. We were two boys alone without a close friend of any kind. We were both very unhappy. Have you ever seen him?'

They shook their heads in unison.

'Well, take a good look at him if ever you get the chance. You know we're related. You'd be surprised to see just how alike Robert and I do look. Sometimes, wearing the same clothes, we could pass as twins. It's the Mayo blood in both of us. As we were both so terribly lonely we thought perhaps we could become friends—and forget our loneliness. My brother James died, you know how, and Grandpa blamed Robert. Really it was all my fault. Since then Robert and I knew we could not hope to be friends because of the terrible past. In fact, boys, I've only spoken to Robert

260

Howard once in all those years and that was recently—but I should not tell your Grandpa that!' he warned them hastily.

Mike, the sensitive one, had been studying his father's face. 'And all that made you very sad, Pa, didn't it?'

Giles slowly nodded, his heart warming to this perceptive son.

'How would you three like to be alone without a friend of your own age?'

They looked at each other, appalled at this thought. To be alone was something so dreadful they had never considered it.

'So Charlton wasn't lying then!' John said later.

'And you hit him for nothing. You'll have to apologize!' George told him. John nodded agreement. He looked at Mike then back at George.

'I think Pa must have had a rotten boyhood!' Mike said flatly.

George nodded agreement.

'I think so too!' added John. 'But I still don't want anything to do with those Howards. I don't like them even if they are distant family. They've caused too much trouble in the past. That Joseph is silly. All he thinks about is painting and music. Girls do that!' he said scornfully.

'David is always reading!' Mike added in some disgust.

'Harry's the best of the bunch. He can ride

261

and shoot nearly as good as us but he's such a kid,' George said.

'What do you mean? He's a year older than you!' Mike pointed out in amusement.

'Well, he doesn't act it at times. He's a bit young!' George sounded a little pompous.

'Listen to him!' roared Mike.

George fell on him, fists flailing like windmills but punches pulled. With a roar John joined in. Within a minute three healthy fine specimens of British youth were wrestling on the ground in a tangle of arms and legs.

'Those boys!' sighed Mary as she looked out of the window.

Helen shook her head. 'I do wish Jane had lived. I'm sure she would have been a steadying influence!'

Giles snorted. 'Nothing will steady those three but work, work and then more work!'

*   *   *

In 1911 Jon took to his bed with a cough and cold. He told them it was nothing to fuss about. Within 24 hours his temperature had risen. Gravely the doctor told them it was this new thing called influenza. They tried everything they knew but Jon developed pneumonia. It was obvious he was dying.

Giles and Helen sat with him one evening, giving Mary a rest. They watched his straining lungs, hearing the fluid rattling inside as he started to drown in his own liquid. He opened his eyes once. His lips twisted in a ghastly smile and he whispered 'Julie! At last!' His heart collapsed under the terrible strain and he died.

The boys were shattered with grief. This was their first meeting with death. They could not imagine Mayo's without their Grandpa. He had always been there. He was as much a part of Mayo's as the foundations. He couldn't, just couldn't, go from them.

For many weeks they were subdued and silent. Then gradually their effervescent spirits returned as their attention turned to a new discovery. Girls! From being gape-toothed creatures they appeared now as luscious creations with swaying hips and tempting bosoms.

They toured the county, having themselves a great time. As they always moved in a threesome and were quick with their fists, this became a little hard on more serious suitors, but the eligible girls adored them.

With their clean shaved faces—all Mayos disliked facial hair—their long, clean limbs and honest eyes, they swept and conquered unmercifully. They did not once get themselves into too serious a tangle which Giles was unable to sort out. Nevertheless, swearing heartily at them, he always deducted monies he had to pay out, from their allowances. He wondered uneasily just how many bastard Mayos these boys were going to be responsible for if they kept on like this.

They were the joy of the girls, the terror of the boys, the bane of the papas and the wistful envy of the mamas. These ageing ladies only wished they had been courted in such a boisterous fashion.

The Mayos and Howards, by mutual sensitivity, took different stamping grounds. The Howards appeared weak, poor creatures against the lusty, virile Mayo boys.

Giles often thought uneasily what Robert made of it all when news reached the area how his three had rampaged through Bristol on a Saturday evening. It was a miracle they had not yet been locked up.

'But I suppose there's time enough for that to happen!' Giles groaned to himself.

Now and again Giles and Robert allowed themselves to meet at the market. It was a safe, neutral ground and though never admitting it they took tremendous pleasure in these casual meetings. They would go and have a drink and exchange safe news like farming versus horse breeding.

Giles thought Robert had aged one Saturday midday. There were distinct lines across his friend's forehead and frequently he appeared to be thinking of other matters far away. Giles hesitated as to whether he should probe.

Robert had always been perceptive to the

point of sharpness. On this particular morning he once again appeared to read Giles thoughts.

'Yes, there is something wrong,' he told Giles abruptly. He paused a second as if marshalling some unpleasant thoughts into an acceptable speech, then, voice faltering a little, he confided in his friend.

'It's Eliza. She's not the best of wives. You see, Giles—oh—to hell with it! This kind of thing can't be said delicately. She's seeing other men and liking it too. From what I've found out it's just pure luck that she's not been landed with a baby!'

Giles was appalled. There had always been something about Eliza which had aroused his distrust. He saw the hurt in Robert's face. He imagined the stab to his pride. How long had this been going on? What did Robert intend doing?

Again Robert answered the unspoken question. 'What am I going to do? I'm going to divorce her for adultery!'

Giles was astounded at first. Divorce was so, and he hunted for a suitable description— divorce was wrong. The church said so. Divorced persons were banned from so much, this action being heavily frowned upon in higher circles. That Robert was contemplating such action showed his desperation. There would be talk, gossip and far worse. His name, even though innocent, would be dragged through the mud. His boys too would not escape uninjured. Divorce was sordid.

Although Giles had never been an avid church-goer he had received sufficient indoctrination as a young boy to flinch aside at the word. Then his logical and reasonable mind came to his aid. How could he pass judgement? What kind of suffering must Robert have undergone? Even *he* had suspected Eliza Howard for a long time. Robert had obviously been the last person to find out as was so often the case. His heart felt for his friend. He wanted to help, to render practical assistance but there was absolutely nothing he could do. Poor Robert, he was having to stand alone and take his blows. First Ferndale and the loss of his horses, then Peter Howard's death and now an unhappy marriage.

'I'll be all right,' Robert told him quietly. 'The solicitors are handling everything and there is adequate evidence. There'll be a smell but I can ride out the storm. The boys will stay with me. Thank God they have faith in their father. Eliza never showed them much interest. I'm glad now otherwise they might have been torn in two.'

'It's a rotten business—and there's nothing I can do to help, is there?'

Robert shook his head. 'It'll all blow over though I expect it will take time.'

A thought struck Giles then with a dart's

penetration. Robert would be free to many again if he wished. Robert—and Mary. His sister with a divorced man? He tossed the idea about for a few seconds. It was against everything bred into him but he knew only too well that true love is the most dangerous force in the world. Did Mary still feel anything for Robert and he for her?

Robert had been studying Giles' face. His sharp, perceptive mind followed the train of unspoken thought.

'I won't say I've not considered the matter because I have,' he stated suddenly.

Giles was taken aback. He could think of nothing to say. 'Where would you stand if?' and Robert left the sentence unfinished.

'I don't know. Honest to God, I just do not know!'

'Why shouldn't we marry—if she'd have me, that is. Shop-soiled so to speak,' Robert added wistfully, 'but through no fault of my own. Why shouldn't we marry? What the hell has convention done for me—or you? We've lost a lot of years but why can't we spend those remaining to us together? We'd not be harming anyone!' he challenged.

'The Church!' Giles objected weakly.

Robert swore savagely. 'And what has the Church done for me—or you? Tell me, did the Church help your conscience when James died? Well, did it? No, you had to battle through on your own. To hell with what people

267

or the Church thinks. We only come this way once. Why shouldn't I take what happiness I can while I'm able.'

'She might not want you,' Giles pointed out softly. 'She's never been out with any man after you.'

'No, and you know why? I'll tell you! It's because she was only made for me and me for her. Eliza—!' and Robert swore another foul oath.

'She gave you your heirs!' Giles pointed out.

'The one decent thing she ever did!' Robert retorted, then he lowered his voice and eyed Giles carefully.

'I still want Mary—if she'd have me. Would you try and stop us?'

'I'd not stop you, old friend. Why the hell should I? I wish you luck but, mark you, Mary's deep and has a mind of her own. It might be too late!'

'In that case she can tell me so herself!' Robert told him grimly, but the telling had to wait. Other far more momentous events were happening.

Hundreds of miles away an insignificant archduke got himself and his wife assassinated. The drums began to roll. Their rumble grew to a thunder and men's hearts beat with the drums. There was far more important news to discuss now than a mere divorce case.

To the Mayo boys this was marvellous. A chance to travel, fight and whore to their

268

heart's delight without parental opposition. This was going to be life itself. They enlisted en masse, refusing to go as officers, knowing they would only be separated. Instead, they donned rough, ill-smelling khaki and flung themselves into the war game with their usual spontaneous frivolity.

They nearly broke Helen's and Mary's hearts. Giles, shocked, but understanding their feelings, gave his reluctant blessing.

'It will all be over by Christmas,' they told him. 'We must go now or we'll miss all the fun!'

It was only the quieter, sober Howard boys who understood the political implications. They appreciated that this would most likely be a long affair. It was no skirmish against mounted farmers. This was the real thing and for keeps. But they were English; they believed in freedom and they had been suitably educated with all the pompous propaganda of the times. Off they went to do their duty for King and Country.

They left behind a broken-hearted Robert and a lonely man. His divorce was absolute. He was alone in Ferndale for the very first time in his life and it hurt deeply.

Giles knew this and made his first call ever, driving his new motor-car. A thing of belching smoke and grinding gears, it moved at the fantastic speed of 25 miles per hour.

Robert, ever conservative, stuck to his horse

and chaise. He was delighted to welcome Giles into his home. It was the first time Giles had entered the house and once inside the two men looked steadily at each other.

'It's taken us a long time to make it!' Robert said as a slow smile spread over his weather-beaten features.

Giles nodded in happy agreement. 'Far too long!'

'And there's no going back now?'

'No!' Giles replied in a strong voice. 'No matter what happens let's enjoy the friendship we lost as boys.'

'So be it! Whisky?'

And so finally began the most wonderful masculine friendship which had taken so many years to turn from bud to blossom. These two men had so much in common, their tastes, though different, melded into each other's. They had sense enough not to hurry things. Both of them still acutely conscious of the past. Like matured wine which had to be sipped slowly for full appreciation, they took their time. Their earlier conversations being about more topical events. They did not mention Mary. Robert was not yet sure enough to move; the war was too powerfully foremost in all thoughts.

'Our boys?' Robert asked hesitantly.

Giles frowned. 'Yes. You have a point. There'll be trouble—because of the past but, quite frankly, the boys can get on with it. I think you and I are both overdue for something for ourselves!'

'I agree!' then Robert's voice became gloomy. 'There will be trouble from our boys. It was all right when they moved in different directions.'

'What do you mean?'

'My three have joined the same regiment as yours!' Robert informed him.

Giles groaned. 'Oh, no! Not that! What possessed them?'

'Well, it's out of our hands,' Robert said philosophically. 'The funny thing is your three are such hellers and don't even look like Mayos. My three are me all over again in appearance yet take after Eliza's parents. Artistic! Breeding's a funny thing. You get much better results with horses. Damned sight more predictable, too!' Robert added glumly.

Giles burst into laughter and slapped Robert on the back. 'You and your horses!'

'Talking about horses, did you know the Army are scouring the country for remounts? I only have some old stock left. All the others have been requisitioned!'

'But that's crazy!' Giles expostulated. 'The horse in war is finished. This is the age of the engine. Fancy taking horses,' he snorted.

'And I've heard that when the weather gets bad in France it really does rain. Vehicles are going to bog down and horses too. What's it going to be like for our lads?' Robert asked

271

unhappily.

Giles stared back steadily. 'One thing's for sure! It's not going to be over by Christmas as so many fools think. This is going to be something long and bad. I can feel it in my bones.'

Robert nodded unhappily. 'My sentiments exactly!'

Giles lifted his glass. 'To our six boys. God grant they all come back to us!'

CHAPTER FIVE

To start with, it was great fun! The Mayo boys thrived on mass masculine comradeship. They drilled, tongues in cheeks, rode, shot and declared unanimously that this was the greatest event in their lives. Their one big fear was that it would all be over before they reached France. They were hell-raisers on a majestic scale. The despair of the drill sergeant. The terror of the meeker men and the idols of every female heart within twenty miles of the camp in all directions.

That men were dying 'over there' meant nothing to them as yet. They were far too egotistical to consider that anything could possibly happen to them. Their spirits were infectious. All the young monied men caroused around them. All except the

Howards.

Their first meeting with their distant relations had been pregnant with possibilities. It occurred one evening after a hard day's training which had not even touched the spirits of the Mayos. The Howards were tired and thoughtful, conversing amongst themselves as they walked through the tented camp. They were thinkers and not at all happy with the future.

The Mayos appeared from around a bend. They saw the Howards and all automatically stopped. The six boys looked at each other with surprise, shock and apprehension.

Mike and George turned to John for a lead, Harry and David to Joseph. Mechanically, the two eldest stepped forward as spokesmen.

Both John and Joseph were unsure of themselves and what was expected of them. In all their young lives they had never been so close to each other. They had instinctive pride in their respective families but also the knowledge that brawling now could mean trouble if an officer appeared. Though this was nothing to what would happen if their sergeant caught them fighting.

The Howards did not care to fight. They were not cowards but all three Howard boys considered brawling to be an undignified way of settling disputes. They preferred to debate an issue like intelligent gentlemen should.

Not the Mayos. They gloried in the sound of

fist smacking bone. They considered it girlish to chatter when muscles could do a job far more efficiently.

John eyed Joseph with great interest, astonished at his Mayo looks. He was suddenly acutely conscious that he did not have one Mayo feature. This irritated him. Scowling a little he stood and waited for Joseph to make the first move. Mike and George closed ranks behind him, fists already clenched. Apprehensively David and Harry placed themselves on each side of Joseph. These relatives looked the hell raisers they were. The Howards noted the clenched fists, jutting jaws and narrowed eyes of the Mayos. They exchanged a flickering glance between themselves. So be it, they said mentally. We would rather talk than fight but if these loutish relations think they can dominate us they have another think coming.

John sneered as he looked at them. For all their Mayo looks he very much doubted whether they had backbone. More than likely they had the same base instincts as their murdering ancestor Joseph who had hidden behind a tree to murder a Mayo. Turning to his brothers his eyes flared his scorn. His sentiments were reflected in his brothers' eyes. In line, they stepped forward, jaws jutting, lips twisted and eyes flashing sparks.

The Howards drew their breaths, sighed and shook their heads at this stupidity. They also stepped forward to battle for their name. Within two seconds six boys were a tangled mass of punching arms and kicking legs. This was a fight without finesse or rules. This was a fight which had been brewing for years. The cry now was for blood.

Suddenly the quiet and peaceful Howards had felt their breeding. They reverted back to that first ruthless Mayo. Their bloodlust rose. They smashed into the astonished Mayos with a venom which would have shocked Robert.

After the initial impact the Mayos fought back in savage silence. It dawned upon them this was not going to be another of their easy victories. They had, at last, met opponents worthy of them. John punched at Joseph who dodged and slipped in a left. David and Mike were closed, arms grappling, as they wrestled to throw each other to the ground. George and Harry stood off one pace and slugged it out without budging an inch. They grunted as blows landed, spat as blood ran from burst lips and cut eyes.

All six had wounds now. Blood flowed copiously on John's and Joseph's faces but neither side had any intention of calling quits. The excited spectators had become subdued. They realized there was more to this fight than met the eye. The boys were vicious. Their blows aimed to cripple and maim. Even boots were used. The fight had degenerated into a very dangerous brawl.

There was a yell of alarm. With incredible speed the spectators disappeared after a cry of alarm rent the air. The warning was not heard by the fighters. The sergeant appeared suddenly, glared horribly, hands on his hips. He stood, feet apart. Opening his mouth he roared a 'Tenshun'! It was the most effective weapon of penetration into the fighters' minds. They halted with a jerk.

'You horrible little men! You disgust me! I've a damn good mind to put you all on a charge: but you want to fight? O.K.! Over there are a few thousand Huns more than willing to oblige! Get yourselves out of my sight! Pack your kit! You have one week's embarkation leave. You leave for France next week and let me tell you, you miserable scum, you're going to wish you'd never heard of fighting by the time you've spent two weeks up at the front. Now get out *of my sight!'*

The Mayos and Howards vanished with an alacrity which astonished them all. Their minds were filled only with one exciting thought. They were going—at last! Now *they* could have a go at clobbering the Hun! Show him what an English gentleman was like! Soon finish these sausage eaters off. With yells and back slapping they raced for their gear, colliding with each other. Mayo slapped Howard in their enthusiasm. Howard grinned back at Mayo. Their eagerness was mutual and infectious.

Only when they walked up the drive to Mayo's did the boys pause uneasily. Their uniforms were smart. Their boots shining, their puttees at the correct angle. They looked three debonair soldiers—except for one thing. Three bruised and battered faces. What were their parents going to say? Uneasily two brothers turned to their leader and, squaring his shoulders, John assumed his rank of firstborn and marched into the living-room where Giles sat reading.

He jumped to his feet with surprise and pleasure. The greeting died in his voice as he regarded them.

'We're home on a week's embarkation leave, sir!' John told him.

Mike fidgeted uneasily, then said, 'We met the Howards!'

George was more blunt. 'We fought 'em!'

'So I see!' Giles said drily as he examined each face in turn.

'Who won?' he asked.

The boys looked at each other when John spoke again. 'The sergeant stopped us but it was a grand fight while it lasted!'

'But who was winning?' persisted Giles in some amusement. What a cut-throat band he had bred himself.

The boys shrugged and George answered him.

'I guess it was about evens, sir!'

'They can fight, those Howards!' Mike said

quietly.

John nodded. 'They're a bit quiet and slow-like to start with but when they get going—why—you'd almost think they were Mayos they're so good!'

Is that so, thought Giles? You young idiots! They're Howards and Mayos combined. The blood is there—and there's never been a yellow Howard yet!

'I don't know what your mother and aunt are going to say when they see your faces but I know what I'll say if the women are upset! You understand me, you three?' Giles asked them, his voice cutting like a whip.

The boys nodded quickly, chorusing together, 'Yes, sir!'

'I want no uproars on this leave, mind you! Stay home, be around the farm—for the women's sake,' he urged them more quietly now. 'Remember, it's always harder for the women who have to wait at home and who don't fully understand.'

They looked at each other again. This was one time when they had better obey their father. No fighting, no drinking and no girls! So for their week's leave they stayed around the property. They devoted their time and companionship to two sorrowful women, whose eyes were often red but who uttered not one word of protest at their prospective going. The boys were fed, coddled and petted like three puppies. It was with unaccustomed sinking hearts they packed their kit, left their home and went to France with the first replacements for the British Expeditionary Force.

Their spirits lifted as their feet touched French soil. Together with the Howards they started to play at war. Between the brothers an unspoken armistice had been agreed. It was not unusual for the six to be seen together. They never discussed their homes or families, knowing these subjects were far too dangerous. Instead they talked about the glory of fighting, the might of England and the stupidity of the murdering Boche who couldn't fight anyhow, being full of sausages!

They soon learned otherwise. They found out the German could shoot a straight rifle, throw an accurate stick bomb and was the very devil himself when he came storming over the shell torn landscape and dropped into their trenches, bayonet slashing.

They discovered hunger. All their lives they had been well fed. Never once had they known the misery of the shrunken stomach when it screams for food. They learned about the great cramps that come with hunger, the physical weakness and the discomfort of the continually salivering mouth. They ate food at which they would once have turned up their elegant noses. They made do with half-warm meals eaten from a dirty mess tin, squatting on their heels, greatcoats dragging in filth, rifles always at their sides.

They learned about cold, real cold, when the bone marrow seems turned to ice. Their fingers became useless appendages and toes were joined together in an icy mass unable to take the body's weight. But most of all they met real fear. They faced that terrible emotion when the heart flutters wildly, the throat burns like fire and the bowels of the strongest men turn to loose water.

They had lost six officers in seven weeks and it frightened them. In their fear they drew together. Six lonely, terrified brothers who, past enmities long forgotten, made a phalanx of comradeship. Each looked after his neighbour whether he be a Howard or a Mayo.

All had suffered minor wounds. John had a bullet in his left arm. Mike and George both suffered shrapnel splinters in their backs. Joseph's left thigh was ripped with a bayonet slash. The wound looked much worse than it was. David and Harry both suffered concussion during one fiendish barrage. They were sent back to the field hospital and finally ended up having leave in Paris. They did not go back home. There was not the time nor could they be spared. Men were short and the Germans were many. The French had been mauled with appalling casualties. It took more than a mere flesh wound to get a soldier home.

They survived long enough to deserve a home leave. In the New Year of 1916 the

Mayos and Howards crossed the Channel together. Six men who were the closest of friends and the greatest of comrades. They respected each other's ability and more—they relied upon each other's action to stay alive. They arrived in Bristol one quiet Sunday morning. They shook hands, smiled and went their separate ways.

Giles and Helen were waiting at Mayo's, with Mary crying helplessly. That telegram had almost killed them. A telegram only ever meant one thing. Giles's fingers had trembled as he opened it. Even when he turned to his women with flashing laugh and shining eyes they had not believed him until they had read that precious message themselves.

HOME ON A WEEK'S LEAVE HOPE TO ARRIVE SUNDAY THE BOYS

Giles thanked God as the three stood in the living-room, while the women broke down afresh. Even Giles himself could feel a prickling behind his eyes. He shook hands with each big son, unable to believe the change in them. Where were those wild hellraisers? Who were these aloof, silent men whose eyes held emotions he could not begin to understand. There was so much he failed to comprehend. One morning he tried to talk to his sons.

'I'd rather not talk about it, Pa!' John told him flatly.

'No! We're on leave. We'll have enough of it next week back there. Civilians can't understand. No one can 'til they get—out there—but I'll tell you this, Pa, those fools at the top, those bloody politicians—they want to go out there and risk their blood! It's the politicians who make the wars but ordinary people who have to fight them. It's all wrong!' quiet Mike told him with a hard, foreign edge to his voice.

'He's right!' George agreed. 'Those bastards in Whitehall juggle around with figures and bits of paper and men die in hell. Blown to bits, gassed, their guts hanging out, skewered on the wire. All the time the politicians—and generals—talk about this movement and that strategic retreat! They make my guts ache!'

'Look what happened Christmas 1914. Blokes on both sides, ordinary English and German soldiers, crossed into No-man's land to fraternize. The Christian spirit and all that. But the blokes at the top they didn't like that, did they? Oh no! That was all stopped very quickly. My God, just think if it could have continued this war would have ended quickly and thousands of men would be alive right now because, as Mike said, it's ordinary blokes like us who have to go out there and do the actual fighting!' John said bitterly.

'Let's drop it, lads!' George told them quietly. 'This kind of talk gets us nowhere. Let's enjoy what leave is left to us.'

And they had dropped it. Giles never attempted to probe again but his heart ached and his blood ran cold. What was happening out there?

He mentioned the matter only once more. 'The Howards?'

The boys spoke in unison. 'They're our mates! They're all right, those Howards!'

They left early one morning while Helen and Mary still slept. The previous evening had been harrowing with the women trying valiantly to control themselves but unable to halt the river of tears. Giles got up to see them off.

He shook hands with each son, looked deep into burning eyes and stayed silent. He had tried to think of something sensible to say as a father should but only the wrong words would form on his tongue.

They stepped back from him as one, saluted him as if he were their general, turned on their heels and stamped down the gravel drive away to war again.

Giles watched them until they disappeared from sight. Unable to contain himself any longer he broke down and wept like a child. Later he drove over to Ferndale seeking Robert's companionship. Together they went out in Giles's noisy car. They found a country pub, bought beer and sat down facing each other.

'I can't go back home yet,' Giles said slowly,

'the women!'

Robert sighed with understanding. His shoulders bent as he nodded. He was suddenly glad that he was free of Eliza. At least he had only himself to consider now. Eliza had remarried and showed no jot of interest in her sons. She was an unnatural female and Robert was heartily glad to be free of her.

'They're not going to come back,' Giles whispered, staring at Robert.

'Don't ever think that!'

'It's true. I'll not be seeing them again. I can feel it in my bones!'

'We can't do anything about it,' he replied heavily.

'That's the worst part of all. We sit and wait while they shed their blood. Oh God, Rob! What'll we do if we lose them?' Giles cried in anguish.

'At least one good thing has come out of this bloody mess. The feud has ended at last. My boys worship those lads of yours,' he told Giles.

'So I've learned. Thank God someone has seen some sense somewhere. I know I can't!'

*   *   *

The boys went back to France, bitter cold men, angry at leaving their homes and determined now on one thing. They would see this stinking mess out and make a land fit for anyone to live in.

During the summer of 1916 they moved up to the Somme area where a vast build-up of troops and equipment was taking place. Twenty-six British divisions lined up with thirteen French ones. Of these, fifteen British divisions were destined to take part in the initial attack planned. The boys' unit was placed on the north flank. On the twenty-fourth of June they crouched down in their trenches as the bombardment began. The noise was unbelievably appalling, being heard even in England. They thought they would die from the noise alone.

On and on the guns fired, getting red hot but there was no pause. This was going to be the real thing, the big push to end it all. When the wind was right, the gas was discharged in a filthy, belching cloud straight into the German lines. The weather, always fickle, became terrible. The bombardment had to cease temporarily, men and equipment being bogged down with their supplies. But the noise started again.

Day after terrible day it raged. All six boys now knew what hell was. Everything which had gone before had been a mere childish prelude to this most awful climax. Still the guns roared on. Their ears closed, their heads split, their bodies trembled without control. They monotonously continued to drop gigantic shells amongst the German lines. It was impossible! No man could live through such an inferno.

At 07.30 hours on the morning of the 1st July 1916 they went over the top, confident that the German resistance would be pitifully weak. After such hell had poured down on them for so many dreadful days there couldn't be anything left.

But the German trenches were deeper and well fortified. The Boche was anything but dead. He was there armed to the teeth and as eager to kill them as they were to slaughter him. It was a slaughter. The raped earth soaked up their blood. It took hold of their mutilated limbs and scattered them about. Crushed legs, torn arms and severed heads were sprinkled in appalling confusion. Still the troops poured over the top and ran stumbling over a land littered with human garbage.

The boys ran to their death.

On the north section of the British front the Germans had massed a veritable armada of machine guns. The men who were slaughtered gave their lives for nothing. The British attack was repulsed. They were beaten down by the machine guns, fields of khaki falling before the reaper's rattling scythe. As one line of soldiers went another took its place, and another, then yet another. Still they died, chopped to bits with the slashing bullets. Their bodies piled high and forced a partial shield for those wounded who struggled to get back into their trenches. Hell on earth. Man's inhumanity to man.

The Mayos and Howards had stood huddled together, waiting for the barrage to stop. They were under no illusions. This was indeed the greatest moment of truth and they were frightened to death. John looked at Joseph, then at the other two Howards and finally at his brothers. In their eyes he read the same stark fear he felt.

The fear they had known before was as nothing to the sheet of agony which raced through their hearts now. John tried to think of something else, anything, but his mind shied violently, reverting to what was coming. He looked up at the wet earth marking the top of their trench. A periscope on both sides of the wooden ladder. His gaze travelled to his right. He saw lines of rigid men, all scared to death, nervously clutching their bayoneted rifles. He saw the spot where the notice was posted warning of a sniper's presence. A spot where, to his knowledge, eleven careless men had been picked off.

Then there was a silence just as horrible as the bombardment had been. A red flare arced upwards. The officer moved, jumped for the ladder, raced up it and over the top. The sergeant followed, then the men jostling after him. John, his brothers and the Howards went over in a straight line and broke into a run. They dodged between the wire, the holes and other unspeakable objects on the ground. They pounded on and the bullets opened up on them. Little specks of deaths which ploughed into flesh and bone with a dull clunking sound, often going through two men at once.

John pressed on, swerving to right and left. A bullet caught him between the eyes. He was dead before he hit the ground. Mike gave a yell of anguish and charged forward, saliva dribbling from his lips. He ran straight into a hail of lead which rattled across his chest from left to right, cutting his torso in half and throwing his head and shoulders in front of George. The stricken brother paused, mesmerized at the head with open eyes, gaping jaws and a bloody mess below. Bile rose into his stomach, his guts churned wildly. Two bullets cracked into him, bowling him over, blood streaming from his leg and chest.

Joseph Howard lasted further. He made another ten paces before his groin took five bullets in rapid succession. He dropped slowly, reluctant to die. David and Harry stared in horror. This carnage, these bodies, their brother, those bullets! No man could get through the lines! They dropped to the ground, firing wildly as the line of khaki wavered. The officer and sergeant were long dead. They were alone and helpless. Men started turning, heading back to safety and the bullets rained into them ruthlessly. The bodies piled high, everywhere was red and sticky with an abominable stench. David turned and a bullet shattered the back of his skull, blowing his brains all over Harry's face. Harry bent double, twisted and turned, jumping a shell hole.

His bullet came when he had almost reached safety. It tore through the muscles of an arm, severing the artery, mangling nerves and shredding fibres.

He fell back into his trench, landing on a heap of tangled bodies, his blood spurting out in a crimson fountain. The limb hung by the merest shred of skin. A quick-thinking stretcher-bearer pounced on him. Fingers probed and tightened, then mercifully he blacked out as a crude tourniquet was lashed around his jagged stump.

George came to when it was all over. Everywhere was black and for a second he thought he was blind. He went to move and pain stabbed at him. Pain of an intensity which he had never known existed. He lay still, listening to sounds which reached him. Moans, groans and screams. He ran his tongue over parched lips thinking of cold, fresh water, then he sighed. He was dying. Oddly enough he found he was no longer afraid. He knew he was the last of them. He had seen both John and Mike go as well as David and Joseph. What had happened to Harry he had no idea. So it was all ended.

He thought of his parents and the house of Mayo. For the first time in many years there would be no heir. He wondered curiously how Ferndale would be placed. Had a Howard indeed survived or were they also extinct? He closed his eyes wearily. He could not think. The pain was too great. He lapsed into unconsciousness and did not emerge again until the next night.

There was little life left in him now. The bleeding had stopped and some of the pain had diminished. Shattered nerves had shut off the supply of feeling to his brain. He listened and there appeared to be fewer voices groaning and certainly less screams. He grimaced and experimentally moved an arm. Pain came back in a flash but he persisted. His mind was surprisingly cool and collected. He was damned if he would die here. He knew he could not be far from the trenches. Anything was better than dying flat on his back with his legs dangling in the mud and water of a hole.

Painfully, infinitely slowly, he inched forward. Six inches was a great feat. A whole foot was stupendous and when he thought he had covered a yard he rewarded himself with a rest. Sounds reached him. Voices, talking normally, not moaning their guts out. A smell wafted to him. Coffee! His mouth dribbled with saliva. He was so thirsty. He had to make it. Gritting his teeth, his eyes flaring his determination, he inched forward another precious yard and then collapsed face down. He could feel the blood running again. A red mist danced before his eyes and he shook as if he had rigor.

'Help!' he whispered, striving to put more sound into his voice. 'For the love of God—get me in!'

'There's some poor bugger out there!' he heard a voice say almost under his nose.

'There's more than one. There are thousands coughing their guts out on the wire. We can do nothing!'

'But he's near, I tell you! I'm going up!'

'You maniac! You'll get your head blown off!'

'I'm still going!'

'I'll come with you!'

They found him within four feet of the trench. With speed they hustled him to safety and laid him gently on their coats.

'Christ almighty! Look at 'is wounds!'

'He's a gonner!'

'Shut up! Can't you see he's conscious?'

'Get the stretcher-bearers! I've seen others like him pull round!'

*   *   *

The telegram came when they were at lunch. It was Mary who went to the door. She returned after a few seconds, white as a sheet of unmarked snow, the envelope held between trembling fingers.

Helen froze while Giles slit the dreadful thing. He read the words slowly. He read it a second time, then lifted blank eyes to his wife.

'Who?' Helen whispered.

'Giles! Tell us!' cried Mary, who could not stand such suspense.

Giles knew there was no way to break such news easily. It was better for them to have it straight from the shoulder. Pray God Helen was made of tougher material than the long dead Julie.

'John and Mike killed in action. George dangerously wounded,' he recited slowly.

Helen sat rigid. The words drumming into her brain. Two of the boys dead and George badly wounded. Now the war was in the house with them. They were no longer civilians standing aloof from it all. Two dead boys and another heading that way? Bold John, sensitive Mike and sensible George. Oh God, she asked herself, why, why, *why?*

Mary sat down slowly. Those laughing, impudent rascals would be no more. It was impossible. There had been a mistake. They would be back again. Then sense returned. They would never be back. They had gone for all time. She must remember them as they'd been in the past. Their three young hellers. She would never see John and Mike again while George—what were his chances?

Giles stood staring morosely out of the

window. He pictured three grim-faced young men standing in a line saluting him, then turning on their heels and stamping away to die. He had known this must happen. He had felt too cold too many times in the last few months.

He saw a chaise turn up the drive. Robert sat back like a ramrod, face white and stern. Oh no, thought Giles, not him too? Not Rob living alone without true companionship!

He met his friend at the door. One look into Robert's miserable eyes told him. Arm on shoulder he took the man into the room. Helen and Mary had not seen him this close in years.

'Who?' Giles asked gently.

'Joseph and David dead! Harry wounded!'

Helen started to weep silently. Mary rose and put her hand in Robert's.

'John and Mike gone. George badly wounded!' Giles told him.

'Oh, my God!' Robert groaned helplessly. 'Our two families all but wiped out in less than five minutes!'

Bending his fine head, hand covering his eyes, he wept as no man should ever have to weep.

Giles stood, holding his shoulder, feeling water trickle down his own cheeks. He looked out of the window again. He was too shocked and frozen in his own grief to comfort his women.

Yet again the house of Mayo encompassed misery. In its turbulent history much grief had entered through the old oak door but never before had two men become wholly united in such grief as the houses of Mayo and Howard.

The grief did more than that. It united a man and woman. Before he left Mayo's Robert looked at Mary. It was a questioning look, silent but understood. It was Mary who went to the door with him. Tactfully, Giles left them alone.

Robert held the woman's hand in his as he looked down into her brimming eyes.

'It's maybe neither the time nor the place but Mary, I love you. God knows I've always loved you and *only* you. Marry me? Will you please marry me?'

She caught at her breath, then slowly reached out and touched his face.

'Oh, my Rob, I thought you were *never* going to ask me!' Then they were in each other's arms. Crying helplessly. The tears rolling for the dead and for their lost years.

CHAPTER SIX

Then came the bad times. The months of worry about George. The many tiring journeys Giles made. To start with, George was far too ill to be transferred back to England. For the first time in his life Giles travelled abroad. He felt lost in France.

When they took him in to see George he failed to notice him and walked past his bed. The French nurse gently caught his arm and took him back.

He still did not recognize his son. George was gaunt and practically emaciated. His leg had been amputated and two serious operations had only just managed to save his life. The bullet in his chest had entered taking with it fragments of his filthy uniform. Only quick and drastic surgery had saved him from gangrene.

He smiled up wanly at his father, fluttered limp fingers, then closed his eyes, too weary to talk. Giles was aghast.

The small, harassed man, who had seen so much horrible human suffering, shrugged eloquently at Giles's blunt question.

'He is alive, monsieur, and I think he will live, but he will not make—how do you say it—old bones! One lung is useless. One heavy cold—and—!' the doctor shrugged his shoulders. 'He will be given an artificial leg. Regretfully, monsieur, we must only hope and pray. No one can do more!'

'When can he return to England?'

Another picturesque shrug and a raising of black, bushy eyebrows.

'Perhaps in a month or six weeks. Understand, monsieur, we need his bed but he is too weak to move yet. Soon, we will have some of your splendid English nurses to help us and they will travel back with your brave soldiers. Sometime before the sea gets too rough. More I cannot tell you.'

With that Giles had to be content. Now he was able to appreciate to the full the loyalty of his men. They ran his farm for him while he made these frequent and tiring journeys. When he returned everything was as it should be. The land in order, his stock milked, fed and prepared for market. His accounts meticulously accurate where Helen and Mary had spent laborious hours on the figures amidst a welter of tears.

Robert was perhaps a little luckier. Harry was able to be shipped back to England more quickly to be looked after by a warm-hearted Mary whom Robert, at long last, had happily installed in Ferndale as its mistress after a quiet civil wedding ceremony.

Mary frequently travelled over to see her brother and ask about George.

Weary weeks passed in slow time and then they heard George had been moved to England. Giles took Helen and Mary to see the surviving son. With admirable fortitude they controlled their tears, talked cheerfully to George and only collapsed in grief when outside the ward.

'Oh Giles, I couldn't recognize him!' Mary wept.

Giles gritted his teeth. What would she have thought of the living corpse he had seen in France?

'My son! My lone son! Oh, Giles! John and Mike—what happened to them?' asked Helen.

Giles had been prepared for this question for a long time. 'They felt nothing. It happened too quickly and that's the truth, my dear, because George saw them go,' he told her gently.

'This bloody god-damned awful war!' stormed Helen in anguish.

Giles halted in shock. Helen had sworn!

'And I bloody well agree with her!' Mary echoed.

Really, I seem to have some kind of mutiny on my hands, Giles told himself. It suddenly struck him that women were a tremendous power in the land. If every wife and mother stood up and shouted they could alter the destiny of the nation. In a flash he appreciated what the Suffragettes were aiming at with their Votes for Women campaign. By heavens, he thought, if they all stood up—and went on strike—shocking thought, England would grind to an immediate halt! The women were the real power behind everything. They produced the family, they raised it. It was in their hands to indoctrinate the young.

Giles was a free thinker and a forward-looking man. When women like this, quiet, highly-bred and beautifully-mannered, were driven to swearing like soldiers, then things were indeed coming to a pretty state.

'I think it's time we went home,' he told them firmly. His eyes twinkled. He was delighted to see them in this militant state. Far better this than to have them swoon in grief.

There were many more visits to George before he was able to come home. Visits which did not end until 1917. When they knew that great day was at hand, tremendous preparations were made to welcome back the son and heir of Mayo's. Giles was rather mystified though to receive a letter from George asking him to call once more before he came home. Puzzled and wondering anxiously if there had been a relapse or some other trouble, Giles hastened to obey. In his fright it did not occur to him that any such news would have come from the hospital authorities.

Giles found George resting in bed. An improved George but also an unhealthy one. His face was that of a man of forty; white, lined and haggard. His once merry eyes were sorrowful. They pictured untold miseries which they had seen and could never forget. Giles felt as a mere child sitting down beside his son. He saw the artificial leg against the bed, then realized George was looking at him, both boldly yet with worry.

Giles grinned light-heartedly, trying to make things easy for him.

'How's the peg-leg?'

'Oh that? Not too bad! Pretty hard on the stump to start with but they've toughened the skin up now. I can manage quite a decent dot-and-carry. The old bellows aren't too good but I guess they'll have to make out. They've not got round to making wooden bellows yet,' he joked a little feebly.

Giles noted his difficult breathing and wondered about the strain on George's heart.

'What's up, George?' he asked him straight out.

His son turned scarlet and lowered his eyes in embarrassment and fear.

'Can't you tell me, George? You know you're all I have now!'

Slowly, speaking in a low voice, George told him. 'It's over eighteen months since I copped this lot, Pa. A year since I came back to England. Well, it's like this. You may have heard that when chaps like me were fit enough we were given days away. To get us used to returning to civilian life and all that—well—I've had a number of weekends away from this place.'

Giles was astonished. 'But you never told us! You never let us know! Why didn't you come home? Where did you go? George— your mother and aunt!' and his voice was reproachful.

George looked his father straight in the eyes. A hard, almost cruel, look which alarmed Giles. My God, he thought, what's he going to come out with?

'I didn't tell you because I was busy with other plans!'

'Such as?'

'Getting married and making a baby!'

Giles was shocked into silence. For a whole minute the men faced each other. George's eyes never left his father's face.

Giles pulled himself together with an effort, shaking his head, lips working soundlessly. He looked back at his son, eyebrows arched.

'I think you'd better start at the beginning,' he suggested slowly.

George nodded, relieved now that it was out in the open.

'She's a nurse. I met her in Paris. She was one of the English nurses sent over to escort us back to this country. Anyhow, she came back with me and—well—we fell in love and I married her,' George ended lamely.

Giles frowned uncertainly. 'How come I've never met her?'

'Because I told her to clear off whenever any of the family came to visit me. We were married two months ago and she's missed twice!' George added bluntly.

'Fast worker!' Giles said drily, then screwing up his eyes he looked at George with a dubious sideways stare.

'But why the mystery? Why not let me, at least, meet her?'

George drew his deepest breath yet.

'Because she's not our type or our class! She's the daughter of a street cleaner. Before she took up nursing she worked in a factory. She's low working-class. She doesn't speak properly, she's no money, manners or breeding but, by God, she was good to me when I needed help. She went far above her duty in taking care of me. No matter where's she's from, she's my wife and carrying my child!'

'All right! All right! Simmer down! Don't get yourself all steamed up, it won't do that lung or your heart any good,' Giles admonished, thinking quickly. He wondered whether George had married for love or gratitude. Who was this low girl? Some fortune hunter? It was easy to find out a wounded man's background, ascertain his social and financial standing. Simple to play upon a sick man and twine him around a little finger. Had George been fooled?

'I'm no class snob, you should know that by now, but—!' and Giles hesitated, trying to frame some tactful questions to ask his son without upsetting him. Already George was red-faced, sweating and straining to breath, his breath rasping horribly in the quiet of the room.

George was no fool. He knew the exact train of his father's thoughts. Sick or not, they had been his too. He was shrewd and careful, having seen so many fellows make asses of themselves during two years of army life.

He was under no illusions about his wife. From her background she would have the most appalling time fitting into the social life and standing of the mighty Mayos. Class distinction was so strong and rife, especially in the country. He had made a firm decision. She was going to be his wife. His chosen mate for what little life was left to him.

Giles was at a loss for words. A city girl from some awful slum, with no speech, manners or education, carrying the heir to the wealthy and powerful Mayos. My God, this was a turn-up for the books. How the county tongues were going to wag!

'Well, Pa?' George barked at him.

Giles stiffened at his son's tone, then controlled himself quickly.

'Do you really love this girl?'

'I married her!'

Giles shook his head. 'You know what I mean, George. Don't fence with me, son. I'm better at that than you. I've lived longer and had more practice. Is this the real thing or the gratitude any wounded man feels for his nurse?'

'It's the real thing—for both of us!' George replied quietly now.

'I see!' Giles murmured. Now what to do. He realized that the ball was once more back in his court.

Then George spoke again. 'We are properly married, Pa! She has the certificate and it was done in church too! Oh, look Pa! I know what you're thinking. You think she's sunk her claws into me because I'm the heir to Mayo's!' George paused unhappily, thinking of his dead brothers. Then his lips tightened. 'It's not a bit like that. I'll tell you straight, here and now. She was dead against us marrying! She said she wasn't good enough for me because of her background! She said I was a nob, one of the gentry and she came from the East End slums. She said it would never work. My family wouldn't want her. People we mixed with would despise her. She'd give me nothing but grief and—well, she said she wouldn't marry me and that's God's honest truth!'

George's voice carried with it the ring of authenticity. Giles believed him.

'What's her name? Tell me about her?' he asked.

'Her name is Susan, Susan Webb that was. She's my own age. She's above average height, black hair, dark eyes and a figure that—!' and George's voice died away in unconcealed admiration. 'I think she's bloody marvellous to give herself to me—like I am!'

'In that case, when do I meet my— daughter-in-law?' Giles asked, smiling.

Apprehension again entered George's voice. 'She's in the visitors' lounge, waiting for you.'

Giles nodded to himself. 'Then in that case I'd better go along and make myself known,' he said, trying to joke.

He left George and with measured tread headed towards the visitors' room. Through the glass door he could see a person's shadow, sitting—waiting for him? He realized he was nervous and anxious. This girl was George's wife, carrying his child. Opening the door he stepped into the room.

The girl lifted her head. Giles was conscious of a pair of firm dark eyes regarding him steadily. She was wearing a white blouse, flowing black skirt and, over a chair, was draped a dark coat and saucy hat. He quickly scanned the clothes, noting their poor quality. She had done her best, obviously dressing up for him with what she had. He advanced towards her, smiling lightly.

'Miss—Susan—I'm George's father,' he managed to get out at last, offering his hand, standing before her.

She gave hers, a long thin hand with palms calloused from rough work. They mutually studied each other, she with a faint blush, Giles feeling himself to be an awkward lout.

'How do you do, Mr Mayo?' she said, speaking at last. She had a soft voice, very low for a woman. Her speech, as George had warned him, told of her low class in life.

Giles slowly sat down and studied her. Frankly she returned the look. My God, she's a real beauty, Giles told himself. Alter that hair style, give her some healthy country air, dress her in good county clothes, remove that frightening London accent, and she would pass anywhere! The girl had a poise which astonished him. She had a dignity surprising in one of her age and if she had been a nurse in France then she certainly did not lack guts. Giles was both surprised and pleased. There was something winning about her. She did not sit trembling before him. She looked with a steady and fearless gaze as if she considered herself equal to him.

'I hope we're going to become good friends,' he said slowly.

'George has told you all about me?' she asked. 'I mean, where I come from—and everything?'

Giles nodded.

'I'm not your class, Mr Mayo. I don't speak like you. I don't know much about dressing either—I've never had the chance to learn and I can learn. I will! I love George!' she told him fiercely.

'I'm sure you do!' he replied, still probing at her with his keen, knowledgeable eyes. Obviously this girl would never have been even remotely considered for a nurse before the war. And even then, by accepting her, the hospitals had demonstrated how desperate they were for girls to go over to France to do the filthy jobs in life. Not ladies for holding hands, writing letters and bathing sweating foreheads. Real, tough girls who wouldn't

305

throw up when a man emptied his guts all over the sheets.

He broke his gaze away and thought of Helen and Mary. They both shared his views and despised snobbery. As for the county? He cared nothing about their opinions. He never had, but it would not be easy for this girl to start with. She would require a lot of moral help. He looked back at her and this time his smile was full and warm. He held out both hands to her, eyes sparkling. There was a good brain here. Given half a chance she would turn out first class.

'My dear child, you are my son's chosen wife. You are my daughter-in-law and I welcome you into my family. Don't worry about anything, it will all come right in the end. George chose you, that's good enough for me!'

She smiled and let out a slow sight of relief, her face lighting up as her apprehension departed.

'And Mrs Mayo?'

'My wife thinks as I do! Now shall we go back and see George? He's probably lying there imagining all sorts of ridiculous things. My arm?'

Her slender hand resting on his muscular arm Giles took her back into George who lifted his head sharply as they appeared. He flashed a glance at his wife, then his father, eyes asking a hundred questions. Giles

306

forestalled him.

'My congratulations son on your choice of lady!' then he paused for a few quiet seconds before continuing. 'This war has wiped out a generation. Here's to the baby and peace for ever!'

*   *   *

Giles returned to Mayo's and, as he hoped, Helen and Mary were delighted with the news. Robert agreed with their logic. 'Times have changed, Giles. Harry says that too!'

'How is he?'

'They've taken the arm away but it's healed well. It's his nerves. I'm worried about him. I only hope he will return to his old self one day.'

'He'll never do that, Rob. No man who was out there will ever return to his previous self. Just as we, who never went, can't hope to understand what they went through. There's a gulf between us which can not be bridged.'

'It's hard to look back—and think what was,' Robert replied sadly.

'I know!' Giles echoed. 'One son instead of three! I'm luckier than you. My boy has married with a youngster on the way. What about your Harry?'

'I don't know. Who'd want him now? He says he's only half a man and at times, his shattered nerves, he frightens me. What girl would take him on.'

'Didn't you once talk about a distant half cousin who was mad keen on him before the war?'

Robert nodded slowly. 'That's true but, as I said, what girl's going to take on a man who wakes up in the night screaming like a child?'

Giles paused a moment, eyeing his friend. 'There's another side to look at, Rob. With all the dead, God help them, the marriage market is pretty limited to put it crudely. At the moment there are few available marriageable men around. The girls can't afford to be too choosy because if they do, they'll miss out altogether! I know you may think I'm speaking in a pretty cold-blooded way, but if this girl is any good and if the interest is there, encourage them to marry. To hell with convention and what people say. I reckon our lads have earned themselves a little happiness. I also reckon that a happily married man will recover more quickly than a man who stays single and only has himself to think about!'

Giles paused to see how Robert was taking all this. His friend sat frowning but listening carefully.

'You have strong views—but then you always did go your own sweet way regardless!' Robert laughed drily. 'I just don't know how keen Harry ever was on young Margaret!'

'Well, throw them together a bit! Nature has to have some help at times. She can't always manage it alone. Go on, go and play cupid! It'll give you something else to think about!'

Both men found life very difficult with their surviving sons. There was so very much which could never be forgotten. Giles was relieved when George was back home with his wife. Susan, as predicted, started to alter with the assiduous help of Helen, who had taken an instinctive liking to this quiet, determined wife of George's.

In 1918, a son was born at Mayo's.

Giles was also desperately worried about George. He coughed a lot, straining away on his one sound lung, causing untold damage to his already overburdened heart. His frame was starting to shrink away. It was as if he was burning up inside with consumption. Their weary doctor could do nothing but wait for the inevitable.

Giles also knew with a sinking heart that the end could not be delayed much longer. The women all knew this too. It was now that Susan showed her true colours. She knew the truth, had known it before any of them. Yet whenever she was with George she was smiling and happy.

How does she do it, Giles asked himself in admiration? My God, and to think I questioned whether she was good enough for us! Can we match *her* courage? He spoke to her about it one evening as they strolled in the garden.

'You know what's going to happen to George, don't you?' he asked her.

She nodded slowly, head erect, eyes dry.

'He'll be dead before the end of the year,' she said calmly in her nurse's voice.

Giles stopped and faced her, holding her hands. 'My dear—' he began, then the words failed him.

They were unhappy months. Any gaiety was forced for George's sake. By comparison it was a happy time at Ferndale. At the end of 1918 Harry Howard quietly married his distant cousin Margaret Johnson who'd had her eye on him for a long time.

Ten months after the wedding Margaret gave birth to a fine daughter. It was a hard birth with complications. Robert told Giles that, once again, the Howards would be a one-child family. He was thrilled with the girl. She was the first break in the male continuity for many years and, Giles told himself in amusement, Robert is going to spoil her outrageously. But he was happy for his friend. No longer would Ferndale be a place of adult loneliness.

Just after, George Mayo's heart gave up the unequal struggle. He died quietly one Sunday morning.

Giles grieved not just for himself but for his daughter-in-law. It was Susan who had to help him. Her young strength wrapped arms of comfort around him and, slowly, he accepted his son's death as he watched the growth of the baby James.

It was George who had given the child his name. Giles mused about it and remarked upon the name when he met Robert one Saturday evening.

'Yes, it's queer. History is repeating itself.'

Giles looked at him in bewilderment. 'What do you mean?'

'Our little girl's name has also been chosen. It's Sarah!'

'So!' murmured Giles in awe, 'as it was in the beginning—'

'So it is in the end!' Robert finished.

The two friends studied each other, both thinking along the same distant track back into history.

'But the feud is over and done with. Dead and gone. Somewhere out there in France,' Giles said soberly.

'That's true. These two babies are another beginning for both of our families. A Sarah and a James—but this time without hatred or greed for land.

'There's been too much hate and death,' agreed Robert. 'Now it must be peace.'

'And unity!' Giles finished.

'Perhaps even love!' and Robert grinned slyly.

Giles smiled back. 'Who knows? Stranger things have happened. Folks are queer; so is life itself. That would be a turn-up for the book. The families joined in matrimony of the two heirs!'

They grinned at each other with self-satisfaction as if they were personally responsible for the respective births.

So the two families were at last united with solid friendship, unquestioning loyalty as well as the bond of Mary's marriage to Robert. The New Year entered and brought peace and hope all round.

Chivers Large Print Direct

If you have enjoyed this Large Print book and would like to build up your own collection of Large Print books and have them delivered direct to your door, please contact **Chivers Large Print Direct**.

Chivers Large Print Direct offers you a full service:

✧ **Created to support your local library**

✧ **Delivery direct to your door**

✧ **Easy-to-read type and attractively bound**

✧ **The very best authors**

✧ **Special low prices**

For further details either call Customer Services on 01225 443400 or write to us at

Chivers Large Print Direct
FREEPOST (BA 1686/1)
Bath
BA1 3QZ